WESTERN FICTION MAGAZINE

MICHAEL P. ROBERTS, Publisher   R. CUSTER, Editor   BEVERLY HARRIS, Art Director

GREAT BOOKLENGTH NOVEL

FIGHTING MAN . . . . Frank Gruber   **2**

It's a tough job to gain the reputation of "fighting man", but it's tougher to keep it!

BETWEEN A ROCK AND A HARD PLACE . . . . S. Omar Barker   **90**

Whether it's a buck fight or a bullfight, Uncle Duff Mason never can stand to miss out on the excitement. That, as you'll find out, is why he happens to be still a bachelor—which doesn't seem to bother him much except when he plays with five-year-old Belinda Wheeler. And it's the strain of choosing in a crisis between the welfare of little Belinda and her big brother that leads to Uncle Duff's "arranging" a match between Ol' Champ, his dun-yellow longhorn, and Jace Wheeler's $500 Hereford bull.

BORROWED BULLETS . . . . **Ralph Berard**   **100**

Cutting sign on a notch-hunter of the Jack Rabbit Kid's calibre any Range City son but Race Gordon would have thought first of the two thousand dollar reward offered for the bandit dead or alive!

TENDERFOOT . . . . **E. Hoffman Price**   **108**

He's only a kid and he has a lot to learn about women but he knows horse flesh and he can make a delayed draw with the speed of a side-winder.

GUN WHIP LAW . . . . **Jack Anderson**   **122**

Bullets were ballots for law and order when young Jeff Hacknew tried to enact a new brand of gun-blazing justice for the down-trodden nesters.

MAY 2020   **A FICTION HOUSE MAGAZINE**   **VOL. 1, NO. 1**

FIGHTING MAN

by FRANK GRUBER

The bullet caught one man squarely between the eyes—

The vociferous West was asking for war, and
these four hundred tough men knew just how
the request could be granted!

—as the cavalcade thundered through the camp.

DO YOU remember what you did in Independence, Jennison? Do you remember, Anthony?

And you, Jim Lane—yes, Senator James Lane. You're not banging on Abe Lincoln's bedroom door this morning. You're not telling him how to run the war. You're home today, home in Lawrence, Kansas.

This is August 21, 1863, a day you will never forget.

It's early morning and you're still in your night shirt, but look out of your window, Jim Lane. Look out and see who's coming.

Yes—it's Quantrell, the man you drove out of Lawrence, three years ago. He's come back—with four hundred fighting men, four hundred of the most desperate, deadliest men this country has even known.

You wanted war, you abolitionists. Well, your war's come home to you!

* * *

CHAPTER I

HE WAS twenty-six years old, a towhead with washed-out blue eyes that had seen too much of life. School teacher, gambler, horse-thief, camp follower, murderer and cannibal; he had been all of them.

And now he was at the crest of his career. Riding into Lawrence, Kansas, the town he hated more than anything in life. He had known hard times here; humiliation and degradation. Men had sneered and jeered at him. They had thrown him in jail and threatened to hang him. And now he was going to pay them back, every mother's son of them.

Lawrence was spread out before him; Lawrence, Kansas, the home of the Jayhawker and the Redleg, the Boston Abolitionist. The home of Jennison and Anthony, and Jim Lane.

Quantrell rode down into the town, four hundred men at his back. Ahead of them, at the edge of the village, was a double row of Army tents, containing not more than thirty—you could scarcely call them soldiers, for they were mere recruits, untrained youths who were waiting to be shipped east where they were sorely needed. The war had not touched Kansas soil; there were no Confederate troops west of Missouri.

Only Quantrell. Quantrell and four hundred guerrillas, armed with Navy Colts, the finest weapon of destruction ever invented, which the Federal Government had not yet got around to buying for its soldiers. But Quantrell had bought Colts and had distributed them so liberally among his followers that each man had a minimum of two and some as many as eight, stuck in their belts.

Those tents in which thirty recruits were sleeping in their blankets. To whom would Quantrell delegate the honor of drawing first blood in Lawrence?

Quantrell's eye ran over his captains. George Todd, Bloody Bill Anderson, John Thrailkill, Cole Younger, Frank James, the ferocious boy, Arch Clements. Fine men, all of them. Ah, but there's Jim Dancer. His father was shot down in cold blood at Independence.

Quantrell nodded to Dancer. "Those tents, Captain."

Young Jim Dancer, nineteen years old, tall and lean and bitter, turned in his saddle and raised his right hand. He swept it forward . . . and his troop left the main body of guerrillas and charged.

Down upon the tents.

A sentry, stupid from illicit sleep, raised himself between two tents, to see what was causing the noise that sounded like galloping horses. His mouth fell open in amazement . . . and then he died.

Captain Dancer's troop struck the tents, trampling them down. Iron-shod hooves crushed out the lives of men. Blue-clad soldiers scrambled out from under canvas and were riddled with bullets. Not one had time to return a shot. Thirty men died and Captain Dancer's troop swept on into Lawrence, only a hundred yards behind the main body of Quantrell's men.

But already the carnage was under way. Guns thundered and roared. Horses galloped down the streets and men yelled and women screamed.

Captain Dancer's men thundered past him, heedless of his commands. The blood lust was surging up in them and they were beyond human reason. They were killing in Lawrence, killing and looting and they wanted their share of both.

THE gunfire in the town became a continual roll of thunder. Flames and smoke shot out of burning houses and store buildings. A bearded man burst out of a house and started to run across the street. A half dozen men charged down on him, a dozen bullets tore through his body and ten more went into his dead body as it lay on the dusty street.

Guerrillas dismounted from their horses, smashed in doors and windows of homes. Sometimes they killed men inside the houses, sometimes they dragged them out upon the street and shot them before the eyes of their wives and children.

And always they burned. A hundred houses were sending pillars of smoke toward the heavens, a hundred and fifty, then two hundred and in a little while three hundred.

Fifty men were slaughtered in their homes, another hundred died upon the streets.

But not Jim Lane. At the first sound of shooting in Lawrence, Senator Jim Lane was out of his home. With the tails of his night shirt flying behind him, he was heading for a corn field. And there he groveled for hours until the holocaust that was Quantrell had departed.

Oh, they searched for him, as they hunted for other men in the town. Guerrillas with sheets of paper containing lists of names rode through the towns and ransacked the houses from cellars to garrets. Sometimes they found men whose names were on the lists. They died horribly. They were the prominent men of the town, or men whom Quantrell or his followers bore personal grudges.

In these things young Jim Dancer took no part. He had led the attack against the soldiers in the tents. They wore uniforms and had taken an oath to fight against the Confederacy. That they were sodden with sleep, that they had no chance when Dancer's men rode them down, was their hard luck. Soldiers had no right to sleep with both eyes closed.

Hate, Dancer had; hate for the North that had spawned the men who had killed his father in cold blood. He killed soldiers because if he did not kill them they would kill him.

But Jim Dancer could not kill unarmed old men, nor those who would not defend themselves.

A guerrilla backed out of a doorway dragging a man by the heels. Behind him came a young girl of not more than fifteen or sixteen. Anguish distorted her face and tears streamed from her eyes.

"Please," she cried in utter panic, "please don't hurt him! Please! please . . .!"

The guerrilla, a filthy, unshaved ruffian,

dropped the legs of the man he was pulling and tugged a Navy Colt from his belt. The girl, seeing her chance, sprang past the unconscious form of her father and fell upon the guerrilla's gun hand.

The man swore a vicious oath and tried to shake the girl from him. She clung with the desperation of a lost soul.

"Let go," howled the ruffian. "Let go, or—"

He suddenly cuffed the girl with his free hand, a savage hard blow. She fell to her knees, but still clung to his wrist. The man took a half step back, braced himself and tore his hand free of the girl's grip.

The hand went up and the gun covered the girl.

"You asked for it," the guerrilla said thickly.

CAPTAIN DANCER stepped up and jammed the muzzle of his gun into the man's back.

"We're not shooting girls, Yancey," he said coldly.

For a moment the guerrilla froze. Then he squirmed and turned. "You, Dancer," he snarled. "I always said you was chicken-hearted."

Dancer struck him in the face with the barrel of the Navy Colt. Blood spurted from the man's face, but he stayed on his feet.

"I'll remember this, Dancer!"

"Do."

The guerrilla stumbled away and Dancer stepped forward to the side of the girl. She was down on her feet, cradling the head of her father in her arms. The older man was regaining consciousness.

Dancer stooped and taking hold of the man's shoulders helped him to his feet. The girl's arms were about her father and she started to help him toward the house from which he had so recently been dragged.

A black stallion shot forward and cut off the sanctuary of the girl and her father. The tow-headed Quantrell looked down upon them and Dancer.

"What's this, Captain Dancer?" the guerrilla chieftain cried.

Yancey appeared beside Dancer, a sneer of triumph on his face.

Dancer said: "Yancey struck the girl."

"Didn't!" Yancey snarled. "On'y pushed her out of the way." He pointed the muzzle of his revolver at the girl's father. "This is Theodore Slocum. His name is on the list."

"No!" cried the girl. "His name isn't Slocum."

"It's no use, Evelyn," said the man.

"No," Quantrell agreed. "It isn't, because I remember you." He nodded to Captain Dancer. "All right."

Captain Dancer remained rigid. Quantrell's terrible eyes bored into those of his lieutenant. "I said all right, Captain Dancer!"

Yancey, the guerrilla, stepped forward with raised gun, but Quantrell's voice crackled. "No, Yancey. I'm going to let Captain Dancer have the honor."

George Todd and John Thrailkill came trotting up.

Dancer said, evenly: "Killing an unarmed old man isn't war."

Quantrell bared his stained teeth. "I gave you an order, Captain Dancer . . ." His eyes went to those of bloody George Todd, merciless John Thrailkill. The guerrilla chieftains flanked young Jim Dancer. Yancey, blood still trickling down his face, was breathing heavily.

Slowly Dancer raised his gun, pointed it at Theodore Slocum. "No—no!" screamed the young daughter of Slocum.

"Fire!" Quantrell ordered.

Dancer pulled the trigger.

CHAPTER II

TWO horses jogged along the old Santa Fe Trail; they trotted side by side and the right hand of one of the men on the horses touched the left hand of the other rider. This was because the two hands were handcuffed together.

One of the men was Jim Dancer, nine years older than he had been at Lawrence, Kansas. He was still lean and hard-bitten and his eyes were slitted and weary. They had seen too much of life and none of it good.

The man who rode beside him was named George Cummings. He was a detective in the employ of the great Pleasanton Detective Agency and he was concluding a mission that he had begun eighteen months before and which had taken him through a dozen states; the pursuit and capture of Jim Dancer.

He was a formidable man, this George Cummings. Dogged determination had brought him up with Dancer but it was sheer luck that had him alive with Jim Dancer a prisoner beside him.

He said as they jogged along:. "I don't know what you've done, Dancer, and I don't give a damn. Yes, I've heard a thousand stories about you, but I believe nothing of what I hear and only half of what I see. I work for Arthur Pleasanton and he sent me out to get you. It's a job of work to me, that's all. I'm turning you over to the Kansas City office, and then I'm going to sleep for eight weeks."

"I guess you've earned your sleep, Cummings," Dancer said. He rode in silence for a moment, then he added: "I haven't slept in nine years myself. Not really slept."

Cummings looked thoughtfully at him. "You were with Quantrell during the war, weren't you?"

Dancer nodded.

Cummings looked straight ahead. "Tell me, was he as bad as they say?"

Dancer said: "You heard about Lawrence, Kansas? That was Quantrell at his worst." He was silent a moment. "But Bloody Bill Anderson and George Todd ran Quantrell out of Missouri afterwards."

Cummings rode in silence for awhile. Then he said: "There's only you and me here; it can't be used against you. Did you ride with Frank and Jesse?"

"No," Dancer replied shortly.

"Then why does Pleasanton want you?"

"I don't know."

Cummings screwed up his face in thought. "I don't mind telling you, Dancer, my orders were to get you. Pleasanton didn't say anything about Frank or Jesse, or Cole or the Miller boys. Only you. He told me to get you."

"Well, you've got me."

Cummings nodded. "I'm not kidding myself, Dancer. I've been around. I've had a few close shaves in my time, but it had to be luck for me to get you."

Dancer thought: *It's still another day to Kansas City. You've got a handcuff on my wrist and a gun in your pocket—on the far side. But watch yourself, Detective!*

TOWARD evening the detective and his prisoner reached the swollen banks of the Wakarusa. A wizened man stood on the river bank, scowling at a flat-bottomed scow which was straining at its mooring.

"Can you take us across?" Cummings asked.

"Yesterday I wouldda been glad to do it,"

retorted the ferryman. "And maybe I'll do it tomorrow. But right. now I wouldn't tackle the job for love nor money."

"Will you do it for this?" asked the detective. He produced a Navy Colt and pointed it at the ferryman.

The man regarded the revolver for a long moment. Then he shook his head. "Mister," he said, "you must want to get somewhere powerful bad."

"I do." Cummings held up his left wrist—along with Jim Dancer's. "I want to reach Kansas City tomorrow."

The ferryman searched the face of Jim Dancer. "An outlaw, Sheriff?" he asked the detective.

"I'm telling you to take us across this river," Cummings said grimly.

The ferryman studied the swirling river a moment, then exhaling heavily, clambered aboard the ferryboat. He caught up a sweep and maneuvered the boat a foot or so closer to the shore.

Cummings said: "We'll dismount, Dancer."

Holding his left hand high in the air, Cummings dismounted carefully, then stood sidewards while Dancer got off his own horse. Cummings moved forward, caught the bridle reins of both horses in his free hand and stepped toward the ferryboat. Dancer, perforce, was compelled to move with him.

Then Cummings tried to urge the horses aboard the boat. They balked, for in spite of the ferryman's efforts with the sweep he could not get the boat close enough to the bank to make boarding easy.

"Get the horses on!" Cummings shouted to the ferryman.

"And who'll hold the boat?" the ferryman retorted.

The sensible thing, of course, was to free Dancer until they were across the river, yet Cummings was loath to do that. But ten minutes of struggling only resulted in all three of the men being soaked from head to foot and at the end of that time the horses were still ashore.

Then Cummings finally drew the handcuff key from a pocket, handed it to Dancer and in almost the same movement drew his Navy gun.

"All right," he said harshly. "But watch yourself, Dancer!"

Dancer unlocked the manacle from about his wrist and the moment it was free, Cummings stepped back. From a vantage point he watched Dancer load the horses on the barge.

Then he clambered aboard himself and the ferryman threw off the rope that held the scow to the bank. At once the boat whirled out into the current, almost upsetting Cummings, who was not quite prepared. When Cummings recovered his balance, Dancer was within five feet of him. There he stopped, his eyes boring into those of Cummings.

"The key," Cummings grated. "Put it down and then move back."

DANCER stopped and deposited the key on the deck, then moved back as far as he could go. Cummings picked up the key and started to put it back into his pocket when the boat was caught in a sudden eddy and whirled almost completely about.

"Hang on!" cried the ferryman.

Cummings plunged forward, down to one knee. The key was jolted from his hand, plunked on the deck and disappeared in the muddy waters.

"Damn!" swore Cummings. He got carefully to his feet. "That means we stay together until we get to Kansas City."

"You'll never get me to Kansas City," Dancer said tonelessly.

"I'll get you there," Cummings said ominously. "Although I may have to carry you. Come over here."

He held out his left hand from which dangled the manacle. His right hand he drew aside carefully, so that he could point the muzzle of the gun at Dancer and fire quickly and accurately.

Dancer came forward.

"Put the cuff on your wrist," Cummings ordered.

Dancer slipped the metal band about his wrist.

"Press it," Cummings continued. "Tight!"

Dancer pressed the cuff until it clicked. And at that moment the ferryman made his move. Cummings' back was to him and the ferryman drew his wooden sweep out of the water and swung at the detective.

The withdrawal of the sweep from the water let the boat out of control. It lurched forward, sending Cummings sprawling—and the sweep missed his head. Cummings cried out hoarsely, twisted about and fired.

He aimed at the ferryman, but the unleashed boat frightened the horses, so that they began to pitch and rear and it was one of the horses that took the bullet. The animal screamed and reared up on his hind legs, causing his mate to begin bucking. The ferryman was struck by a plunging hoof and knocked overboard.

The wounded horse reared up so high that it went over backwards into the river. The removal of the horse's weight from the one side of the scow shot it high into the air, completely out of the water and Dancer and Cummings skittered across the deck, got embroiled with the remaining horse and all

three scudded into the waters of the Wakarusa.

CHAPTER III

THE stagecoach schedule was a flexible one. The coach left Topeka at a definite time but its stops along the route depended entirely upon the weather and the temperament of the driver. So, for that matter, did the route.

The ford at Eel's Bend was six feet under water and therefore no ford, so Joe Partridge swung to the left and followed the winding Wakarusa. There was a ferryboat eight or ten miles up the river and it ought to be able to take the stage across, provided the coach and horses were taken over in relays.

Only there was no ferryboat. The rutted trails that served as a road led up to the water's edge and could plainly be seen on the far bank, but the ferryboat was gone.

Joe Partridge, who had been a muleskinner under Sherman, pulled up his horses and swore roundly.

The right-hand door of the stage opened and a man stepped to the ground. He was a lean, sardonic-looking man wearing a Prince Albert and a flowered vest.

"What's the trouble, driver?" he asked.

Joe Partridge shot out a stream of tobacco juice. "It's the gosh-danged ferryboat, Mister."

The lean man surveyed the river. "What ferryboat?"

"That's it—there ain't none. But there oughtta be."

"What's become of it?"

"Don't know. Busted its rope and went down the river, I guess."

Another man stepped out of the coach, an enormously fat man of about forty.

"If the ferry's gone how are we going to cross?"

"Your guess is as good as mine, Mr. Kerigan," retorted Joe Partridge. "I was supposed to cross by the ford, eight-ten miles back, but there was six feet of water there. I oughtta change these horses about now, but don't see how I'm goin' to, with the station on t'other side of the river."

Kerigan frowned. "Is there any other place to cross?"

Partridge scratched his head. "There is another ferry 'bout ten miles downriver, but that means back about eighteen before I c'n change horses. Twenty-eight miles." He shook his head. "We'll have to rest them."

"They're resting now," said Kerigan.

"Yeah, sure. I'll give them ten minutes." Partridge scrambled down from his perch. "Anybody want to stretch for ten minutes c'n get out," he called.

The passengers descended from the coach.

First came Florence Peel. She was in her mid-twenties and her beauty caused every man she met to breathe a little faster. But when they looked into her eyes they were always repelled. They were green and as cold as ice. Florence's father had been a famous Mississippi River gambler, whose derringer caught in his vest pocket when Florence was twelve. That was in 1860, the year before the war, and Florence had supported herself ever since.

The fat man, Kerigan, was a cattleman from Texas. A herd of his was coming up the Chisholm Trail, but Kerigan had taken steamship passage to New Orleans, then come up the Mississippi to St. Louis and west to Kansas City by trail. He was going south now to meet the railroad that was building west. It was a long, roundabout trip, but it lacked the rigors of the overland Chisholm Trail route and Kerigan, who had been shipping cattle since 1867, was rich enough to indulge himself.

The fifth passenger's name was Paul Hobson, although he had given it to none of the other passengers on the coach. In fact, he had spoken less than a dozen words since the beginning of the trip.

IT WAS Dave Oldham, the lean sardonic man in the Prince Albert who discovered the two men down by the river bank. They were a hundred yards from where the stagecoach had stopped and they must have seen the coach, but had not acknowledged its presence by rising or calling.

One of the men was seated on the river bank; the other lay close beside him.

Dave Oldham started toward them, then thought better of it. He turned back and catching Joe Partridge's eye, indicated the men downstream.

Partridge looked and exclaimed, "Be damned!" He put his hands to his mouth and using them like a megaphone, called: "Hey, you . . .!"

The men made no reply, nor did either of them get to their feet. They couldn't, although those at the coach did not know that.

"What's the matter with them?" Kerigan exclaimed. He started forward, but was stopped by the stagecoach driver.

"Just a minute!"

Partridge stepped to the side of the coach, reached up to his seat and brought down a double-barreled shotgun. "Might be a trick," he said.

Kerigan unlimbered a short-barreled revolver. "Come on, there's only two of them."

He started downstream, with Joe Partridge at his side. Dave Oldham fell in behind them and Hobson followed after a moment. They were halfway toward the men down by the river bank when Florence Peel suddenly decided to hurry after them.

When they were twenty feet from the strangers, Joe Partridge stopped. The two men had not changed position since they had first been observed.

"What's the trouble?" Partridge cried.

The sitting man held up his right hand and by doing so brought up the limp hand and forearm of the other man. The two wrists were joined together by a pair of handcuffs.

"He's dead!" ejaculated Kerigan, referring to the man lying on the ground.

Partridge stepped forward, the muzzle of his shotgun pointed at the sitting man, but it was Oldham who reached him first. His right hand hovered near his vest where he could reach his derringer in a swift draw.

Oldham's eyes bored into those of the man seated on the ground.

"How long've you been here—like that?" Oldham asked.

"Last night," was the reply. The man was lean and hard-bitten and his eyes were slitted and weary. They had seen much of life and little of it good. They looked past Oldham and Partridge at Kerigan and Hobson who were coming up, and beyond them to Florence Peel.

"Where's Bart Huggins who runs the ferryboat?" Partridge demanded.

The man on the ground indicated the river. "That's how this happened. He was taking us across the river when the horses got panicky and capsized the boat." He looked down at the man who was handcuffed to him. "One of the horse's hoofs caught him on the head."

Joe Partridge grunted. "Surprised Bart ever took a chance crossing the way the river

must have been yesterday. Never saw a more cautious man in . . ." Then he suddenly inhaled sharply. "Say . . . which one of you two is—?" He broke off, but his eyes were filled with suspicion.

The stagecoach passengers exchanged glances. Then Hobson asked softly: "What's your name?"

The man on the ground looked at him steadily. "Cummings, George Cummings."

"Marshal?" asked Partridge. "Never heard of any by that name in this territory."

"I'm not a marshal," Cummings replied. "I work for Arthur Pleasanton."

"A Pleasanton man," exclaimed Joe Partridge. "I'll be damned. Didn't think you fellows ever got out this far." He pointed to the dead man. "Who's he? Soom poor devil whose wife got the Pleasanton Agency after him?"

Cummings said: "I don't know what he's done, for sure. His name is . . . Jim Dancer!"

Joe Partridge cried out in horror. "Jim Dancer!"

Dave Oldham shot a quick look at Cummings' face, then took a step forward and peered down into the cold dead face on the ground. "You never got Jim Dancer," he said thinly. "No Pleasanton man ever got Jim Dancer, not like this."

"Say," said Kerigan warmly, "I've heard of this Jim Dancer. He's a curly wolf." He nodded to Oldham. "I side with you, pardner. No city detective will ever take Jim Dancer."

"Dancer's the most desperate man in the West," Paul Hobson added.

THE Pleasanton man shook his head wearily. "I don't know anything about Jim Dancer. Yes, I've heard a thousand stories about him. They say he's killed a thousand men and made two hundred orphans. I believe nothing of what I hear and only half of what I see. But I work for Arthur Pleasanton and he sent me out to get Jim Dancer. That was a year and a half ago. I followed Dancer to Montana Territory, to Oregon and California. He went to Mexico and I followed him and then he came back and yesterday—" he stopped for a moment, then said: "He had to sleep sometime."

"Yes," Oldham said bitterly. "Sometimes a man gets tired. And then he's got to sleep." He exhaled heavily. "And Jim Dancer went out like that, handcuffed to a Pleasanton man."

These people lived within the law: Kerigan, Leach, Hobson, Florence Peel and Joe Partridge; yes, even Dave Oldham. But the ignominious end of a notorious outlaw affected them all. They should have been respectful to the detective who caused the death of Jim Dancer, but there was no friendliness in any eye. Only aversion.

George Cummings drew a deep breath. Then, looking at Partridge, he said: "Have you got such a thing as a steel file in your coach?"

"No," replied Partridge. "I don't carry tools on this run, what with stage stations every three-four hours." His eyes smoldered. "Where's your key?"

Cummings nodded to the river. "When the boat was capsizing, Dancer made a play. I threw the key into the water to keep him from getting it."

Florence Peel said: "You'll have to cut off Jim Dancer's hand."

Paul Hobson shuddered and turned suddenly away. The others exchanged uneasy glances. The suggestion had occurred to all of them, but none had wanted to express it.

Joe Partridge worked at his chewing tobacco for a moment. Then he draw a huge

clasp knife from his pocket. "If it's gotta be done I guess it's gotta be done."

CHAPTER IV

BERTRAM SLOCUM turned in at the three-story brick building and climbed the stairs to the second floor. Near the head of the stairs he saw a ground glass door on which was stenciled:

PLEASANTON DETECTIVE
AGENCY
NEW YORK   CHICAGO   LONDON
Kansas City Office

Slocum, a tall well-built man of about forty-five, with slightly greying hair, drew a deep breath and opened the door. In the small outer office a sharp-faced man took his boots off a desk.

"Mr. Pleasanton?" Slocum said. The sharp-faced man grunted. "You mean the gent that owns this here deteckative agency? He ain't never been in this office, far's I know."

"I received a telegram yesterday asking me to come here." He drew it from his pocket. "It's signed Captain Travers."

"Oh, sure, Cap'n Travers," was the reply. "He runs this here branch."

"Can I see him?"

"Don't see why not. But you said Mister Pleasanton an'—"

Slocum cut the man off coldly: "My business in the past has been with Arthur Pleasanton and when I received a telegram I assumed he would be here."

"You assumed wrong, Mister. The old man with the whiskers don't bother about little things. What's it you want us to do for you? I c'n probably take care of it myself."

"I want to see Captain Travers!" Slocum snapped.

The Pleasanton man got to his feet. He shrugged. "Well, whyn't you say so in the first place?"

Muttering to himself he opened a door and went through, closing the door behind him. He reappeared almost instantly and nodded to Slocum.

Slocum went through the door, through an empty office and beyond, entered another door. A lean, black-moustachioed man got up from behind a desk.

"Mr. Slocum," he said, "I'm Captain Travers."

Slocum nodded. "I got your telegram. Is it . . . about Jim Dancer?"

"Yes," replied Captain Travers. He paused a significant moment. "We've got him."

For just a second Slocum stiffened. Then his entire body relaxed. "How?"

Captain Travers pulled out a drawer and took from it a telegraph form. "This came from our Chicago office last night. Cummings reported there, as he was working under direct orders of Mr. Pleasanton."

He handed the telegram to Slocum. The latter scanned it quickly. It read:

Have just received despatch from George Cummings filed from Bower Springs, Kansas. He reports that he is bringing in Dancer. Am unable to come to Kansas City myself, so contact Bertram Slocum, Lawrence, Kansas, at once, as operation was for his account. Have wired Cummings to proceed to your office with prisoner.

Arthur Pleasanton.

SLOCUM lowered the telegram. There was an odd yellow glow in his eyes. He said: "Bower Springs is only about forty miles from here. This—this Cummings should be here by now."

Captain Travers took the telegram from Slocum and put it back in the drawer. He closed the drawer and seated himself in a creaking swivel chair. Then he said deliberately: "He should have been here this morning."

Slocum stared at the detective for a moment. "You don't think that Dancer got away?"

Travers evaded a direct answer. "Mr. Pleasanton considers George Cummings the best operator he's had since the war. He gives him the hard ones."

"I've paid Pleasanton twelve thousand dollars in all," Slocum said bitterly.

"That's a lot of money," Captain Travers conceded. He paused a moment. "What did Dancer do to you?"

"He killed my brother."

Travers' eyes searched Bertram Slocum's face. "Your brother was killed during Quantrell's raid on Lawrence during the war."

Slocum nodded. "He was shot down in cold blood—by Jim Dancer."

"How do you know it was Dancer who did the actual killing? Were you an eye witness?"

"No. As a matter of fact, I was living in St. Louis during the war. But my brother's daughter, my niece, saw the killing. And it was murder, cold-blooded murder. My brother was unarmed, offered no resistance. He was dragged out of the house by the heels and shot down in cold blood, right before the girl's eyes."

"But how did she know the killer's name was Dancer?" Travers persisted.

"Because Quantrell himself called him by name. I assure you, Captain Travers, my niece has ample cause to remember every detail of that horror. She was only fifteen years old at the time and the tragedy made an indelible impression on her." He frowned. "As a matter of fact, it was my niece who urged me to employ your agency to bring Dancer to justice."

"Mr. Slocum," said Captain Travers, "this happened nine years ago, during the war. I doubt if you could get a jury to convict a man today for something that was done during the war."

"They haven't forgotten in Lawrence," Slocum said angrily. "Besides—there is Dancer's record since the war."

"Just what is that record?"

"I should think you would know it better than I."

"I wonder," Travers said thoughtfully. "Yes, I know all the things Dancer's done. He's held up stagecoaches, banks, trains. He's murdered a hundred men and he's supposed to be Jesse James' lieutenant. But could you prove any of those things in a court of law?"

"Bring him to Lawrence and you won't need any proof. Jim Dancer'll never appear before a judge."

Travers grunted. "I can believe that."

There was a knock on the door and the sharp-faced operator who had engaged Slocum in verbal jousting opened the door a few inches. "George Cummings is here, Cap'n."

Captain Travers kicked back his chair and leaped to his feet. "Send him in!"

THE door was pushed open and George Cummings came into the room. He was haggard and drawn, his clothing wrinkled and foul from immersion in dirty water. He was alone and Slocum got the significance of that at once.

"Where's Jim Dancer?" he cried.

Cummings looked briefly at Slocum, then at Captain Travers, who was behind his desk. "You're Captain Travers?"

Travers nodded. "Yes. Mr. Pleasanton sent word that. . ." He jerked his thumb at Slocum. "It's all right, Mr. Slocum is the client for whom we've been working on this—this matter."

"Slocum," said Cummings and looked at Slocum. "I thought it was Theodore Slocum who was—"

"I'm his brother," Slocum snapped.

"Ted was killed by—" He scowled at the open doorway as if still expecting to see Jim Dancer materialize.

Cummings said flatly: "Jim Dancer's dead."

"Dead!" cried Slocum. "Where . . . how?"

Cummings addressed Captain Travers. "I sent the telegram from Bower Springs and I waited there until I got a reply from Mr. Pleasanton. He told me to bring Dancer here to you."

He paused and Slocum prodded savagely. "Go on, man!"

"The Wakarusa was in flood," Cummings continued. "We tried to cross on a ferry and the boat capsized. The ferryman drowned and Dancer—well, he died, too."

"What about his body?" Slocum asked.

"Joe Partridge, who drives the Holliday stage, helped me bury it."

Slocum swore. "Damn it, man. You should have brought it in. I've got to know for sure that it was really Dancer." He appealed to Captain Travers. "I've paid enough money to have positive identification."

There was a slight frown on Travers' forehead, but he nodded agreement. "Mr. Slocum's right, Cummings. You brought Dancer that far, you should have brought him the rest of the way."

Cummings reached into his pocket and brought out a wallet. He took from it a thin packet wrapped in oilskin and dropped it on Travers' desk. "My credentials," he said. "I'm turning them in."

Travers exclaimed, "You're quitting?"

"I quit this morning," Cummings said, "along about sunrise. After I sat all night on the river bank, handcuffed to a dead man."

"What?"

"Dancer made a play," Cummings said. "I threw the handcuff key into the water so he couldn't get it. Well, I won, but the stage-coach driver had to cut Dancer's hand off . . . with a pocket knife."

Even Bertram Slocum shivered.

Cummings went on tonelessly: "You can send in my resignation to Arthur Pleasanton." He reached into his pocket and brought out a pair of handcuffs. "And you, Mr. Slocum, can have these."

He turned and walked out of the office.

CHAPTER V

CHARLES LANYARD, vice-president of the Missouri, Kansas & Pacific Railroad was seated in his Kansas City office, reading the stock market quotations in the Kansas City Standard, when a clerk came into the room and handed him an embossed calling card.

"Bertram Slocum," Lanyard read. "Who is he?"

"He says he wants to see you on an important personal matter."

Lanyard grunted. "A salesman?"

"He doesn't look like one."

"They very seldom do." Lanyard shrugged. "All right, I'll give him a minute."

The clerk went out and a moment later Bertram Slocum entered the office. He shook hands with the railroad man and seated himself in a convenient armchair. Lanyard regarded him coolly.

"Mr. Lanyard," Slocum began, "I understand that you are in charge of construction on the M. K. & P."

"That's right."

Slocum nodded and rising, stepped to the wall on which hung a large map of Missouri and Kansas. A red criss-cross line stretched from St. Louis to Kansas City and westward across Kansas to the borders of Colorado. Superimposed upon three-fourths of the red line was a green one.

Slocum took a pencil from his pocket and touched the point of it to the map where the green line stopped. "Your road is now at this point, isn't it, Mr. Lanyard?" he asked.

Lanyard was watching Slocum narrowly. "What if it is?" he demanded truculently.

Slocum moved his pencil a little ahead of the green line and about a quarter inch below the continuing red line. He drew a small square on the map.

"I own a bit of land here. Not very much, as land goes out West, but still—" He smiled blandly. "Twelve thousand acres. I bought it from the government, two years ago for fifty cents an acre."

"A pity," Lanyard said coldly. "If it were a few miles further north it might become worth something."

Slocum turned and smiled at the railroad man. "That's what I came to see you about."

"I don't get you."

Slocum turned back to the map and tapped the red line with his pencil. "This point here is exactly ninety miles from the town of Potter, back here—" He indicated a dot several inches closer to Kansas City. "It will therefore be a division point on your railroad where you will build repair shops, etcetery. Am I right?"

"We figure a division as ninety miles—yes. But I still don't understand what you're driving at."

"Why, it's simply this, Mr. Lanyard," Slocum said. "My property is exactly eight miles south of this point and your division headquarters isn't going to do me any good at all."

Lanyard smiled frostily. "Quite." Then he added: "There's a little place called Bruno eight miles north of your property. Now *that's* going to be quite a town."

SLOCUM again touched his pencil to the map. He drew a slight curve from the red line, down through the penciled square that indicated his holdings, then up to the red line.

"Suppose," he said, "your road made a slight southward curve—like this—what would happen to my land then?"

"And why would we do that?"

"Because of the topography of the country. There's a river running right through my land which would give you water facilities."

"There's water at Bruno."

"Ah, but I just told you—I don't own Bruno."

"And because you own that land you think we should swing the road down? Increasing our trackage about six miles—"

"Seven. I've had it surveyed."

"Seven miles,", said Lanyard grimly. "At forty-two thousand dollars a mile."

"Two hundred and ninety-four thousand dollars," Slocum said blithely. "Not a great deal of money—to a railroad."

Lanyard got to his feet. "Goodbye, Mr. Slocum."

Slocum made no move to go. He said, almost lazily, "Are you a rich man, Mr. Lanyard?"

"What concern is that of yours?" Lanyard snapped.

"None, really," Slocum admitted. "But I've been hearing a bit of talk, something about your getting caught in that New York Central deal—"

"Get out of here!" Lanyard roared.

"Two hundred thousand it was you dropped, wasn't it?" Slocum went on.

His face purple from rage, Lanyard strode around his desk and crossed to the door. He jerked it open. "Get!"

Slocum stepped to the door, took hold of the edge and swung it shut. "Don't be a fool, Lanyard," he said coldly. "Do you think I came here with empty pockets?"

Lanyard stared at him. "What—what do you mean?"

"I have fifty thousand dollars in my pocket."

Lanyard recoiled as if struck. For a long moment he looked at Slocum, then he walked slowly back to his desk. He stood there for a moment with his back to Slocum, then slowly turned.

"You . . . you're offering me fifty thousand dollars as a . . . a . . ." He could not bring out the word, but Slocum said it.

"Bribe."

He let it sink in a moment, then he went on. "The water facilities at Bruno aren't adequate, Mr. Lanyard. This town is going to be the closest point in the entire state to the Chisholm Trail and cattle drovers are going to bring their herds to it. You're going to need unusually large shipping pens—and plenty of water that you'll get from the river. You're a far-sighted man, Mr. Lanyard . . . and you're the vice-president in charge of construction."

Lanyard suddenly drew a deep breath. He

walked to the map on the wall, studied it a moment, then turned to Slocum.

"Yes," he said, "I'm in charge of construction. And I'm also a substantial stockholder in the railroad."

"More or less," Slocum corrected, "you've pledged most of your stock to cover your losses on the New York Central deal."

"Oh, you know that, too?"

"I know everything about you, Mr. Lanyard."

"Then you also know that my brother-in-law is president of the road?"

Slocum nodded. "But your brother-in-law didn't lose any money on the New York Central."

"If he had I suppose you would have gone to him."

"N-no, I don't think so."

"Why not?"

"Well, frankly, because I believe your brother-in-law is a man of greater, shall we say, integrity?"

The insolence of that no longer affected Lanyard. He had made up his mind and he was going to play out his hand. He said: "He would have thrown you out of his office. As I almost did."

"Yes, as you almost did."

"Slocum," Lanyard said, "I admire your gall. You come in here to bribe me with a piddling fifty thousand dollars on a proposition that's going to make you one of the richest men in the West."

"That's what I thought," Slocum conceded.

"The proposition is worth millions, properly handled."

"Oh, I expect to handle it properly."

"Exactly. So, shall we consider the fifty thousand dollars merely as an—an advance?"

"Advance against what?"

"One half of your deal."

The good humor left Slocum's face and it became as cold as Lanyard's. He said thinly: "One quarter."

It was Lanyard who had the upper hand now. "You've investigated me thoroughly, Slocum. You know that I'm a man of very little integrity. And you know that my brother-in-law is president of this railroad and possesses those qualities that I lack. But he is my brother-in-law and between us we run the M.K. & P. You've got to do business with me or you don't do business. Is it one half . . . or is it—nothing?"

Slocum exhaled heavily. "It's one half."

CHAPTER VI

THERE were ceremonies when the railroad reached Lanyard, Kansas. A committee of citizens met with a group of railroad officials and following the precedent set at Promontory Point in Utah, three years before, a gold-plated spike was driven into a tie.

The M.K. & P. would build west of Lanyard, but not for awhile. There was a little matter of financing that would have to be done in St. Louis, Chicago and New York. More bond issues would have to be floated.

George Cummings, because of the letter "C," was one of the first track layers to be paid off. He walked from the railroad pay-car to the single street of the town of Lanyard and stopping there for a moment, marveled what men could do.

Two months ago, there had been only buffalo grass here. Now there was a town—a row of false-fronted buildings, a few of which had even been painted. And beyond the buildings, stretching out into the prairie, were rows and rows of white painted stakes, indicating building lots.

There was a block of wooden sidewalk, raised from the prairie soil some eight inches. Cummings strolled along this sidewalk, past the Bon Ton Hat Shop, the Eldorado Saloon, the Boston Dry Goods Store, the Lanyard Saloon & Gambling Hall, the New York Bazaar, the Trail Drivers' Saloon, the St. Louis Barber Shop, the Texas Bar, the Cattleman's De Luxe Bar & Gambling Saloon and finally to the Drover's Hotel, a two-story frame building—the biggest in the town.

Here he turned in. There was a tiny lobby, off which was a saloon that ran the length of the building. Paul Hobson, in Prince Albert coat, was behind the desk. He looked at Cummings and handed him a pen.

Cummings wrote his name on the register. Hobson swung it around and read aloud, "George Cummings." He looked up. "Late of the Pleasanton Detective Agency."

"Late of Track-Layers Gang, Number Nine," Cummings retorted.

"You quit the detective business?"

"Nine weeks ago. . . . How much for the room?"

"Two dollars."

Cummings put two silver dollars on the desk. That was as much as he had earned in a day on the railroad. But he wanted to sleep in a bed.

Hobson handed him a key. "Number Eleven."

Cummings nodded and clumped up the stairs to the second floor. There was a long hall running down the length of the building and a shorter one across the front, so that the rooms were arranged in the shape of a T. Number Eleven was the last room on the left, in the front corridor. It was about six by eight feet in size, had bare, unpainted walls and contained a cot, a porcelain wash bowl and

pitcher, a small unpainted stand on which the last two items reposed, and an ordinary unpainted kitchen chair. There was a thin mattress on the cot and a moth-eaten Civil War blanket.

Cummings locked the door on the inside, hung his coat on a nail in the wall and taking off his boots, stretched himself out upon the bed. For a moment he stared at the bare ceiling, then he closed his eyes and let the air out of his lungs.

OUT on the street a gun banged. Cummings winced a little but did not open his eyes. Another gun banged, then another. The last shot was punctuated by a loud scream that brought Cummings up to a sitting position on the bed. He had heard that sound before; it was the wild Confederate yell.

A fussilade of gunfire followed and the Confederate battle cry went up and down the street.

Someone had made a mistake.

There were fourteen Texas trail herds grazing on the plains near Lanyard; they had been awaiting the arrival of the railroad. That was all right, the railroad wanted the business. The mistake was in paying off the railroad men. They were Northerners and the cowboys were from Texas, where the carpetbaggers still controlled. You couldn't mix Northerners, Texans and whiskey.

A dozen cowboys were drinking in the Texas Bar, when a score of railroad men entered. There wasn't room for all at the bar and there was some crowding. A railroad man bumped a cowboy's elbow and the cowboy promptly threw his whiskey into the railroad man's face.

The fight that followed wrecked the interior of the Texas Bar. The railroaders drove the cowboys out upon the street, where the

Texas men mounted their horses and galloped them up and down the street. They challenged the railroad men to come out upon the street. A few accepted and were promptly driven back to shelter by a volley of gunfire.

It is hard to put guns away once they have been drawn and the Texas men now amused themselves by shooting out store and saloon windows. They had a lot of powder and lead and quite a lot of whiskey, which they replenished periodically from saloons, without paying for it.

In short, Lanyard was treed.

In his room, George Cummings abandoned the thought of sleep. He put on his boots and leaving his room, clumped down to the lobby. There were a half dozen men crouched behind the desk, whose thick planking gave protection from stray bullets.

As Cummings came down, Paul Hobson was having an altercation with a heavy-set, mustachioed man. "I've had just about enough of this nonsense, Simmons," he was snarling. "You'll get out there and stop them or you can turn in your badge."

The man called Simmons unpinned his nickeled badge and dropped it on the counter. "The marshal's job is open, Hobson," he said.

Although he had issued an ultimatum and it had been accepted, it wasn't what Hobson wanted. "You can't quit now!" he cried.

"I ain't in the mood for committin' suicide today," Simmons declared.

"He's right, Hobson," said one of the other men behind the desk. "There are fifty Texas men out there."

"If we let those crazy Texas men get the upper hand, they'll take over the town," Hobson protested.

"They've already taken it over," the other man said, "and there ain't a thing we can do about it."

DURING the discussion, there was a lull in the shooting outside and one of the men ventured out from behind the desk. He looked out upon the street through a broken window and suddenly cried out hoarsely,

"That girl. She'll get killed!"

Cummings stepped quickly to the window and saw a girl across the street. She had apparently just stepped out of a dry goods store and was moving toward a buckboard nearby. Even as Cummings looked a gun banged and a bullet kicked up dirt inches from the girl's feet.

She came to a stop and a horseman galloped up. He swung down from his horse and advanced upon the girl.

Sober, there was no greater respecter of women than the Texas man, but these cowboys had been drinking all day. Moreover they were in a fighting mood and they were in the stronghold of what was to them, the enemy. Perhaps their respect of women did not extend to Northern women.

At any rate the cowboy suddenly grabbed the girl and tried to kiss her. She struck him in the face, which merely served to enrage the cowboy and he began wrestling with her.

George Cummings jerked open the door of the hotel, stepped out upon the street and started across at a dead run. He heard the thunder of horses' hooves as he ran, but paid no heed. A bullet whistled past him.

He reached the girl and the cowboy, just as the latter was forcing his unshaven face against the girl's. He caught hold of the cowboy's left arm, jerked him away from the girl and drove his fist into the man's face. The cowboy reeled back and Cummings, stepping in, smashed him again in the f ace.

The cowboy hit the ground and his gun was knocked from his hand. Mouthing savage oaths he scrambled for the gun, got it and came up to his knees.

Cummings, moving in, was caught. The only thing he could do was hold his hands clear of his sides to indicate that he was unarmed:

"I'll kill you," screamed the cowboy.

"I haven't got a gun," Cummings said quickly.

It would have made no difference to the enraged cowboy, except that another Texas man spurred his horse in between Cummings and the cowboy on the ground.

"Hold it, Ben!" the new arrival cried. "You can't shoot an unarmed man."

Ben got to his feet, shook his head and stepping around the man on the horse, faced Cummings. "Get yourself a gun," he snarled. "Get yourself a gun and come back."

"We can settle it without guns," Cummings said calmly.

"Nothin' but guns'll finish this," the cowboy cried. "I'll give you ten minutes to get one or by God, I'll come and pistol-whip you."

BY THIS time a dozen cowboys were surrounding the group on the ground. There was hostility on every face. One of the cowboys expressed the general sentiment. "You heard what he said. Get yourself a gun or start runnin'."

Cummings turned away. For a moment he looked into the wide eyes of the girl he had rescued from the drunken cowboy, then he walked past her, across the street to the hotel.

Inside, Paul Hobson caught his arm. "That's Bert Slocum's niece you saved, Cummings!"

"Yeah, and that was Ben Slattery you hit," exclaimed Simmons, the forner marshal. "He's lightning with a gun—killed a man day before yesterday."

Hobson looked narrowly at Cummings. "There's a horse behind the hotel."

"Why would I want a horse?"

Grudging admiration came to Hobson's eyes. "You've got guts, Cummings, but you can't go up against a gunfighter."

"It doesn't seem as if I've got much choice in the matter." Cummings looked at the marshal. "You've got a Navy gun. Wonder if I could borrow it."

"You're going to face Slattery?"

Cummings held out his hand and the former marshal gave him his gun. Cummings hefted it to get the feel of it, spun the cylinder and examined the caps on the nipples. Then he took off his coat and dropping it on the hotel desk, stuck the Navy gun in the waistband of his trousers.

He stepped to the window and looked across the street. More than a score of cowboys were assembled. Ben Slattery was the only one afoot.

Cummings opened the door and stepped out upon the wooden sidewalk. A man across the street yelled: "There he is!"

The distance between Cummings and the cowboys was almost two hundred feet, too far for accurate shooting. Cummings stepped down from the sidewalk into the dust of the street. He started across, walking deliberately, but at a fast pace. His eyes never left the face of Ben Slattery. The cowboy was suddenly alone, although he had not moved. It was the mounted men who had backed off to give Ben all the room he needed.

The distance between the two men narrowed to less than a hundred feet, but it was Cummings alone who walked. Slattery remained by the hitchrail in front of the building that housed the Lanyard Land Company.

Seventy-five feet.

"All right, Slattery," Cummings called. "Make your play."

But Slattery remained as if frozen to the ground. His arms were slightly crooked and his right hand was within two inches of the gun in his holster, whereas Cummings' were hanging loosely at his sides.

Fifty feet and Cummings could see that Slattery's mouth was working nervously. He wasn't sure, but he thought that Slattery's face had broken out in perspiration.

"Wait a minute!" Slattery suddenly cried. "Wait a —"

And then he went for his gun.

WITHOUT breaking his stride, Cummings whipped out the borrowed Navy gun. He thrust it out before him, thumbed back the hammer and pulled the trigger. The motions were continuous, performed with incredible speed and accuracy; the work of a man who knew what he was doing and had absolute confidence in himself.

Both guns roared, Slattery's as well as Cummings', but it was the latter's which went off first. The bullet struck Slattery dead center in the forehead, knocked him off balance, so that his own gun merely fired into the sky.

Slattery was hurled backward to the ground. Before he touched, Cummings was pointing his gun at the mounted cowboys.

"Was it a fair fight?"

The cowboys were stunned by the unexpected defeat of their champion. They exchanged bewildered glances, looked at the unwavering gun in Cummings' hand.

There was a man in the front of the crowd, the same one who had come between Slattery and Cummings before. He saw the gun muzzle pointed at him. He said quickly: "It was a fair fight," and turning his horse, galloped it off.

A cowboy followed, then another and then the entire lot of them. They rode down the street and out of Lanyard.

Before they had gone very far, Bertram Slocum sprang out of the door of his office. He strode toward Cummings, giving only a brief glance at the dead cowboy.

"I saw it from the window," he said. Then he looked again at Cummings' face and exclaimed. "Cummings! The Pleasanton detective!"

"Former detective," Cummings corrected.

Then he stepped to one side to watch Hobson and the men from the hotel come up. In their van was Simmons. Cummings held out the Navy Colt, butt first.

"Here's your gun, Simmons," he said. "It shoots straight."

"If there's a good man behind it," Simmons replied in a tone of respect.

Cummings walked past him, heading for the hotel. Paul Hobson halted, wheeled. "Cummings, wait a minute, we want to talk to you."

"Later," Cummings called back over his shoulder. "There's some sleeping I've got to finish, first."

CHAPTER VII

IT WAS a few minutes after seven when Cummings came down from his room. It was getting dark outside and in the hotel lobby a pimply-faced youth of eighteen or nineteen was lighting lamps. New glass had been put into the front windows.

The saloon adjoining the lobby was doing a rushing business. The noise from it had awakened Cummings in his room overhead.

Cummings opened the door and stepped out upon the wooden sidewalk. Sounds of revelry came from the saloons, but otherwise Lanyard seemed reasonably peaceful. Nobody was galloping horses up and down the street and there was no shooting.

A sign next door to the hotel caught Cummings' eye: *China Cafe.*

He walked over to the building and peered through the window. The interior seemed clean, although only sparsely patronized for what should have been the dinner hour.

Cummings entered and sat down at a table. A pig-tailed Chinese came padding up. "Got nice beefsteak," he said smiling.

Cummings nodded. "All right."

A man got up from an adjoining table and crossing, seated himself opposite Cummings. It was Dave Oldham, the lean man who had been a stagecoach passenger that day when Cummings had been found, handcuffed to a dead man.

"That was quite a stunt you pulled this afternoon," Oldham said. He shook his head. "Violence seems to follow you around."

"I imagine you've seen your share of it," Cummings retorted.

Oldham shrugged. "I'll never have a grey beard." He pursed up his lips. "They say you quit the detective business, Cummings."

"Who're 'they'?"

"Everybody in town. Hobson. Slocum."

"This Slocum," Cummings said. "What does he do in this town?"

"He's manager of the Lanyard Land Company which owns the townsite. The girl, for whom you killed Ben Slattery . . . she's Slocum's niece. Evelyn Slocum."

Oldham, looking into Cummings' eyes at that moment, saw that they were oddly

masked. He dropped his own eyes to the table.

"This is a new town," he went on. "Nobody knows much about anybody, but there's talk about Slocum being more than just the manager of the land company."

Then he stopped and pushed back his chair. "I'm late."

He got to his feet. "Stop in at the Eldorado if you feel like it." He left the cafe.

Cummings stared unseeingly at the far wall. Evelyn Slocum, the girl who had paid the Pleasanton Detective Agency twenty thousand dollars to get Jim Dancer. And because of her, this afternoon, Cummings had killed a man.

THE Oriental brought the dinner and Cummings ate, but scarcely tasted the food. He paid for it and leaving the restaurant, stood outside and looked across the street at the narrow building that housed the Lanyard Land Company.

Then, after awhile, he drew a deep breath and walked up the street to the Eldorado Saloon & Gambling Hall. It was one of the biggest places in the block and when Cummings pushed open the swinging doors he saw that it was doing a thriving business.

A bar almost fifty feet long ran down one side of the room. Six bartenders were working behind it. The rest of the room was given over to a few tables and gambling layouts.

Cummings pushed his way through until he came upon Dave Oldham dealing faro. The gambler caught his eye and nodded slightly. Then he inclined his head to the right and Cummings, looking in that direction, saw another old acquaintance: Florence Peel, the girl with the green eyes who had also been on the stage that memorable day.

Her blonde hair was combed high upon her head and in striking contrast to the low-cut green velvet evening gown she was wearing. She was weaving her way in and out among the tables and Cummings watched her for a moment as she came closer.

Then her eyes suddenly caught his and she stopped. She recognized him but her face remained inscrutable.

A cowboy, beside whose table she had stopped, reached out drunkenly to grab her, but she brushed away his hand without even looking and came forward.

"Mr. Cummings," she said.

"Hello."

She smiled impersonally and said under her breath, "My office is in the rear." Then smiling again, she walked past him, talking to a man here, another there.

Cummings watched a faro game for a moment, then headed aimlessly toward the rear of the room. An anaemic-looking man with a cigarette in his mouth was playing a tinny piano beside a door and gave Cummings a shrewd look as he opened the door and entered a small room, furnished with a roll-top desk, a couple of chairs and a small steel safe.

Cummings pulled up one of the chairs and started to seat himself when the door opened and Florence Peel came in. He got to his feet again.

"It's all right, sit down," she said. She crossed the room to the desk and sat down in the swivel chair.

"You own the Eldorado?" Cummings asked in surprise.

She nodded briefly and leaning back in the chair, studied Cummings thoughtfully. A little frown creased his forehead, but he remained silent, waiting for her to speak.

Then she said suddenly: "You almost gave yourself away this afternoon."

"What?"

"The fight with Ben Slattery. You were too good."

He regarded her steadily. "How can a man be too good in a gun fight? I had to kill him or be killed."

"Detectives aren't gun fighters. You beat Ben Slattery to the draw."

HE SEATED himself and drew a slow breath. "I don't get you."

"I think you do."

He shook his head. "I don't."

"Would you understand if I called you by your real name . . . Jim Dancer?"

Without hesitation, he exclaimed softly, "Jim Dancer's dead!"

"Is he? When did he die?"

"That time we met down by the Wakarusa. When you told them to cut his hand from mine." And then he looked into her green eyes. "When did you know?"

"Then. Your right hand was handcuffed to his left."

"The others didn't notice that."

"I think Dave Oldham did, although he's never mentioned it. But then Dave's one of us."

"Us?"

"Us," she repeated clearly.

He shook his head slowly. "Oldham's a gambler."

"And so am I," she said quietly. "In a little while you can go out there and watch me deal faro, or poker—or three-card monte."

"And tomorrow morning," he added, "you can walk down the street and people will talk to you. They don't talk to . . . Jim Dancer."

"Jim Dancer!" she exclaimed. "Who's

Jim Dancer?"

"A man who rode with Quantrell."

"And who's been riding ever since. Why, Jim Dancer?"

"Because they wouldn't let us come in. Yes, I know all Confederate soldiers were given amnesty. Some of the boys who rode with Quantrell tried to surrender in '65. They were murdered." He shrugged. "So some of us are still riding."

She looked at him narrowly. "Are you here in Lanyard alone?"

He jerked up his head. "I haven't ridden with anyone since the war. No matter what they say."

There was a knock on the door. Florence Peel looked at Dancer, then called: "Yes?"

The door opened and Dave Oldham slipped into the room. He closed the door before he spoke. Then he addressed Jim Dancer. "Paul Hobson and Bert Slocum want to see you."

"What about?" Florence Peel asked sharply.

"They didn't say."

Dancer got heavily to his feet. "All right."

Dave Oldham left the room as cautiously as he had entered and Dancer started to follow, but Florence called to him. "Mr. Cummings!"

Dancer turned.

Florence Peel said: "That's all I wanted to say—Mr. Cummings. Watch yourself with Hobson; he's tricky."

DANCER nodded and left the room. Out in the gambling hall he discovered Slocum and Hobson seated alone at a table. Hobson had a glass of milk before him. He saw Dancer approaching and signalled.

Dancer pulled out a chair and sat down.

"We've got a proposition to make you," Slocum said bluntly. "But first I want to ask you a few questions."

"Yes?"

"Do you have any objections to my telegraphing the Pleasanton Agency?"

Dancer looked carefully at Slocum. "Why?"

"I want to make sure that you really quit the agency."

"You were there at the time."

"I know, but how do I know you didn't retract later? If you're here in Lanyard on detective business there'll be no proposition."

"Why don't you tell me what the proposition is?"

Hobson nodded to Slocum. "Why not?"

Slocum's face showed annoyance, but he shrugged. "We want you to be the marshal of Lanyard."

A little shiver ran through Dancer. In his wildest dreams he had never thought of himself as a law officer. He looked from Slocum to Hobson, then back to Slocum.

"You're offering me the job of marshal of Lanyard?"

"Yes," said Slocum. "There's no actual city government in Lanyard, but a number of the merchants have chipped in to pay the marshal's salary. However, we're having a city election the day after tomorrow. Simmons' name has been down for marshal but we're going to take it off. After what you did today you won't have any trouble being elected."

Dancer began to shake his head and Hobson exclaimed: "So you are still with Pleasanton?"

"I'm not. It isn't that."

"We haven't told you what this job will pay."

"I imagine it'll be as much as the M.K. & P. paid me these past nine weeks."

"You've been working on the railroad?"

"Laying track."

Slocum snorted. "A common laborer, at two dollars a day! We were going to offer you three hundred a month . . ."

"Which is a lot of money," Hobson offered.

"And three dollars for every arrest you make," Slocum added angrily. "If you're the kind of marshal I think you are, you can make five hundred a month. You can't refuse that kind of money."

Dancer leaned back in his chair and studied the two men for a moment. Then he said slowly: "You can get a lot of good men for five hundred dollars a month."

"Wild Bill Hickok asked for the job," said Slocum. "He's a killer, but only when the breaks are in his favor. John Wesley Hardin, a seventeen-year-old boy backed him down in Abilene. Nobody would have blamed you for backing down this afternoon. But you didn't." Slocum paused. "Besides, the whole West knows by now that you're the man who got Jim Dancer."

Hobson said, "That alone will make those Texas men behave in Lanyard."

Dancer pushed back his chair and got to his feet. "I figured I'd had enough of manhunting when I turned in my badge to Pleasanton. I don't intend to start being a killer, not for pay."

He walked away from the table and left the place. Outside, he walked to the Drovers Hotel and climbed up to his room. He locked the door on the inside and, undressing, went to bed.

But it was hours before he went to sleep. Nor was it the noise from the saloon on the first floor that kept him awake.

CHAPTER VIII

IT WAS the middle of the morning when Dancer came down from his room. The youthful clerk was in attendance behind the desk and he was spared having to talk to Paul Hobson. Outside he walked to the China Cafe and taking a stool at the counter, ordered his breakfast.

He was starting on his eggs when Dave Oldham entered and sat down beside him.

"Up rather early, aren't you?" Dancer asked, to make conversation.

"I don't sleep well," Oldham replied. He gave his order to the waiter, then said: "There's talk that Slocum offered you the marshal's job."

"I refused it."

Oldham was silent awhile, then asked: "Why?"

Dancer knew that Oldham was pressing the matter for reasons other than idle curiosity, so he said, "It's not the kind of work I'd like."

"Because your sympathies are with—" Oldham smiled thinly, "—the underdog?"

Dancer hesitated. "Perhaps."

Oldham nodded thoughtfully. "They will probably hire a man like Wild Bill Hickok or Johnny Tancred, who shoots first and asks afterwards if the man was guilty."

"In other words, you think I ought to take the job."

"I think it'd be a good job for the man who got Jim Dancer."

Dancer finished his eggs and mopped up the remaining yolk with a piece of bread. When he had eaten it, he said: "You've talked to Florence Peel?"

"No," Oldham said quickly. "But I served under Colonel Plumb in Clay and Jackson Counties. Man for man, we got licked by the guerrillas every time. It took me a long time to figure it out. Our men were good soldiers.

They were willing to die if they had to, but they wanted to go home again."

"They had homes to go to."

"I saw you fight that Texas man yesterday. He knew he was fast and he'd won some fights. He thought he had the edge. He didn't expect to be killed . . . and when he finally figured that out, he went to pieces. Quantrell went into a fight to kill and be killed. We to kill or be killed. That one little word makes all the difference in the world. We cared, you didn't."

"You may be right," Dancer said slowly, "but sometimes a man gets tired of killing. And there comes a time when he can't run any more."

"Then you've got to compromise," Oldham said. "Florence Peel's father worked the river boats. He took her along with him because a man with a child is above suspicion. Well, his luck ran out when Florence was twelve. She had every reason in the world to hate cards and what goes with them, but she found out after awhile that no matter how bad a thing is, there's something worse. She was a drudge, worked in the homes of the rich. And always there was a man around because she was poor and a poor girl can't fight a rich man. So at last Florence knew that she had to be rich and she turned back to the one thing she hated more than anything else."

HE STOPPED and began eating. Dancer, who had finished his own breakfast, watched him for awhile. Then he said, "And you, Oldham?"

Oldham shrugged. "I'm a gambler because I was no damn good as a lawyer."

"You know that I'm Jim Dancer?"

"Dancer's dead," said Oldham. "I helped bury him."

"All right, Oldham," Dancer said.

"This is Lanyard, Kansas," Oldham went on. "It's a new town and it's raw, just like all the country west of the Missouri. It's a strong man's country and the weak are going to give up or die. But in a few years the country'll be civilized and the ones who've lasted from the beginning, the strong ones, are going to own it . . . You're as strong as any of them, Cummings."

"Fighting's all I know," Dancer said. "Fighting and losing. We fought in Missouri and lost and then after it was over I went down to Mexico with Shelby and fought with Maximilian. And after that I went with the French to France and we fought the Prussians and lost again. I've been in a few of these trail towns and I've seen some pretty good marshals; they never stood a chance to win. Sure, I got Ben Slattery yesterday, but what about today and tomorrow when a hundred Texas men come back to get revenge for Slattery? I can't fight them all."

"If someone doesn't," Oldham said, "you might as well set fire to Lanyard, because this is going to be the roughest, toughest trail town of them all. It's the closest to Texas and all the herds and all the trail drivers and what comes with them will come here."

Dancer was silent for a moment. Then he shook his head slowly. "This man, Slocum—does he own the town?"

"Why, yes. He pretends to be the local manager for the Lanyard Land Company, but he's the land company. He owns the townsite and all the country round about. He's selling it off piece by piece and he isn't taking all his pay in cash. He's got an interest in almost everything in town, the dry goods store, the barber shop, the bank—most of the saloons."

"The Eldorado?"

"No, Florence had enough money to buy her site outright."

"Where does Hobson come in?"

"Slocum's front man. He's going to be the mayor tomorrow. There's talk that Slocum and Hobson were in business together during the war. Selling rotten beef and weevily flour to the Union Army."

Dancer said carefully: "What sort of a woman is Slocum's niece?"

There was just the shade of a pause before Oldham replied. "I don't know her and as far's I know, nobody does." He stopped, then, looking out of the window.

Dancer's eyes followed and he saw Evelyn Slocum walking past on the opposite side of the street.

He put a silver dollar on the counter and rising, said to Oldham, "If I don't see you again—so long."

"You're leaving?" Oldham asked.

"I usually do," Dancer replied and left the restaurant.

OUTSIDE, he saw Evelyn Slocum turning into a shop. He walked down the wooden sidewalk until he was directly across from the shop and he could read the sign on it: *Carrie Brown, Milliner.*

Beyond a few doors on Dancer's side of the street was a livery stable. He walked down to it and found the liveryman shoeing a black gelding and not enjoying the task, for the horse had spirit.

Dancer watched for awhile until the man finished nailing down the shoe. Then he looked up irascibly, but his annoyance disappeared quickly.

"'Morning, Mr. Cummings," he said.

Dancer nodded. "Good horse. Yours?"

"Until I can find someone to take him off my hands."

"He can run a bit, I imagine?"

"He can run like hell," snorted the liveryman, "but so can every goddam Texas pony and the people in town don't want to rent a horse that don't like to be rid."

"What were you figuring to ask for him?"

The liveryman wiped his mouth with the back of his hand. "Well, Mr. Cummings, if there's one thing around this barn I got too much of, it's horses. And one thing I ain't got much of, it's money. So what do you figure you'd want to pay for a horse that ain't much good for nothin' but runnin' and buckin'."

Dancer thought a moment. "He's worth more, but I can pay only fifty."

The liveryman shook his head. "I couldn't accept fifty dollars—not unless you took this-here saddle and bridle along with him, which ain't much good, anyway."

He pointed to a saddle and bridle that hung over a stall.

"The saddle alone's worth fifty," Dancer snapped.

"To who? These fool cowboys sell them for ten dollars when they're drunk and want to get more drunk. The demand sets the price, Mr. Cummings and out here there are more cows and horses and saddles than there are prairie dogs on the prairie. I figure I ought to board the horse for you a month for that price."

"Well," Dancer said, "I want you to keep him here a little while at least." He took out a roll of greenbacks and counted out fifty dollars and then he saw Evelyn Slocum come out of the shop across the street and hurriedly left the livery stable.

On the sidewalk, however, he showed no haste. He crossed the street leisurely and was setting foot on the board sidewalk just as the girl came along.

She started to pass him, then suddenly

stopped. "Mr. Cummings, isn't it?" she asked.

"Why, yes."

Her color was rather high. She was embarrassed—but that was all. "I—I didn't thank you yesterday," she said, "for what you did."

"It's all right, Miss Slocum," Dancer said stiffly.

"Oh, but it isn't. You were forced into that terrible—" She shuddered and could not finish the sentence, so shifted to another. "What I meant to say was, well, my uncle suggested I ask you to dinner." And then she suddenly threw up her chin and attempted a wan smile. "Tonight?"

"Why, thank you, ma'am," Dancer said slowly, "but I'm afraid I can't make it. You see, I'm leaving town in an hour."

"Oh!" She squinted a little as if in pain. "I'm sorry. I—I mean, I didn't know. At any rate, I want to thank you." And with that she nodded and walked past him.

DANCER remained standing a moment where he was, then began walking back toward the hotel, clumping heavily along the wooden planks. His eyes were straight ahead, so that he didn't see Florence Peel, who had just dismounted from a horse in front of the Eldorado. She spoke to him and he took another step before the words penetrated his brain and he wheeled.

"I'm sorry," he apologized.

"Day-dreaming, Mr. Cummings?" Florence Peel asked calmly. She was wearing a green riding habit and carried a quirt.

He grimaced wryly. "I was just thinking about the horse I bought. The liveryman didn't recommend him very strongly."

Florence Peel's eyes were looking past him, down the street. "A filly, Mr. Cummings?"

He turned and followed her eyes. Evelyn Slocum was just disappearing into another store. He said: "No, I haven't found fillies good for the kind of traveling I do."

Her green eyes regarded, him inscrutably. "You're riding on?"

"Yes."

She nodded and slapped her quirt into her gloved left hand. "I suppose there are still some hills you haven't crossed?"

"No," he admitted, "there aren't. At least, the other side always looks the same. But what can I do in Lanyard?"

Dave Oldham was crossing the street from the China Cafe. Florence Peel looked at him broodingly and said to Dancer: "I don't know, Mr. Cummings."

Oldham came up and stopped. "Have a good ride?"

"Yes," she said. "Mr. Cummings and I were just discussing work. Have you heard of any jobs that are open in Lanyard?"

Oldham looked closely into Dancer's eyes. "No," he said, "I don't know of a thing."

Florence pointed across the street with her quirt. "Maybe Mr. Slocum knows of something? He's got his fingers in a lot of pies around town. Why don't you go over and talk to him, Mr. Cummings?"

Dancer said: "Perhaps I will."

HE SMILED bleakly at Oldham, nodded to Florence Peel and started across the street. There was a heavyset man with a black spade beard in the office with Slocum, but the latter saw Dancer through the window and was on his feet when he came in.

"Ah, Cummings," he greeted Dancer. "Shake hands with Carter Bullock." He smiled. "Mr. Bullock's president of the bank."

The banker shook hands with Dancer.

"How are you, Mr. Cummings? There's been quite a bit of talk about what you did yesterday. Mr. Slocum was just telling me that he suggested your running for the office of marshal, but that you couldn't accept."

"I've changed my mind," Dancer said.

Slocum blinked quickly. "Darn it, I told Paul not to be in such a hurry." He pulled out his watch, a massive gold stem-winder. "The stage has gone by now. It's carrying a letter to Johnny Tancred."

Dancer suddenly knew disappointment. "That's all right, Mr. Slocum, I should have spoken sooner."

"No," Slocum exclaimed. "I'll send another letter telling Tancred not to come. He was a last resort. The job's yours, Cummings."

Bullock coughed gently. "By all means, Mr. Cummings; you're the sort of man this town needs. A—uh--firm hand, you know . . ."

Slocum reached for his hat that was lying on a chair nearby. "I'd better run over to the printer's; he was going to start on the ballots. I want your name on it." He smiled thinly. "Better if it's legal, you know."

"Yes, yes," agreed Bullock. "It ought to be legal."

That afternoon the Texas men hurrahed the town, but Dancer remained inside the hotel, despite a pointed remark or two from Paul Hobson.

"You could take over today, Cummings," Hobson suggested at one point, after a window of the hotel had been smashed by a stray bullet.

Dancer shook his head. "Mr. Slocum likes things legal."

He went to bed early that night, but sleep was almost impossible. Every ten or fifteen minutes a drunken cowboy came out upon the street and emptied his gun at the moon.

And generally he let go a few rebel yells to accompany his bullets.

CHAPTER IX

THE next day the voters of Lanyard went to the polls. This was an amazingly simple matter. A large wooden box with a slot in the top was set up on the desk of the Drovers Hotel. It was guarded by Paul Hobson, a clerk from Bullock's bank, and a man named Meeker, who dealt faro in Hobson's gambling hall. Hobson himself handed out the ballots to whatever citizens were in the mood for coming into the hotel and voting. It was Hobson, too, who decided who was a qualified voter, since the oldest resident in point of time was Hobson himself and he had been in Lanyard just a few days over sixty.

When Dancer came down from his room, Hobson extended a ballot to him. "For voting," he said.

"But I've only been in town two days."

"What of it? You're a resident of Lanyard, aren't you? Not many people have been here a great deal longer."

Dancer examined the ballot. Paul Hobson was down for Mayor, Chandler Leach, Justice of the Peace, Kenneth Vedder, Prosecuting Attorney and George Cummings, City Marshal. There were three other names on the ballot: Bertram Slocum, Martin Bullock and Jason Walcott, who were running for City Council. No space was provided on the ballot for writing in candidates. You either voted for the people on the ballot or you didn't vote.

Dancer borrowed a pencil from Hobson and put an X in front of all the names, including his own. Then he folded the ballot and deposited it in the box.

Hobson nodded in satisfaction. "All right, you're marshal of Lanyard."

"Before the ballots are counted?"

"A mere formality." Hobson reached under the counter and brought out a nickeled badge. "Put this on and go down to Keller's store and pick yourself out some guns—whatever you think you'll need."

"A couple of things I have to know," Dancer said. "If I arrest someone, what do I do with them?"

"Why, you throw them in jail."

"There's a jail?"

"Of course there's a jail," exclaimed Hobson. "At the end of the street on this side, the two-story log building."

Dancer nodded. "And after I throw them in jail?"

"Judge Leach and Prosecutor Vedder will try the prisoners every morning in the courtroom over the jail."

"What about a man to guard the prisoners, or am I supposed to do that?"

"I don't see why you can't hire a man for about fifty dollars a month."

"I pay him myself?"

"I guess you'll have to, since there's no provision for such a job. The same goes for a deputy marshal, if you feel you need one. You can hire him, but you'll have to pay his salary yourself." Hobson suddenly smiled wolfishly. "A good man would earn his pay from the fees."

"He probably could," Dancer said, "but I think I'll try the job alone until I see how it goes." He started to turn away, then stopped. "Suppose I step on the wrong toes?"

"What do you mean?"

"I mean, can I be fired?"

"Who's going to fire you? You're elected by the voters." Hobson looked narrowly at Dancer, then added, "Of course, you're re-sponsible to the city council, which includes all the names on this ballot."

"Including myself?"

"You're a member of the city government, so you'll have a vote." Hobson pursed his lips. "There's just one thing you want to keep in mind: it's the business men of Lanyard who pay your salary."

"And a very good salary it is," Dancer said, and left the hotel.

OUTSIDE, he walked to the gun shop of Keller, a few doors up the street. Keller greeted him by name as he entered the store.

"Good morning, Mr. Cummings."

"Good morning. Mr. Hobson suggested I stop in and pick out some guns.

"Certainly, Mr. Cummings. Here's a very fine .44 .. ."

"Have you got a second-hand Navy gun?"

"I've got a dozen of them, but surely you'd rather have something new."

"I wouldn't. No better gun was ever made than the Navy Colt and I'd prefer a gun that's been used."

The gunsmith took a couple of guns out of his showcase. Dancer picked up a .36 Navy Colt, tried the action and spun the cylinder. He hefted it for the grip, twirled it once or twice and examined the nipples to see if they showed any signs of wear.

"That gun's been taken care of," Keller said, as he watched Dancer handle the gun. "This other one would make a mighty fine mate for it."

"One's all I'll need," Dancer replied. "Although I think I'd like to have a good shotgun."

"A shotgun, or a rifle?"

"A shotgun." Dancer pointed to a fowling piece that was hung on the wall. "What sort of a shotgun is that?"

Keller got it down. "It's an English gun, Mr. Cummings. Double-barreled and uses a brass shell." He broke the weapon and handed it to Dancer.

The latter examined it closely. It was a beautiful weapon of fine tempered steel and a carved walnut stock. Keller brought out a boxful of brass shells and Dancer tried a couple in the gun. They slipped in smoothly and when he broke the gun again, after closing it, the shells were thrown out.

"That's all right," Dancer said in satisfaction. "I'll take this and the first Navy gun."

He bought a supply of shotgun shells, a couple of hundred caps for the Navy gun and enough paper cartridges to go with them. He completed his purchases by buying a worn holster and broad belt to hold it.

He wore the holster and gun and carried the shotgun under his arm when he left the shop.

A FEW minutes later he stopped before the town jail. It was a log building, well constructed, of two stories. A staircase on the outside led up to the second floor.

The door on the lower floor was unlocked. Entering, Dancer found a room some eight by twelve feet, which contained a wooden table and three or four chairs. A barred door, standing open, led into another room twelve by twenty feet—the jail. A single iron-barred window lighted up the interior.

He found a couple of large keys in a drawer of the table in the marshal's quarters and put them in his pocket. Leaving the building he climbed the outside stairs and found the door of the second floor also unlocked. He opened it and looked into the courtroom, which was merely a single room covering the entire second floor. A chair and table at one end comprised the furniture.

He closed the door and started down the stairs. A whiskered man, riding a mangy horse, was passing the building. He went twenty or thirty feet, then turned his horse and rode back, reaching the foot of the stairs just as Dancer came down to the street level. He peered into Dancer's face.

"I know you," he said suddenly.

"You'll know me a lot better if you don't behave yourself in this town," Dancer retorted.

"I ain't makin' no trouble," the man on the horse said in a whining voice. "But I do know you from somewheres." He scratched his whiskers. "I can't just remember where."

"When you remember come and tell me," Dancer said sarcastically. "You'll find me right here in the jail."

He walked away from the man and entered the marshal's office where he deposited his shotgun on the table. And then he looked at the table for a long moment and exhaled heavily.

The man out on the street had known him, all right. And Dancer knew the man. His name was Yancey and because of him Dancer had murdered a man in cold blood . . . Evelyn Slocum's father.

It was nine years since Dancer had seen Yancey, for the guerrilla had deserted during the black days following the Lawrence Massacre. General Ewing had issued his infamous Order No. 11 and his troops, under Colonel Plumb, had burned every home in three and a half Missouri counties; they had killed every head of livestock in that territory and destroyed the crops in the fields so that no guerrillas could exist.

The scorched earth policy had scattered Quantrell's guerrillas; many had deserted and the rest had retreated to Texas where they remained inactive for the rest of the war.

Dancer went to the door, opened it and stepped out upon the street. Yancey was gone, refreshing himself in some saloon, no doubt.

CHAPTER X

DANCER walked down the street and entering the China Cafe, had a breakfast that he scarcely tasted. Leaving the restaurant he stood outside a moment and watched a half dozen Texas cowboys ride up to the Drovers Hotel and, tying their horses to the hitch-rail, go in.

The time of day apparently meant nothing to the wild Texas men; they could drink as well at ten in the morning as ten at night. Then Dancer remembered that the Drovers Hotel, today was the polling place.

He went quickly toward the hotel and even before he entered heard blustering voices. He pushed open the door and stepped into the lobby.

Paul Hobson spied him instantly. "Here, Marshal!" he called. "Get rid of these men."

The Texas men faced Dancer. "Look— he's got a tin badge," one of them jeered.

"Get out!" Dancer snapped.

"Who's going to make us?" a second Texas man challenged.

"I am," Dancer said calmly.

The Texas men exchanged glances; they apparently knew that this was the man who had killed Ben Slattery two days ago and they were a little worried, but they had evidently discussed this subject before riding into Lanyard and had probably come on a dare.

Their bluff had now been called and it was up to the Texas men to make the next move.

Only Dancer didn't wait. He took a quick step forward, half turned so that his left side was toward the closest Texas man, then with his right hand whipped out his newly purchased Navy Colt and laid it along the side of the nearest man's head. The man fell like a log but before his body hit the floor, Dancer had leaped back and was covering the others.

"Reach!" he said.

The Texas men were caught flat-footed. They cursed wildly, but as Dancer's eyes narrowed, they began raising their hands.

Dancer signaled to Hobson. "Get their guns."

Hobson and one of the poll workers came out from behind the counter and collected the weapons of the Texas men. Then Dancer holstered his own gun and stepped to one side.

He pointed to the unconscious man on the floor. "Pick him up."

The Texas men shuffled about for a moment, then two of them picked up the buffaloed man, one by the shoulders, the other by the legs.

"Outside," Dancer ordered.

He herded the group out to the street where they waited for further directions. Dancer nodded up the street in the direction of the jail.

Half the population of Lanyard came to doors and windows as the little procession passed and a half dozen men joined in, among them Dave Oldham.

"Well, how's the job?" the gambler asked.

"Six head, at three dollars each," replied Dancer grimly. "Not bad."

IN THE jail, Dancer herded the prisoners into the back room and locked the door on them. As he left, curses followed him. Dancer and

Oldham walked silently back to the Eldorado. At the door of the gambling hall, Oldham stopped.

"What made you change your mind?"

Dancer had had ample time to figure out an answer to that; he'd been thinking about it since the day before. "I guess you convinced me that this is my job, Dave."

Oldham looked at him in sudden embarrassment. "A man does the job he's cut out for."

"And you think I'm cut out to be a law man?"

"You've just proved it, haven't you? Simmons wouldn't have tackled those six men—not if he knew that they'd come primed for him."

Up the street, Yancey, the former guerrilla, came out of the China Cafe. He saw Dancer and came over.

"Saw you leadin' those boys to the calaboose," he said. "Nice work." He cocked his head to one side. "Was it Cheyenne we met, Marshal?"

"No," Dancer replied shortly. "I've never been in Cheyenne."

"I have," Oldham said calmly.

Yancey sized up the gambler. "Yeah, I seen you. Dealin' faro in French Jack's, wasn't you?"

". . . The time you got run out of town," Oldham finished.

Yancey scowled at Oldham and trotted off at a shuffling gait.

"Dirty bushwhacker," Oldham muttered.

"He thinks he knows me," Dancer said.

"Does he?"

"Yes. He can't remember from where." He paused a moment, then added: "It'll come to him."

"Run him out of town," Oldham suggested. "It'd be good work, too, for he's a sneak thief and cutthroat."

"He'd still remember."

"Oh, it's like that."

"He was at Lawrence."

Oldham whistled softly.

Either the voters of Lanyard had all voted by noon or Paul Hobson judged that enough votes had been cast to make it legal, for he announced that the polls were closed and that all the candidates had been elected.

An hour later Dancer got his first taste of what it meant to be a politician.

Arch Kerigan rode into town from his camp five miles out on the prairie. He sought out Paul Hobson, the newly-elected mayor of Lanyard, and talked to him for ten minutes. Then the two men went to look for George Cummings, the marshal. They found him standing on the walk outside the barber shop.

"Cummings, this is Walter Kerigan who's got a herd of six thousand Longhorns south of town."

"We've met before," Dancer said quietly.

Kerigan exclaimed. "Of course, you're the Pleasanton man who killed Jim Dancer."

"That's right," Hobson said. "You were on the stage-coach with me that day." He nodded. "Cummings, those men you arrested this morning work for Kerigan."

"That's too bad."

The fat cattleman grunted. "I want you to turn 'em loose."

Dancer looked at Hobson. "That's not within my province, is it?"

"It's all right. The boys didn't really mean any harm."

"They meant to kill me."

"Oh, say," expostulated Kerigan. "That's pretty strong. They came to town to have a little fun, that's all. You're making too much of this business."

"You've got a judge," Dancer said to Hobson. "If he says turn loose the prisoners, I'll turn them loose."

The mayor of Lanyard made an impatient gesture. "That won't be necessary, Cummings. I've vouched for Mr. Kerigan and it's all right to let his boys out."

Dancer said deliberately: "You told me the procedure was to deliver the prisoners to Judge Leach in the courtroom."

"Ordinarily, yes, but not this time."

"Oh, there are exceptions to the rule?"

Kerigan blustered. "Looks like your marshal doesn't know who's boss around here, Hobson."

Hobson flushed. "This is Cummings' first day on the job, Walter. You'll have to excuse him."

"I'll excuse him as soon as he lets my boys out of his calaboose."

"That'll be when the Judge says to let them out."

"Now look, Cummings," Hobson said ominously, "let's not have trouble right at the start."

"All right, let's not," Dancer replied. "So just get Judge Leach to tell me to let the prisoners go."

Angrily, Hobson turned away and strode to a narrow building between two saloons on which was a sign: *Chandler Leach, Lawyer.* He disappeared inside. Kerigan followed Hobson, but waited outside the building.

DANCER walked to the jail a block away. As he reached it he turned and saw Hobson, Kerigan and a tubby little man coming toward him. He waited in the doorway.

Chandler Leach, Justice of the Peace, was about five feet four inches tall and about two-thirds of that distance wide. He affected a goatee and a black slouch hat.

"Marshal Cummings," he snapped briskly as the trio came up, "what are the charges against these men?"

Dancer looked at Hobson. "What are the charges?"

"How should I know?" Hobson said testily.

"You told me to throw them out of your hotel."

"They weren't doing anything."

"Case dismissed," Judge Leach said. "Lack of evidence."

Dancer went into his office and unlocked the jail door. The man he had buffaloed was on his feet with his friends. "You're free, boys," Dancer said to them.

They filed out of the jail, each man in turn giving Dancer a dirty look. Outside, they began complaining to Walter Kerigan.

"It's all right, boys," Kerigan soothed. "The marshal got a little uppity. You've had a long trip from Texas and you're entitled to a little fun. Go and enjoy yourselves."

Dancer came out. "Without your guns," he said.

"Are you crazy, Marshal?" Kerigan demanded. "A Texas man isn't dressed without his gun."

"Then he'll have to do his celebrating outside of Lanyard," Dancer said, "for I'm not going to permit the wearing of guns inside the town limits."

Hobson bared his teeth. "You're going too far, Cummings. There's no ordinance against carrying guns."

"I'm making a personal one," Dancer told him. "And I'm going to arrest every man who carries a gun."

"And I'll turn them loose," barked the justice of the peace.

"In that case," Dancer said calmly, "you can hold a new election for a town marshal."

He closed the door of the jail and walked away from the group. But before he had reached the Drovers Hotel Hobson caught up to him.

"Don't be a fool, Cummings," the mayor said. "You're making a mountain out of a molehill."

"I didn't ask for the job," Dancer replied. "You asked me to take it."

"I know," Hobson said. "And personally I agree with you about that gun-toting business. After what happened yesterday such an ordinance might be a good thing. I'll bring it up before the council."

BERT SLOCUM was cutting across the street from the land company office. Dancer saw him coming and stopped.

"What's the trouble?" Slocum asked before he reached the two men.

"Cummings has threatened to quit his job," Hobson said surlily.

"I haven't threatened—I've quit."

Slocum shot an angry glance at Hobson. "What's this about, Paul?"

"Just a misunderstanding, Bert. Cummings arrested some of Walter Kerigan's men and Kerigan got all hot and bothered so I asked Cummings to let the men go. He—uh—insisted he couldn't let them out without an order from Judge Leach."

"What was wrong with that?"

"Nothing." Hobson frowned. "But you know Kerigan. He brings four-five herds up the trail every year and—well, he's an important man. Bert, you know that as well as I."

"True, he spends a lot of money here and the railroad gets a lot of his business, but if we're going to have law, Paul, it's got to be the same law for everyone." Slocum clapped Dancer on the shoulder. "You were quite right, Marshal. Of course in the case of a man

like Walter Kerigan, you could have taken the men before Judge Leach right away."

He smiled. "Is that all that this is about?"

Hobson hesitated. "He also thinks we ought to pass an ordinance against gun-toting within the town limits."

"An excellent idea. I was going to bring that up at the first meeting of the council. You saw what happened here a couple of days ago. Such a thing couldn't take place if we had such an ordinance and enforced it."

"You're right, Bert, I agree with you."

Slocum beamed at Dancer. "So it's all settled then, eh, Cummings?"

Dancer shrugged. "We'll try it."

"Good. Paul, have you told him about tonight?"

"Clean forgot. There's a party tonight at the hotel, Cummings. Sort of celebration. We expect you to be there."

CHAPTER XI

THE Texas men began coming into town around noon, but Dancer, in view of the promise of a forthcoming ordinance prohibiting the wearing of firearms, decided to forego the disarming of the cowboys until he could do so legally.

There was some carousing during the afternoon, but no shooting. Some of the Texas men left town before dark, but their places were taken by others who had been riding herd during the day.

Dancer had his dinner at the China Cafe around seven and then went to his office in the jail building and got the shotgun. He left it with the clerk at the Drovers Hotel. The hotel was centrally located and if he needed the gun he could get it more quickly here than from the jail.

He made a leisurely tour of Main Street

afterwards, going down one side of the street and returning on the other. He stopped in at two or three saloons and gambling halls and received the hostile stares of a few Texas men.

Dancer didn't like it; things were too quiet. At eight o'clock he stopped in at the hotel and found Paul Hobson freshly shaved and wearing his best Prince Albert.

"You're going to the party, aren't you, Cummings?" Hobson asked.

"I intend to look in."

"Make it before nine; we're going to have a little meeting and I'd like to get started before there's too much drinking."

Hobson left the hotel with Dancer and they walked a half block to a big frame building which had a wooden sign over the door: Masonic Hall. The front door was open and the interior brightly lighted. A small orchestra at the rear was tuning up its instruments. Fifteen or twenty people, including several women, were already inside.

"I'll see you later, then," Hobson said as he left Dancer at the door. Dancer nodded and started down the street. As he was crossing to return on the other side he met Bert Slocum and his niece, Evelyn, just crossing to the side on which the Masonic Hall was situated.

"Evening, Marshal," the land company man greeted Dancer. His niece nodded.

"Good evening," Dancer responded. He finished crossing the street and looked in at the Panhandle Saloon. Two or three cowboys were having a warm argument with a bartender and Dancer lingered for awhile, but when the argument subsided he left.

As he came opposite the Masonic Hall, music came across the street, the lilting strains of Sweet Betsy From Pike. Dancer stopped and listened for a moment, then crossed the street.

There was a small crowd standing outside the hall. All were well dressed indicating that they were business men of the town. One or two greeted Dancer and he responded. The door was partly closed now so that he could get only a glimpse of the interior, but since it was already eight-thirty or later, he opened the door and stepped inside.

THE room was a large one, with a staircase at the far end leading to the second floor. Just inside the front door was a plain table behind which sat a middle-aged man with flowing white mustaches. Behind him was a row of nails upon which hung revolvers and pistols of all sorts.

"Check your gun," he said to Dancer, then recognized him and grinned. "Guess we'll make an exception in your case. And you won't have to buy no ticket neither."

"I don't mind buying a ticket," Dancer said. "How much is it?"

"Dollar, but we can't take money from the marshal. Go in and dance." He winked. "Some mighty nice-looking women folks here."

Dancer had already seen one: Evelyn Slocum. She was dancing with a paunchy middle-aged man whose Prince Albert dragged below his knees. She was smiling but it was a forced smile.

The music stopped and Evelyn's escort said something to her and walking off, left her in the the middle of the floor. Evelyn shook her head and started for the side of the room, then suddenly changed her course and came toward Dancer.

"Well, Mr. Cummings," she said as she came up. "What do you think of our society? They're all here—the best people of Lanyard."

"They're good people, I imagine," Dancer said.

"Until the men get liquored up." She nodded toward the staircase at the rear. "We're not supposed to know why the men keep going upstairs." She smiled. "Well, I'm keeping you from joining the procession."

He shook his head. "I don't drink."

"You don't—drink? A Southerner . . ."

"I'm not a Southerner."

She seemed surprised. "I wonder what made me think you were?"

At that moment the four-piece orchestra started playing and Evelyn looked at Dancer questioningly. For just a second Dancer stiffened, then he drew a deep breath.

"Are you engaged for this dance, Miss Slocum?" he asked hesitantly. For answer she smiled and held up her arms. Dancer placed his right hand in the small of her back and took her right hand in his left. He started to lead her awkwardly. Fortunately the piece was a waltz and he could concentrate upon the steps, for it was ten years since he had danced.

They made a half circuit of the room without speaking, then Evelyn broke the silence. "You're an improvement over my last partner."

"Not much, I'm afraid. It's some time since I've danced."

"Well, you are a little stiff," Evelyn admitted. "It might help if you relaxed a little."

A fine film of perspiration was already covering Dancer's face. "Would you rather sit it out?" he asked.

"Oh no, I'm enjoying the dance." She looked up at him. "Besides, I've wanted to talk to you ever since the—the other day. You say you're not a Southerner, Mr. Cummings. I was almost certain you were because I can't imagine a—well, a Northerner risking his life

to help a woman. What made you do it?"

"I don't think I stopped to think of a reason."

"You acted instinctively?"

DANCER didn't like the trend of the conversation, but did not know how to change it, so remained silent. A little frown of annoyance flitted across Evelyn Slocum's features.

"I understand you're not supposed to question a man about his past out here," she persisted, "but I'm curious about you, Mr. Cummings. Where are you from?"

"Hasn't your uncle told you about me?"

"Why, no," she said. "I asked him but he said he knew nothing about you."

Dancer was surprised. "He didn't tell you I was a . . . a detective?"

She exclaimed. "A detective!"

"That was my qualification for the marshal's job."

The music stopped and Dancer released her, but for a moment she stood with her arms half raised, frowning at him. "Is there . . . some reason my uncle hasn't told me about you?"

"I can't think of any. I was a detective for Arthur Pleasanton." He paused to let that sink in, then added: "I'm the man who got Jim Dancer."

She recoiled as suddenly as if he had slapped her. "You . . . you . . . got him? You mean Jim Dancer is *dead?*"

"Didn't you know?" Dancer asked tonelessly.

Around them the couples had left the floor, but Evelyn Slocum seemed not to have noticed. She stared at Dancer with burning intensity.

"I'm sorry," Dancer said stiffly. "Your uncle probably had a reason for not telling you."

Her lips parted a little and her tongue

came out to moisten them. Her eyes remained wide open. Dancer bowed. "Thank you, Miss Slocum, for the dance."

He walked off, heading for the stairs at the rear. It wasn't until he was climbing them that he risked a quick glance back at the dance floor. Evelyn Slocum was walking to the side of the room, her legs carrying her as stiffly as if she were an automaton.

Dancer swore under his breath. "Ah, Cummings," Hobson called from the top of the stairs. "I was just coming down to see if you'd showed up. We're ready to start."

There was a little room at the top of the stairs where there was a table on which stood a half dozen bottles of various brands of whiskey. Several men were sampling them, but Hobson took Dancer beyond to another room.

Here were gathered around a table the rulers of Lanyard. In addition to Leach, Justice of the Peace, there was Kenneth Vedder, the prosecuting attorney, a lean consumptive-looking man in his early thirties and the members of the city council, Bertram Slocum; Walter Bullock, the banker, and Milo Meeker, who owned the biggest dry goods store in the town. With Hobson, the mayor, and Cummings, the marshal, they comprised the "elected" public officials.

HOBSON introduced Cummings to those members of the council whom he had not yet met, then they seated themselves at the table.

"We might as well get right down to business," Slocum began, then. "Paul, as mayor of Lanyard, you have the chair."

Hobson pursed his lips. "What'll it be first—money matters?"

Walter Bullock chortled, but found that his humor received no support and quickly sobered. "Money's always interesting," he said lamely.

"If you've got it," Vedder, the prosecuting attorney, said drily.

"We haven't," Slocum said testily. "A few of us have been digging down into our own pockets, but we've got a regular government now and I think we ought to make it self-supporting." He frowned at Vedder. "How much pay d'you figure you ought to have?"

"That depends on how much time I'll have to give to the job."

"I think you'll find that it'll take just about all of your time," Slocum said grimly. "I want Lanyard to be the kind of town where a respectable woman can walk down the street at any time of the day or evening without being in danger of her life, or—"

"Or dignity?" Vedder suggested.

Slocum scowled at the prosecuting attorney. "Or dignity!"

Hobson hastened to say, "A good town means business for all of us. Lanyard's the fastest growing town in Kansas. Another two years and it'll be a city."

"Danged near a city now," declared Judge Leach. "If you don't mind, I been doing a little thinking. I can make my office self-supporting."

"How do you figure that?" Slocum demanded.

"The fines. Marshal Cummings arrested six men this afternoon." He looked furtively at Paul Hobson. "I could have fined those men ten dollars apiece for disorderly conduct."

"Which amount you expected to keep for yourself?" Slocum asked witheringly.

"That's the way they do it in a lot of towns," Leach said defensively. "The Justice of the Peace keeps the money he takes in."

"You'll get twenty-five per cent," Slocum snapped. He turned to Vedder. "And another twenty-five per cent goes to you. The other fifty goes to the town treasurer."

Kenneth Vedder smiled mockingly. "And who'll be the treasurer?"

"Bullock. He's used to handling money." Slocum took a slip of paper from a pocket, unfolded it and studied some notes. "Now, there's taxes."

"Taxes!" exclaimed Vedder. "Isn't that a county matter?"

"We haven't got a county government. Lanyard's the county—except for Bruno, that wart on the prairie, up north. But we don't have to consider them. I'm in favor of taxing the business men of this town."

AND then Milo Meeker spoke his first words. "Wal, now, Mr. Slocum," he began.

"Yes?"

"Wal, I dunno, don't they usually tax the property owners afore they do the business men in a town?"

Slocum's eyes glowered angrily. "A man makes money off business, not land."

"Correction," interposed Vedder. "The first money around here is made by the land-owner who sells the property to the business man."

Slocum fixed Vedder with a cold glance. "Seems to me you're making a lot of suggestions, Mr. Vedder."

"Oh, am I?" Vedder said, not at all abashed. "I apologize. I'll let some of you other gentlemen talk. What do you think, Mr. Bullock?"

"Oh, quite," said the banker of Lanyard. "I agree with Mr. Slocum. Don't you, Mr. Mayor?"

"What Mr. Slocum says makes sense to me," Hobson said. "It's the merchants of this town who'll get the benefit of the—ah—civic improvements and I, for one, expect to pay for them."

"Then it's agreed that we tax the business men of this town?" Slocum said.

"Objection!" cried Vedder.

Slocum banged the table with his fist. "What the hell are you objecting to, Vedder? You don't own any business."

"I'm objecting to what you objected to a moment ago, Mr. Slocum," Vedder said coolly. "Too many *suggestions* by one man. I think we should have a vote."

"A vote on what?" Slocum demanded.

"Your *suggestion* of taxing the business-men instead of the property owners."

Bertram Slocum leaned back in his chair and looked around at the faces around the table. "All right," he said finally. "What's your vote, Meeker?"

"How much would the tax be?" Meeker asked fidgeting.

"No more'n you could pay."

"I'd like to know how much. I paid quite a lot for my store building and I'd like to get it back."

"You'll get it."

Meeker still did not seem too certain. "Business has been all right so far, but you can't tell what it will be like in winter when the herds stop coming to town."

"Taxes won't be as high in winter."

"How you going to determine just how much a man's to pay—and when? Some businesses are bigger than others. And more profit in them. You take a saloon—or a gambling hall—it's nearly all profit. But I sell merchandise that costs a lot of money. My prices are low."

SLOCUM pounded the table again. "Let's not get into that or we'll be here all night. My idea is that the tax will depend on the size of a man's business, but we can thrash that out later. Let's just decide now who's going to be taxed: the business man or the—the property owner. Mr. Vedder thinks we ought to vote on it. All right, let's vote."

"I vote that both the property owner and business man should be taxed," Vedder said promptly, and received a glare from Slocum.

"Hobson?" snapped Slocum.

"The business man."

"Meeker?"

Meeker swallowed hard. "I vote like Mr. Vedder."

"All right, what about you, Bullock?"

"I cast my vote with yours, Bert."

"That leaves the judge and the marshal."

Judge Leach cleared his throat. "I'm afraid, Mr. Slocum, that I'll have to agree with Vedder. The property owner—"

"All right, you've said it," Slocum cut in. "That makes it three to three, with the marshal yet to vote."

"I know very little about city governments," Dancer said, "but what the prosecutor said seems to make sense—those who get the benefit of a government should pay for it and it strikes me that the property owner gets as much benefit as the business man. . . ."

"Very well," Slocum conceded, "the majority votes that the property owner pays a tax along with the business man. That takes care of the city finances. We'll work out the details later. Now, Marshal, you suggested a special ordinance prohibiting the carrying of guns in Lanyard. Suppose we passed such an ordinance? Do you think you could enforce it?"

"I could try."

"You can't be on duty day and night, though. I think you ought to have a deputy marshal."

Chandler Leach suddenly brightened. "A town this size really needs two law officers

and three mightn't be a bad idea."

"Two ought to do it, for the time," Slocum said. "I propose that the council employ a deputy marshal to assist the marshal, at—say, a hundred dollars a month. And a percentage of the fees would only be fair, wouldn't it?"

Dancer saw that he was being penalized for having voted against Slocum on the other proposition and he could foretell the vote on this new issue: the more peace officers in the town, the more arrests . . . and cases brought before Judge Leach—at twenty-five per cent.

CHAPTER XII

THE vote was a unanimous one, for Dancer surprised the others by voting in favor of it. Kenneth Vedder hesitated over his own vote, but when Dancer announced his own decision, Vedder went along.

Two or three minor matters were brought up by Slocum and disposed of, then Slocum pushed back his chair. "I guess we've about covered everything now. Shall we join the ladies downstairs?"

They filed out of the room, but Vedder catching Dancer's eye, held him back. Then, when the others had gone out, Vedder held out his hand.

"Didn't really get a chance to say hello before," the prosecutor said.

Dancer smiled. "Hello."

"I'm glad we're to be friends," Vedder said, "for it looks like you and I are going to be on the same side in a lot of things." He grinned. "We forgot to give a vote of thanks to the mayor for the way he conducted the meeting."

"The mayor?"

"Isn't Slocum the mayor?" Vedder asked

innocently.

Dancer chuckled. "Well, it's his town, isn't it?"

"That's why I thought he ought to pay for its upkeep," replied Vedder.

They left the room. Judge Leach was in the ante-room with a bottle tilted over his mouth, but the other members of the city council had gone downstairs.

Vedder indicated the liquor. "A snort, Marshal?"

Dancer shook his head.

"Guess I'll have a short one," Vedder said.

Dancer left him with his colleague, the judge, and proceeded on down the stairs. At the foot of the stairs he stopped and surveyed the dance floor. It was considerably more crowded than it had been before and it seemed to Dancer that the character of some of the guests had changed.

He got it after a moment. Some Texas men had filtered in. Two or three were even dancing with the wives and daughters of business men. And the latter were not exactly showing approval. Several were gathered in one corner in a spirited huddle. Bert Slocum, one of the group, spied Dancer and started across the room.

Dancer, seeing him coming, tried to ease along the far side of the room, but was blocked by the dancers so that Slocum caught up to him.

"Look here, Cummings," Slocum said angrily, "I want you to get rid of these Texas men."

"Sure, replied Dancer, "if you'll point them out."

"I don't have to point them out," snapped Slocum. "You can pick them out by their clothes."

"Oh," said Dancer, "I get it. The ones wearing old clothes are Texas men." He suddenly reached into the dancers and caught hold of a man wearing a suit of rusty broadcloth. "Here, you, Mr. Slocum says to get out of here."

SLOCUM lunged forward and grabbed Dancer's arm. "Not him," he cried. "He owns the Lanyard Hardware Store. Excuse it, Chester . . ." He stabbed his forefinger at a man in soiled levis and high-heeled boots, who was dancing nearby. "There's one."

The cowboy saw Slocum's pointing finger and released his partner. "You pointin' at me?" he demanded truculently.

"Throw him out," Slocum ordered Dancer.

Dancer went up to the cowboy. "This is a private party, Mister."

"Who says so?"

"I do."

"And who the hell do you think you are?"

"I'm the man who's going to break your thick skull if you don't get out of here quietly," Dancer said.

The Texas man started to bluster but Dancer grabbed his arm and twisted it around behind the man's back in a savage hammerlock. He propelled the man through the dancers toward the door and was shoving him out of the hall when he heard pounding footsteps behind him. He released the man and whirling, faced three charging cowboys.

Dancer stepped quickly to one side and dropped his hand to the butt of his gun. That brought up the cowboys, for they were all unarmed.

"Out," Dancer said coldly.

"It's a Yankee trick," one of the men snarled. "We have to check our guns and they keep theirs."

"I'm the marshal," Dancer said. "There's

a law against carrying guns in Lanyard."

"Since when?"

"Since ten minutes ago, when the city council passed it."

"One of the cowboys suddenly winked at his friends. "Okay, we're leaving town now. Give us our guns." The last sentence was spoken to the white-mustached custodian of the checked guns.

Dancer blocked the table of the gun checker. "You'll get your guns tomorrow."

"We ain't comin' into town tomorrow."

"Then you'll have to wait until you do come in."

"Oh, yeah?" sneered one of the Texas men. He made a sudden lunge for Dancer— and reeled back as Dancer smashed him in the face with the barrel of his Navy gun.

"Now you go to jail," Dancer said.

The man at the door, the one whom Dancer had brought out from the dance floor, ducked outside. But the other three men were caught and Dancer herded them out of the Masonic Hall and up the street to the jail where he locked them in.

Leaving the jail he returned to the Masonic Hall, but found that whatever other Texas men had been there had left. And quite a few of the townspeople were leaving.

Dancer caught a glimpse of Evelyn Slocum with her hat on, but she either did not see him or saw him and kept her eyes averted. He left the hall and walked down the street to the Eldorado, where he turned in.

THE place was doing a land office business and Dancer saw Florence Peel herself presiding over a faro table. She did not see him as he approached the table.

"Place your bets, gentlemen," she was droning. "The house pays Number 7—eighty

dollars to the man with the hat on."

She manipulated the cards in the box. "The king wins and the deuce loses."

She looked up then and met Dancer's eyes. "Are you playing, Marshal?" she asked mockingly.

"Not during working hours," he retorted.

"A drink on the house?"

"Yes."

She shoved the card case toward the house man beside her, and came around the table. Touching his arm lightly she led the way through the crowds to the bar.

"Bourbon, Marshal?" she asked.

"A bottle of beer."

"You fight on beer?"

He grinned. "I do my best killing on water. I've just come from a meeting of the city council—that's why I need the beer."

"As bad as that?"

"You'll find out when you get your tax bill."

"What taxes?"

"City taxes. That's what the meeting was about." He shook his head. "You can't run a government without taxes, you know."

"Then let Bert Slocum pay taxes. He owns everything around here."

"Oh, he's going to pay taxes. We outvoted him on that—four to three."

"Who voted against him?"

"The prosecutor, the judge, Milo Meeker and myself."

Florence's lips curled contemptuously. "And Bullock and Hobson voted with him? . . . How much are these taxes going to be?"

"It wasn't decided. I have a hunch Slocum's going to decide that without bringing it up in another meeting."

"And then who's going to do the collecting?"

"Not the marshal of Lanyard. Oh—that

reminds me, there's going to be an assistant marshal."

Dave Oldham came up and dropped his hand on Dancer's shoulder. "Evening, Marshal. How long are you supposed to be on duty?"

"Don't know's there are any special hours. Why?"

"Thought you'd be turning in by now."

"What's up?"

Oldham shook his head. "Nothing. Just thought you'd be tired along about now."

"Don't try being subtle, Dave," exclaimed Florence.

Oldham said in a low voice: "Just overheard something. They're getting together a crew to break some of their friends out of jail." He smiled and signaled to a bartender. The man brought a bottle of whiskey and a small glass. Oldham filled it and tossed off the whiskey in a single gulp.

"What's the difference, Marshal? The judge let six of them go this morning."

"I can't help that," Dancer said. "But you're right, I can't stay up all night. Think I'll turn in." He nodded to Florence, smiled at Oldham and left the bar.

HE MOVED leisurely toward the door, but once through it, walked swiftly toward the Drovers Hotel. The pimply-faced night clerk was dozing in an armchair behind the desk and Dancer got his shotgun without awakening him.

Leaving the hotel he crossed the street and strode quickly toward the jail. By striking a couple of matches inside he found a lamp, which he lighted and by its light examined the front door. It was a sturdy one, made of planks two inches thick, and would withstand any assault less than a battering ram. But looking about the room Dancer saw only one window and that was on the side. The architect of the building had made an error there. If he locked the door on the side, Dancer would be a prisoner himself—until the door was broken down and then the fighting would be at extremely close quarters.

He shook his head and stepped out of the jail. He walked to the edge of the building, noted the stairs going to the second floor and returning to the front door, pulled it shut and locked it with the key.

Then he ran lightly up the stairs and unlocked the courtroom door. He stepped through the door and closed it to within two or three inches. He leaned the shotgun against the wall and seated himself beside it.

For a mob, the Texas men were pretty quiet. Dancer, his ears cocked, had expected to hear loud talking and shouting as they approached the jail building, but the first he was aware of their presence was when the doorknob was rattled down below.

A voice called: "Hey, Marshal, there's a man been hurt at the Texas Bar."

There was of course no reply from inside the jail. Upstairs, Dancer got to his feet and picked up the shotgun.

Down below and around in front, a Texas man banged on the door with his fist. "Open up, Marshal!"

After that wrangling began among the Texas men. Dancer swung open the courtroom door and stepped cautiously out upon the stair platform. Boots pounded and a man came running around the corner. He was headed for the rear of the building.

"Looking for something?" Dancer called down.

The man cried out and skidded to an abrupt halt. His eyes darted about on the ground for a moment before they turned upwards and picked out Dancer, who was silhouetted in the moonlight.

"It's the Marshal!" the Texas man cried out hoarsely.

By that time there was a rush from the front of the building. Eight or ten Texas men pounded around the corner of the building in a solid body and like their vanguard came to a halt and searched for the whereabouts of their enemy.

Dancer called down from the head of the stairs: "I've got a double-barreled scattergun here."

A man shouted, "We want those prisoners!"

Moonlight gleamed on a revolver down below. "Drop that gun!" a man cried.

"I've got my finger on the trigger," Dancer said calmly. "Even if you get me, half of you'll die."

THE truth of that was apparent to the Texas men, for the range was not more than fifteen or sixteen feet. It was merely a matter of nerve and the men on the ground had seen his stand against Ben Slattery a few days ago when Dancer had gone against almost certain death.

A couple of the Texas men began edging backwards so that they could spring around the edge of the building for protection, but Dancer saw them move.

"Stand still," he warned.

He started down the staircase, taking each step with deliberate care.

When he was halfway down so that he stood about six feet above the men, he stopped.

"All right now," he said, "start unloading your hardware."

From the middle of the street a cool voice called: "Do what he says!"

And they obeyed, nine Texas men who had been a mob only a few minutes ago. Dave Oldham moved forward from the gloom of the street with a derringer in his left hand and a full-sized six-gun in his right.

Dancer came down the rest of the stairs then, and moving up beside Oldham, handed him the key to the jail. "Unlock the door, Dave."

A couple of minutes later the jail held an even dozen prisoners. At twenty-five per cent of ten dollars a head, Judge Chandler Leach would make a nice profit on his next day's work.

When the Texas men were locked up, Dancer and Oldham stepped out upon the street. "Thanks, Dave," Dancer said.

"I didn't do much," Oldham replied. "You had the situation well in hand before I showed up." He paused. "As a matter of fact, it was Florence who suggested I go and see if you'd really gone to sleep."

Dancer was silent for a moment. Then he said: "I'm going to bunk down here tonight."

"I'll keep you company."

"That won't be necessary. I doubt if they'll try anything else tonight."

Oldham hesitated, then nodded. He walked off into the night. Dancer watched him until he was out of sight, then locking the door of the jail, climbed up to the courtroom. He locked that door on the inside and stretching out on the floor, was asleep inside of two minutes.

CHAPTER XIII

JUDGE CHANDLER LEACH, accompanied by the prosecutor, showed up in the courtroom a few minutes after eight.

"Hear you got some prisoners, Marshal," he said, with satisfaction in his tone.

"An even dozen."

The judge rubbed his hands together. "Fine, fine. Bring them up, please." Dancer went down to the jail and unlocked the inner door. "All right, boys," he said, "the judge is ready for you."

The Texas men filed out sullenly. Out on the street a group of Lanyard residents had gathered and watched the prisoners climb up to the courtroom. They followed Dancer up the stairs.

Judge Leach surveyed the prisoners. "Well, Marshal, what's the charge?"

Dancer picked out the three men he had arrested first. "Disorderly conduct for these three."

Vedder said: "What'd they do?"

"They were at the dance last night and Mr. Slocum wanted me to throw them out. I asked them to leave and then—well, there was some argument . . ."

"The charge is disorderly conduct and resisting arrest, Your Honor," Vedder said.

"Good, good!" exclaimed Judge Leach, then caught himself. "How do you plead—guilty or not guilty?"

The three men looked at each other, then all said, simultaneously, "Not guilty."

"Guilty!" snapped Judge Leach. "And you're fined twenty-five dollars each."

"You go to hell!" cried one of the Texas men.

"Twenty-five dollars for contempt of court," snapped Judge Leach. "That's fifty dollars for you and if you say another word it'll be another twenty-five."

The Texas man glared at Judge Leach, but swallowed hard. "I haven't got fifty dollars."

"Then you'll go to jail."

The three sentenced prisoners got together in a huddle and produced some money. "We got sixty-two dollars," one of them announced.

"Try again," the judge instructed.

This time the trio went into a huddle with the other nine men and the hundred dollars was raised. Judge Leach accepted it and thrust the money in a pocket. Then he nodded to Dancer.

"Next case."

Dancer indicated the nine men. "These men tried to break the other three out of jail."

"Jail breaking, eh? That's a serious charge. Guilty or not guilty?"

"Not guilty," cried a couple of the men.

Leach surveyed the prisoners coldly. "I find you guilty and fine you twenty-five dollars apiece."

Howls of rage went up and there was considerable calling of names, but when the contempt of charges had all been slapped on, Leach was holding out for a total of four hundred dollars from the nine men.

They scraped together one hundred and eighty dollars of the amount. Judge Leach singled out four of the men, along with the three whose cases had been disposed of first. "You men can go; the others stay here until the fines are all paid."

OUTSIDE, boots pounded the stairs and Paul Hobson and Walter Kerigan came into the courtroom.

"Just a minute, Judge," cried Kerigan. "I've hired an attorney for these men—he'll be here in a minute."

"Too late; I've already sentenced them."

"You can unsentence them," roared Kerigan.

The judge pounded the table with his fist. "Mr. Kerigan, I must warn you, you're liable to be in contempt of court. I've already had gan to make up the balance of the fines—"

"I'll see you in hell first," roared Kerigan.

Leach pounded the table. "Fifty dollars for contempt of court!"

Kerigan began to sputter. "Why, you, goddam two-bit imitation. . ."

"One hundred dollars!" thundered Judge Leach.

Kerigan's lawyer grabbed his arm. On the other side Paul Hobson took hold of him and between them they propelled Kerigan out of the courtroom, out upon the stairs. Then, after a couple of moments, Hobson returned, his face flushed.

"What's the total amount, Judge?" he asked.

She whipped the quirt squarely across his face

"It was two-twenty and I fined him one hundred for contempt of court—three-twenty all told."

Hobson took out a large roll of bills and counted out the money.

"All right," Leach said to the prisoners, "you can all go now."

They left with a good deal of mumbling and muttering. As soon as the door was closed, Hobson strode to the judge's table. "Now look here, Leach, you've gone too far!"

"Have I?" Leach asked grimly.

"Kerigan is the biggest cattleman in the Texas Panhandle," Hobson cried. "He's brought two herds to Lanyard already and he'll bring five a year."

to fine several of these men for that very thing."

A stocky, middle-aged man came into the room. "Your Honor," he said, "I've been retained to defend these men . . ."

"You're too late, Counsellor," said the judge. "But you're in time to advise Mr. Keri-

"Then it's a good thing he learns about law and order," Leach snapped.

Hobson whirled on Charles Vedder.

"That twenty-five per cent stuff was a mistake. You two have cooked this up between you."

"Oh, no, we haven't," retorted Vedder.

"This is the judge's own idea." He chuckled. "Although it's not a bad one, if you ask me. The town's cut is three hundred."

Hobson choked down more angry words and fled the courtroom.

THE judge took out all the money he had collected in fines. "Six hundred dollars," he said gleefully. "Not bad, not bad . . . That's one hundred and fifty for me, the same for you, Prosecutor." He was sorting out the money. Vedder watched him in complete astonishment.

"Aren't you going to turn it over to the city?"

"What for? The agreement was twenty-five per cent to you and me, so why shouldn't we take it when we get it? And you, Marshal, you get three dollars per arrest. Here's your thirty-six dollars. Keep up the good work and we'll make ourselves a nice little pile here."

"I think you'd better turn mine over to the city treasurer," Dancer said. "I'd prefer to collect it from him all at one time . . ."

"That goes for me, Judge," Vedder said.

Leach shrugged. "Just as you say, but I'm taking mine now."

Dancer left the courtroom, but before he had reached the ground, Vedder was coming down the stairs after him.

"I'll walk with you, Marshal," Vedder called.

They walked side by side a moment, then Vedder said, "Well, what do you think of justice in Lanyard?"

"About the same as yesterday." Vedder grinned. "Yes, but Leach is going to be on our side—he's so hungry for money he'll defy even Bert Slocum."

"Do you think Slocum will take it?"

"Slocum's in a pretty good spot. He owns the town site and Lanyard is a hundred miles closer to Texas than any point on the railroad; that's a saving of ten days' travel with a herd and the drovers will come here whether or not they like the town."

"Yes, but Slocum's money comes from selling business lots. And merchants do a better business if the town is wide open. So by tightening up Slocum hurts his own interests."

"That's the part I'm wondering about," Vedder said. "Slocum's got some angles I haven't figured out. I'm convinced that he owns the Drovers Hotel and most of the bank and he's got some sort of influence with the railroad."

"Are you guessing about that?" Dancer asked. "Or do you know?"

"Look at the map," Vedder replied. "The road was originally surveyed to go through Bruno, eight miles north of here, but suddenly the route was changed—the road made a neat little curve to run through Slo-cum's prairie lands. It cost the railroad quite a bit of money to do Slocum that little favor."

"Maybe Slocum owns part of the railroad?"

Vedder shook his head. "I don't think Slocum's that rich." Then he added, "Although he'll be before Lanyard is much older."

At the China Cafe Vedder left Dancer and the latter entered and had his breakfast. Leaving the restaurant he went to the Drovers Hotel.

As he climbed the stairs to go to his room, a big man who had been sitting in the lobby his face concealed by an open newspaper, folded the paper and followed.

DANCER unlocked his door on the second floor and entered, closed it. He was starting to take off his coat when there was a light tap on the door.

"Yes?" Dancer called. He dropped his right hand down to the butt of his gun.

The door opened and the big man stepped into the room. He was well over six feet in height and weighed more than two hundred pounds. He wore a neat suit of heavy black serge.

Dancer stared at the man in utter astonishment.

"My name is Harrison," the big man said quickly. "Stanley Harrison."

Dancer stepped forward and gripped the big man's hand and at the same time reached past him with his free hand and closed the door.

"It's been a long time," Dancer said.

"So it has," Harrison replied. "I saw you last night at the Eldorado. I couldn't believe it was you because we were so sure that you were dead."

"I took the Pleasanton man's name."

"Isn't that risky?"

"It was the only thing I could do at the time. I even rode into the Kansas City office where Cummings wasn't known and resigned his job for him, so there wouldn't be so much mystery if he disappeared."

"Being marshal of a boom town isn't such a good way of disappearing."

"I was forced into this job." Dancer motioned to the chair. "Sit down."

Harrison seated himself on the chair and Dancer sat down on the edge of the bed. "Yancey's here in town," Dancer went on.

"Yancey?"

"He was with us for a few months."

"Oh, yes, I recall him now." The big man's nose wrinkled distastefully. "Scum!"

"He hasn't placed me yet."

Harrison looked at Dancer thoughtfully for a moment. "What about this marshal job, Jim?"

"It's a strange story."

"Feel like telling it?"

"It goes back to Lawrence."

Harrison grimaced. "You had some trouble with Quantrell there, I seem to recall."

Dancer nodded. "There was a name on the list—Theodore Slocum. Yancey was dragging him out of the house by the heels and Slocum's daughter, a fourteen- or fifteen-year-old girl, was trying to help her father. Yancey slapped her around and I interfered. He ran off for Quantrell and came back with him—and Thailkill and Todd. Quantrell ordered me to shoot Slocum. And—well, I did."

He was silent a moment and Harrison prodded gently: "I don't think any of us feel very proud at all about Lawrence."

"There's a little more to the story than that. Either Yancey or Quantrell called me by name and the girl never forgot it. About two years ago the Pleasanton Agency got on my trail. George Cummings followed me to the Northwest to California and then Mexico and back here to Kansas. He was a good man and—he caught up with me."

"Pleasanton's a bloodhound," said Harrison. "He may get us all one day." His eyes narrowed suddenly. "You think this young Slocum girl got Pleasanton after you?"

"Yes. She spent twenty thousand dollars with Pleasanton. Her uncle was in the Kansas City office when I came in to resign as George Cummings. His name is Bertram Slocum."

Harrison exclaimed: "The man who owns this town!" Then he whistled softly. "And he knows you as George Cummings, the former Pleasanton man!"

"Yes. Last night I danced with his niece, Theodore Slocum's daughter."

"She didn't recognize you?"

"It's nine years and she was only a child at the time. She remembers a name—Jim Dancer . . ."

HARRISON leaned back in his chair and studied Dancer thoughtfully. "But you're sitting on a keg of powder, Jim. She may suddenly remember you, or . . ." He snapped his fingers. "Yancey! You were only nineteen at Lawrence and you've changed a lot since then, but Yancey hasn't—he was over thirty then."

"I've thought of that."

Harrison's eyes narrowed. "Maybe I'll look up Yancey."

"You're not here with him?"

"Good lord, no!" There was disgust in Harrison's tone. "You don't think we'd let a scurvy chicken thief like Yancey ride with us?"

"I didn't think so, but—well, what are you doing here in Lanyard?"

Harrison's mouth opened to reply, then suddenly he grinned. "How serious are you about this marshal business?"

Dancer was silent a moment. "I'm going to play it out, Cole."

"I wondered about that." Harrison exhaled heavily. "What have you been doing all these years, Jim?"

"You knew that I went to Mexico with Shelby?"

Harrison nodded. "Yes, but Maximilian was killed in '67. That's five years ago."

"There was a war over in Europe I got mixed up in. I got back about two years ago and since then I've been running. A man gets tired of that. Although I guess you know that as well as I do."

"Yes, Jim, but what else can we do? It's too late."

"Is it, Cole?"

"For us it is."

"Is that why you're here in Lanyard?"

"Do you remember Jesse?"

"Yes, although I knew Frank better. We're about the same age. I haven't seen either Frank or Jesse since '64. They stayed with Quantrell, you know, when you and I went south with Bloody Bill."

"Jesse was only sixteen then," said Harrison. He shook his head. "He's changed."

"You mean he really is the leader?"

"There's some difference of opinion about that. Frank has matured; he's got about as fine a brain as I've ever seen."

"Yours wasn't so bad."

Harrison smiled wryly. "Book stuff. Well, Frank's got that, too, but he's got more. I guess the reason they haven't got us yet is Frank. But Jesse; there's no man in the world like him."

"How do you mean?"

"Well, it's not that he's so very fast with a gun, although he's fast enough and Donny Pence could shoot rings around all of us, and Jesse hasn't got any more nerve than Clell Miller. It's just that he's—desperate. No one will ever take him alive."

"He's here, Cole?"

"N-no."

"Why are you here? The bank?"

"I don't think I'd better answer that one, Jim."

Dancer shook his head slowly. "Don't . . ."

Harrison nodded. "I'd hate to think that you and I were looking at each other across guns. And Frank thinks a lot the way I do."

"Jesse?"

Harrison sobered. "You can't ever tell about him. If it wasn't for Frank he and I would have tangled long ago. Frank can handle him most of the time."

Cole Younger, alias Stanley Harrison, got to his feet. "We'd better not be seen together around town."

"You're staying awhile?"

"I thought I'd have a talk with Yancey. Oh, it won't be about you, Jim. I'm just going to put the fear of the Lord into him, that's all. He always was chicken-hearted." He held out his hand. "It's been good seeing you again."

"Good luck, Cole."

"The same to you." Cole Younger stepped to the door, but stopped with his hand on the knob. "I hope you can see it through." Then he opened the door and went out.

CHAPTER XIV

AFTER Younger had gone, Dancer stretched himself out on the bed, but it was a long time before he slept and then it was only fitfully. Toward noon he got up and, stripping to the waist, washed himself in cold water.

A few minutes later he descended to the lobby. The place was deserted except for Paul Hobson, who was behind the desk.

"Cummings!" exclaimed the hotel man. "I was just about to come up and see if you were in."

"Why?"

"Mr. Slocum would like to have you step over to his office. He's got a man with him he thought would do for a deputy marshal."

"He hasn't wasted any time."

"Don't you think we need another man?"

"We may need a bigger jail," Dancer said as he went out.

He crossed the street to Bert Slocum's office. With Slocum was a lean young man of twenty-four or -five, who wore a gun on each hip. He had deep brown eyes, one of which had a slight cast. Jim Dancer thought him the most vicious-looking man he had ever seen—and he had seen many in his time.

"Ah, Marshal," exclaimed Slocum as Dancer entered, "I want you to shake hands with your new deputy—Johnny Tancred."

"H'arya, Cummings," said Tancred, although he made no move to extend his hand.

Dancer nodded shortly. "Hello, Tancred."

"Johnny left Abilene before he got my second letter," Slocum explained. "He came here expecting to have your job, Cummings." He coughed. "He's quite agreeable to being deputy, however. I've told him you'd split the fees."

"Hear you got twelve last night," said Tancred. "Not bad, but we ought to get twice as many in a day—especially with that no gun-totin' ordinance." He winked.

"That worked out fine in Abilene and Wichita. Towns're too tame now, though."

"We want a tame town here, Johnny."

"You'll get it."

"The quicker the better. All right, Cummings, I'll let you two get acquainted."

Taking that as a dismissal, Dancer and his new deputy left Slocum's office. Outside, Johnny said: "Guess we might as well start earning some of those fees, eh?"

"Go right ahead, Johnny."

Johnny Tancred grinned wickedly at Dancer. "Don't care much for me, do you?"

"Slocum hired you."

Tancred squinted at Dancer. "What'd you ever do, Cummings, outside of drowning Jim Dancer?"

"You and I are going to get along fine, Johnny," Dancer said.

"Look, Marshal," said Johnny Tancred, "I know this business. I've been doing it in other towns. It takes something that you don't find in Chicago—plain nerve, see? I'll show you what I mean."

ACROSS the street two cowboys had come out of a saloon; both were wearing guns on their hips. Johnny Tancred started across the street and when he was a dozen feet from the men he whipped out both of his guns.

"All right, hombres!" he cried. "Reach!"

The hands of both men shot up into the air. Tancred stepped up to them. "There's a law against gun-totin' in this town," he sneered. "You're both under arrest."

He holstered his left gun, then stepped up to the cowboys and relieved each of his six-gun, which he tossed away contemptuously. Then he struck one of the men in the face with the back of his hand. "When you get out of jail you can tell your friends that Johnny Tancred's running this town."

Dancer crossed over and handed Tancred the key to the jail. "Nice work, Johnny," he said. "Now you can lock them up."

"Sure, and they'll have company in a little while." He fired at the boot of one of the men, missing by about a half inch. "Get movin'!"

The Texas men started down the street, their hands still in the air. Johnny Tancred swaggered after them.

Dancer drew a deep breath and sought out the local print shop, where he learned that the printer, a man named Anderson, was about to issue the first edition of a weekly newspaper to be called: *The Lanyard Lance.* Dancer ordered a dozen placards, to read:

PUBLIC NOTICE
The carrying of guns within the limits of this town is prohibited by a town ordinance. Please deposit all firearms at designated places immediately upon arriving in town. They can be retrieved when leaving,
Signed: CITY COUNCIL
Lanyard, Kansas

The printer promised the placards for that evening and Dancer began a tour of the saloons and gambling halls. In every place he told the proprietors of the new ordinance and asked them to accept the guns of the Texas men as they entered their places. There was some grumbling on the part of one or two of the saloon keepers, but all agreed to act as gun repositories.

The job took Dancer almost two hours to complete and twice as he came out upon the street he saw Johnny Tancred heading for the jail with prisoners. His last port of call was The Eldorado, where he found Dave Oldham playing solitaire at a table.

"Sit down, Marshal," Oldham invited as Dancer came up to the table. "Tell me how you like your new deputy."

"I don't," replied Dancer, seating himself opposite the gambler.

"Do you have to keep him?"

"I've been wondering about that, Dave. Slocum figures he made a mistake making me the marshal and he hired Johnny Tancred to keep me in line."

"That's what I gathered. But just what could Slocum do if you refused to have Tancred?"

Dancer shrugged. "I'm not worried about that. I'm just wondering what Slocum's game is. He's certainly doing his best to antagonize both the cattlemen and the business men of the town."

"Maybe he just hates everybody."

"It goes further than that."

"He'd better not go much farther," said Oldham. "He's sold a lot of property here at pretty stiff prices. The buyers have got to make out on their investments or there's going to be hell to pay." Oldham began laying out the cards for a new game of solitaire. "Did you know that there's a private railroad car on a siding at the depot? President of the M. K. & P., or maybe just the vice-president. Slocum spent most of the morning with him . . ." He broke off as two shots sounded on the street.

DANCER kicked back his chair and ran to

the door. He sprang through, drawing his gun, and saw Johnny Tancred standing over a man in the middle of the street.

As Dancer approached, Tancred put his foot against the man on the ground and turned him over. Dancer needed but a glimpse of the staring eyes to know that the man was dead.

"He drew against me," Tancred said briefly.

"While you had your gun on him?"

"Sure. There's always some damn fool who doesn't know when the score's against him."

"How about you, Johnny? Do you know when the score's against you?" Dancer raised the muzzle of his Navy Colt to the level of the deputy's stomach.

Tancred stiffened. "What's the idea, Cummings?"

"You're through. I'm firing you, Johnny."

"You are like hell," retorted Tancred.

"Drop your gun, or try to beat my bullet, Johnny—like the Texas man tried to beat yours."

Out of the corner of his eye, Dancer could see Bertram Slocum striding toward them, but he continued to concentrate on Johnny Tancred.

"You can't fire me," still protested Tancred.

"Maybe not, but I can kill you," Dancer said grimly. "And I will if you don't drop that gun."

Tancred let the gun fall to the ground and then Bert Slocum reached them. "What's going on here?" he cried.

"Cummings says I'm fired," Tancred said quickly.

Slocum fixed Dancer with a cold look. "You have no authority to do that, Cummings."

"You had no authority to hire Tancred," Dancer shot back at him.

Slocum's eyes blazed. "You know very well that the city council authorized the employment of a deputy."

"I know," Dancer said grimly. "I voted for it myself. But nothing was said about you doing the hiring. You forget that I was elected marshal. I'll hire my own deputies."

"What's the matter—afraid I'll get your job?" Tancred taunted. Then he appealed to Slocum. "I've arrested eighteen men in less than two hours."

"And you murdered one," Dancer added,

"I did like hell—he drew on me."

Slocum said: "You killed a man the other day, Cummings."

"In a fair fight," Dancer retorted.

"I fail to see the difference," Slocum said. "Slattery drew on you and you beat him to the draw. This man drew against Tancred."

"While Tancred had his gun on him. And Tancred drove him to it."

"What the hell do you mean?" Tancred cried. "He was violatin' a city ordinance and I told him he was under arrest, that's all."

"Just like you told the eighteen men you've already arrested."

"Yes."

"All right," said Dancer. "I won't argue the point. But you don't work for me."

"Now look here, Cummings," exclaimed Slocum, "you're carrying things too far." He glared at Dancer a moment, then suddenly capitulated. He signaled to Tancred. "Johnny, I want to talk to you."

Tancred stooped to reach for the gun he had dropped, but Dancer kicked it away. "You'll carry no guns in Lanyard."

"I'll take custody of his guns," Slocum said quickly.

Johnny Tancred started to protest, but

Slocum shook his head warningly. He picked up Tancred's gun, then drew the other from his holster.

"And now," Dancer added, "you can remove this body."

"What'll I do with it?" Tancred asked sullenly.

"That's your lookout."

Tancred was spared that, however. A couple of sullen-looking Texas men who had been listening to the proceedings from the doorway of the Eldorado came forward and relieved Tancred of his job. They loaded the dead man on a horse and rode out of Lanyard.

AT SLOCUM'S office the land company man found a man in the uniform of a trainman awaiting him with a note. It read: "Come and see me—now!"

Slocum thrust the note in his pocket. "I've got a new job for you, Johnny," he said, "but I haven't time now to tell you about it. I'll be back in a half hour."

"I'm not going to hang around here a half hour without any guns," Johnny Tancred cried.

Slocum put the guns down on his desk. "The law's against wearing the guns, Johnny. Nothing says you can't sit inside here, near guns."

Johnny Tancred chuckled wickedly and Slocum left the office. He walked to the end of the street to the railroad depot and then another hundred yards to the siding where the private car was standing.

A trainman, who had a big bulge in his side coat pocket, was sitting on the little observation platform. "It's all right, Mr. Slocum," he said. "Mr. Lanyard is waiting for you."

Slocum pushed open the door and stepped into the car. The rear half was fitted out as a luxurious office, and Lanyard was seated behind a desk dictating to a secretary.

"Ah, Mr. Slocum," he said; then to his secretary, "I'll be occupied for awhile."

The man got up and went into the other section of the car. Lanyard reseated himself, took a fresh cigar from a humidor and took some time biting off the end and lighting it. Slocum, meanwhile, seated himself on a sofa and waited for the railroad man to speak.

CHAPTER XV

LANYARD took a couple of puffs on his cigar. Then he finally said: "All right, Slocum, lay your cards on the table."

"I haven't got any cards," Slocum replied calmly.

"No?"

Slocum shrugged and made no further reply. Lanyard took three or four puffs on his cigar. "You hired a notorious killer as a deputy marshal this morning. I understand he's arrested over a score of men in the last two hours."

"Something like that, Lanyard. And a few minutes ago he killed a man who resisted arrest. However, he isn't working for the town any more; the marshal fired him."

"Good!" snapped Lanyard. "But you should never have hired the man in the first place."

"What else is on your mind, Lanyard?" Slocum asked.

The railroad man looked narrowly at Slocum a moment, then he grunted. "I said, put your cards on the table."

"And I told you I haven't got any cards," Slocum retorted. "But maybe you've got some."

"I have, Slocum. I've got a half interest in

the town of Lanyard."

"What did you pay for it?" Slocum asked insolently.

"Seven miles of a railroad."

"And how much freight has this town given your railroad in two months?"

"Quite a lot—but it would have had the same amount if the railroad had gone through Bruno. But stop beating about the bush, Slocum. If this is a showdown, let's have it."

"*You're* making the showdown, Lanyard."

"All right, so I am."

Slocum nodded. "What were the terms of our deal?"

"I don't think you've forgotten, but I'll remind you. I built the railroad here, instead of through Bruno and for that I was to cut in for one half of all the money you made out of this town."

"That's right, Lanyard—and haven't you gotten your half? It seems to me that I've paid you something like ninety-five thousand dollars in less than sixty days."

"I haven't complained about that part of it."

"Then what do you want?"

"I want half of *everything* you've got here."

"Correction, Lanyard. The deal was for you to get half of whatever money comes out of the town."

"What's the difference?"

"The town site measures a mile by a mile."

"I still don't see your point. The town, including the railroad right of way and the loading pens, doesn't take up the entire town site. Even if it grows it'll be some time before the mile is built up."

"That's right, Lanyard."

"Then what are you quibbling about?"

"I'm not quibbling; you are."

"You've got something up your sleeve," Lanyard said, screwing up his face.

"Uh-uh," said Slocum. "You can come down and look at the books anytime. I've sold town lots to the amount of one hundred and ninety-thousand dollars. There are roughly three hundred lots left in the town site."

"What about our interest in the hotel and bank?"

"You'll get your share, but it'll be awhile before there are any profits from them." Slocum hesitated a moment. "I'll tell you what, Lanyard, if you're dissatisfied, I'll buy you out."

"Not a chance!"

"Then how would you like to buy me out?"

Lanyard exclaimed in surprise. "What?"

"I'll sell you my half interest in the town site, the hotel and the bank."

"For how much?"

"Make me an offer."

Lanyard looked at Slocum narrowly. "Seventy-five thousand?"

"Why not make it ninety-five—the amount you've taken out so far?"

LANYARD pushed back his chair and came to his feet. He walked around his desk and looked down at Slocum. "You'll pull out of here?"

"I didn't say that."

"What would be the point in your hanging around if you sold out your interest?" Lanyard asked musingly. "All you'd have left is some prairie land." His eyes suddenly widened. "Just how much prairie land have you got?"

"Quite a lot." Slocum smiled like a wolf about to devour a jack rabbit. "I had twelve thousand acres to begin with."

"And the town site occupies only six hundred and forty acres. That leaves you more than eleven thousand."

"Oh, no, it leaves me about twenty-one thousand. You see, I spent most of my ninety-five thousand for more land. Among the right of way. Cost me quite a bit of money—some of it four dollars an acre."

"You've got twenty-one thousand acres of land—along our right of way?"

"A mile and a half on each side of your track, for about fourteen miles. The town site is right in the middle of that land."

"In other words you've got the town surrounded?"

"That's what it looks like on the map."

"And anyone who wants to get to the town would have to cross your property?"

"Unless he came by train; I deeded a strip ninety feet wide to your railroad, you'll remember."

"It's still a blockade; we need those ninety feet for trackage." Lanyard leaned back against the edge of his desk and chewed the cigar that had gone cold in his mouth. "So you've had an ace in the hole all the time!"

"An ace in the hole is a good thing to have."

Lanyard's face was suddenly very pale.

His tongue came out and licked his lips. "It rather looks as if your ace wins the pot, Slocum."

"I don't see any stronger hands, do you?"

LANYARD shook his head slowly. "What are you going to do?"

"Why, we were talking about freight awhile ago, Charlie," Slocum said genially. "According to my figures close to one hundred thousand head of cattle have been shipped from here since the railroad came. There are about that many head out on the range now, grazing on my land and the way the herds are coming in, I wouldn't be a bit surprised if another half million head are shipped from here by the first of November."

"I'm not arguing the figures, Slocum," Lanyard said tightly.

Slocum nodded. "I've given the railroad a lot of freight business. Don't you think the railroad ought to give me a commission?"

Lanyard swallowed hard. "How much?"

"I thought about a dollar a steer."

Lanyard cried out hoarsely, "You're mad, Slocum!"

"Oh, I don't think so."

"My brother-in-law would never stand for it."

"You sold him on swinging the road south of the original survey."

"And I had a hard time doing it. It cost a quarter million dollars."

". . . Of the stockholders' money."

"Harley Nelson is the principal stockholder, a fact of which you're undoubtedly quite aware."

"Yes, he owns about twenty-five per cent and you've got ten—only your stock is pledged to a couple of St. Louis and Chicago banks because of the beating you took in the New York Central."

Slocum regarded Lanyard steadily for a moment. "As you said awhile ago, Charlie, I've got you blockaded—not a head of cattle will go into your loading pens unless I let them." He paused. "But if I raise the blockade the cattle will have to cross the town site of Lanyard . . . and the original agreement is that we split share and share on what comes out of that."

Lanyard grabbed at the lifeline. "You mean—?"

"Get the road to pay that dollar-a-head commission and we split fifty-fifty."

Lanyard widened his eyes and began to breathe a little faster. "Fifty-fifty . . . straight down the line?"

"A quarter million dollars apiece . . . inside of four months!"

Lanyard whistled softly and Slocum drove in the last nail. "More than enough to redeem your stock in the M. K. & P."

Lanyard straightened from leaning against the desk and took a quick turn up and down the private car. Then he suddenly stopped and faced Slocum.

"I'm going to have trouble with Harley over this . . ."

"A man can stand a lot of trouble for a quarter million dollars."

"I know—I need the money. Harley's pretty tough, but so is his wife . . . my sister. I might swing it."

"Why don't you tell him the truth? That a dirty dog named Bert Slocum's got the railroad over a barrel." He chuckled. "Although I don't think you'll want to tell him that you're the dirty dog's partner."

AFTER Slocum was gone, Lanyard sat at his desk staring out of the window. His secretary came into the room and seeing that Lanyard was in deep thought tiptoed out again. But after a time Lanyard struck a bell on his desk and the secretary re-entered.

"Russell," Lanyard said, "I need a man to solve an important business problem and I find that I don't know how to go about getting the right man for the job."

"What is the business problem, sir?"

"I want to rob a bank."

The secretary gave a start of surprise. "I beg your pardon!"

"I'm serious, Russell. A pipsqueak who's suddenly gotten too much money is trying to destroy me and the only way I can stop him is to take away some of his money. He keeps it in a bank, where he can get at it quickly. I don't want his money myself, but I want it removed from this man's reach. Now, the problem is to find a man who can remove it."

"I'm afraid that's a rather large order, sir," said the secretary.

"Aren't you from Missouri, Russell? I thought that's where all the bank robbers come from."

"As a matter of fact, sir," said Russell slowly. "My home is at Independence . . ."

"Independence!" exclaimed Lanyard. "Isn't that the home of—?"

Russell cleared his throat. "As a matter of fact, sir, I—I have a cousin, a distant cousin, who—"

A gleam came into Lanyard's eyes. "As a matter of fact," he said, slowly, "I've been thinking of visiting Independence. You—ah—might happen to run into this cousin—the distant cousin . . ."

CHAPTER XVI

MOUNTED on the horse he had bought his first day in Lanyard Jim Dancer rode beside Dave Oldham, who was astride a rented gelding. On the right of them was a herd of at least fifteen hundred Longhorns, grazing on the rich buffalo grass. Off to the left was an even larger herd, and straight ahead, the prairie was dotted with cattle.

"You wouldn't think people could eat that much beef," Oldham said.

"There are a lot of people in the East," Dancer replied, "and beef is cheap." He pointed straight ahead. "There's a sodhouse up there."

"Could be the place we're looking for."

They put their horses into a canter and passed through the herd of Longhorns. The sodhouse seemed to be about a half mile beyond and, once through the herd, Dancer and Oldham picked up a rutted wagon trail.

They rode at a trot to within four hundred yards of the house, then Dancer pulled up his horse. "That's a barbed wire fence around the place," he said to Oldham.

"Why would anyone want to fence in a place like that?" Oldham asked.

"To keep out the cattle . . . maybe."

A sharp whining sound penetrated Dancer's ears. He was already flattened down behind his horse's head when the boom of a rifle came over.

He looked sidewards at Dave Oldham, who sat erect in his saddle, his revolver in his hand. "Careful, Dave!" he cautioned.

"That was only a warning shot," Oldham said. "Seems like they don't want visitors. What do we do?"

Dancer sat up. "We can't charge because he'd pick us off with that rifle before we got in revolver range."

"Then we go back to town?"

"I'd rather ride back than be carried back."

But even as Dancer said that a man came out of the sodhouse and vaulted into the saddle of a horse that stood inside the fence. He rode toward a gate, leaned over and unfastened it, then sent the horse through the gate and putting it into a gallop came toward Dancer and Oldham. "Oh-oh," said Dancer.

He drew his Navy Colt, holding it carelessly across the pommel of his saddle. Near him, Oldham suddenly exclaimed: "That isn't a man!"

Dancer had already discerned that. "I know. It's Evelyn Slocum . . ." He holstered his gun.

Evelyn Slocum, wearing boots, Levis, flannel shirt and a black, flat-crowned Stetson, pulled up her horse, a spirited young filly. "I recognized you through the glass," she exclaimed. "I'm sorry about that shooting."

"You did it?" Dancer asked.

She shook her head. "No, it was Bill Harmer."

"Who's Bill Harmer?"

"A former buffalo hunter who works for Uncle Bert. He lives there."

DANCER and Oldham exchanged glances. She caught the look and laughed. "My horse threw a shoe and Bill offered to nail it on. Uncle Bert couldn't wait, so he and Johnny rode on."

"Johnny?" Oldham asked.

"Johnny Tancred. He works for Uncle Bert, you know."

"I hadn't known," Dancer said. "I thought he'd left town."

"Oh, he has; he works out on the ranch."

Dancer nodded toward the sodhouse. "Is that the ranch?"

Evelyn half-turned. "Oh, no, that's just a sort of storehouse."

"Must be storing something valuable," Dave Oldham observed, "if the caretaker shoots at anybody who comes close."

"I'm sorry about that," Evelyn said. "I had no idea what he was going to do until he fired." A frown creased her forehead. "Isn't it rather unusual for you to be riding out here?"

"Just getting a little exercise," Dancer replied.

Oldham gathered up his reins. "We rode out farther than I expected to. Do you mind, George? I've got to get back."

"Not at all."

Oldham nodded to Evelyn and Dancer, turned his horse and put it into a swift trot, in the general direction of Lanyard, five miles away. Dancer knew that Oldham was in no hurry to get back to town; he was merely riding ahead because he thought that Dancer wanted to be alone with Evelyn Slocum.

And that was one thing that Dancer did not want. Or thought he did not want.

Evelyn fell in beside Dancer and they began to ride easily. For a moment they rode in silence, then to make conversation, Dancer said: "I didn't know Mr. Slocum was going in for ranching."

"He's got all this land," Evelyn said, "he thought he might as well get some use out of it."

"That was quite a shipment of barbed wire that came out this way, a few days ago."

Evelyn started to nod, then suddenly looked sharply at Dancer. "Aren't you unusually—well—*concerned*, about my uncle's activities?"

Dancer shrugged. "There's been a lot of talk that he's fencing the range."

"What if he is?" exclaimed Evelyn. "It's *his* land."

Dancer nodded. "So it is, but you see, your uncle made the town and he brought the trail herds to Lanyard. He sold a lot of townsites to people who depend on those herds. They're a little nervous now that fencing in this grazing land will interfere with the herds."

Evelyn showed sudden relief. "They've got nothing to worry about. Uncle isn't fencing in that much land."

"I hope not."

"But why should you be worried?"

"I'm not."

"Isn't that why you rode out here?"

Dancer nodded reluctant assent. "Yes."

"Well, now you know."

"I know your uncle's fencing in some land," Dancer said. "I don't know why he has an armed guard to shoot at anyone who comes in rifle range. And I don't know why your uncle has hired a man like Johnny Tancred."

Evelyn's color was several shades deeper than normal and her eyes were blazing. "What's the difference between a man like Johnny Tancred and you? You're both—killers!"

DANCER jerked his horse to an abrupt halt. For a moment he stared at the girl. Then he exhaled slowly. "I'm sorry," he said and raked the horse's flanks with his spurs.

The animal leaped forward and went into a gallop. Dancer let it run for awhile, but had to slacken speed as he passed through a herd of cattle. Through the herd, he saw Dave Oldham, jogging along a few hundred yards ahead.

He put his horse into a gallop again and Oldham stopped his horse when he heard the drumming of hoofs. The gambler looked at him sharply as he came up, but as Dancer glowered at him, he made no comment. Not for a half mile.

Then Oldham said, with the ghost of a smile playing about his lips, "Maybe I shouldn't have gone ahead."

By that time Dancer was in better humor. He grinned wryly: "I guess it was kind of a dirty trick to pump her about her uncle."

"Just the same," said Oldham, sobering, "there's something awfully fishy about Bert Slocum. Aside from Johnny Tancred, have you noticed some of the people that've been coming into town, staying a few hours, then riding out this way?"

"There've been quite a few salty-looking lads lately," Dancer admitted, "but I haven't paid much attention to the direction in which they've been riding." He paused a moment. "You think Slocum's hiring a crew of gun-fighters?"

Oldham shrugged. "That sodhouse couldn't hold a half car of barbed wire, let alone six full cars."

"The wire goes farther?"

Oldham nodded. "I'd say the lad with the rifle is stationed at the sodhouse to discourage anyone from *going* any further." Then he added: "And I notice, Slocum's niece didn't get past the sodhouse, either."

"She said her horse threw a shoe."

"That's what she *said*," Oldham agreed, although the emphasis on the word "said" was not lost on Dancer.

They rode into Lanyard and returned their mounts to the livery stable. Then Oldham went to the Eldorado and Dancer walked to the jail, over which a middle-aged ex-mule-skinner, named Romeike, now presided. Dancer paid him fifty dollars a month, out of his own pocket. In the jail proper, a man named Chadwick was serving out thirty days in lieu of his refusal to pay a twenty-five dollar fine for disorderly conduct.

"Hello, Marshal," the jailer greeted Dancer. "There was a fella here lookin' for you."

"Who?"

Romeike scratched his head. "He gave his name, but doggone if I can remember recollect it now. Harper, or something like that."

"I don't know anyone by the name of Harper. What'd he look like?"

"Tall, pretty well set up. Black whiskers. Seemed anxious to talk to you. Stranger around here. Leastwise, I never saw him before."

Dancer nodded and started to leave, but with his hand on the door, turned. "The name couldn't have been Travers?"

"That's it!" exclaimed the jailer. "Travers. And I remember now, he said he'd be staying at the Drovers' Hotel."

CHAPTER XVII

DANCER left the jail and walked down the street. He was nearing the Eldorado when he saw the tall figure of Captain Travers of the Pleasanton Agency come out of the barber shop. The detective recognized him at a distance, but waited until Dancer had come up before speaking. Then he held out his hand.

"Hello, Marshal," he said, in a conversational tone. "How are you?"

"Good enough," Dancer replied. "And you?"

"Couldn't be better. Like to buy you a drink."

Dancer nodded toward the Eldorado. "Here's a good place."

They entered the saloon and Dancer headed for the bar, but Travers touched his arm. "Could we have it at a table?"

"Of course."

It was mid-afternoon and there were only a few patrons in the place. Oldham was watching a desultory poker game in the far corner, but Dancer was sure that he had spotted him coming in.

He signalled the bartender and led Travers to a table, at the near side of the room. They seated themselves.

"Been reading about you," Travers said, as he rested his elbows on the table and leaned forward. "There was a piece in the Kansas City paper last week that said you'd tamed this town."

"It's a job of work," Dancer said.

The bartender came up. "What will you drink, Cummings?" Travers asked. "Beer."

"Make it two, bartender."

Travers leaned back and surveyed the room until the bartender brought the beer. Then he raised his glass.

"How!"

He drank about half of his beer, although Dancer barely wet his lips on the glass. Travers set down his glass and smiled. "You should have left a forwarding address, Cummings," he said.

"I didn't have any, not for quite awhile."

"So we discovered, when our mail come back from your old Chicago address." Dancer raised his glass and drank beer slowly. It was coming now and Dancer had to guess at the right answers.

"Your brother was quite worried about you," Travers said.

Dancer said: "My brother?"

There was a shade of hesitation before Travers replied and Dancer knew that he had guessed correctly. "Why, yes," Travers said.

Dancer shook his head. "I haven't got a brother."

Travers looked at him in surprise. "Why, I'm sure the chief said it was your brother."

Dancer nodded. "Probably. That's why I didn't leave an address."

Travers exclaimed. "You don't mean—?"

"I guess even Dancer had friends."

TRAVERS leaned back in his chair and regarded Dancer steadily. "The chief thought that might be a possibility. But after I sent him that piece from the Kansas City paper—well, he wondered if you'd use your right name out here." He half smiled. "It's outlaw country, you know, and Dancer's friends . . ."

"I think a couple of them have looked me over."

"Lately?"

"About' a month ago."

Travers frowned. "We've got a lot of men devoting their full time to Jesse's outfit. We came pretty close in Omaha, a couple of weeks ago."

"Just a little late, though."

"As usual." Travers sighed. "Mr. Pleasanton said you could name your own salary to come back."

Dancer shook his head. "I'm afraid not."

"What difference is there, whether you work for the agency, or work as a marshal."

"I sleep in a bed here."

"And you're a walking target. The average life of a peace marshal is pretty short. Yes, I know, you've tamed this town, but Tom Smith tamed Abilene and he was dead in three months."

"A man's got to play out his hand," Dancer said, doggedly.

"But he can draw new cards."

"No," said Dancer. "Whatever's going to happen is going to happen here."

Captain Travers drank the last of his beer. "The chief's coming down to Kansas City; you'll go in and talk to him?"

"I haven't got anything to talk to him about."

Poorly suppressed rage began to darken the detective's face. "There's no chance of you changing your mind?"

"None whatever."

Captain Travers pushed back his chair and got to his feet. "Goodbye, Cummings," he said angrily and stalked off.

Dancer remained seated at the table and after awhile Dave Oldham came over. "An old acquaintance, Jim?"

"Captain Travers of the Pleasanton Detective Agency."

Oldham whistled softly.

"Pleasanton sent him out from Kansas City. George Cummings disappeared a little too completely."

"Disappeared? They were able to find you."

"Most people have relatives somewhere. Although I know one relative Cummings didn't have. A brother." Dancer traced a design on the table top with his finger. "Captain Travers was very cute about it." A frown flitted across his features. "Or maybe he wasn't cute."

"Another month," Oldham said, "and there won't be a Texas man in town. Half the business places in Lanyard will board up their windows until next year. I'm thinking of going to New Orleans for the winter."

"The Eldorado'll close?"

"No point keeping it open for just the townspeople. Besides—Florence has been talking about selling."

Dancer looked up in surprise. "I thought the place was doing well?"

"It is—too well, perhaps. That may be the trouble. Some nights she doesn't even come out of her office."

"Why not?"

"She's lost interest. Or maybe her heart isn't in it."

Dancer looked steadily at his friend. "You're in love with her, Dave?"

Oldham looked at his lean, flexible hands. "I'm a gambler, Jim. Florence is the daughter of a gambler."

"And for that reason she wouldn't marry a gambler?"

"I mean," Oldham said evenly, "Florence isn't in love with me."

DANCER, looking past Oldham, saw the door of Florence's office open and Florence come out. His eyes on her, he said to Oldham: "How do you know, Dave?"

Oldham, who saw that Dancer's eyes were focused on the office in the rear, pulled out a chair and seated himself across from Dancer. He took a pack of cards from his pocket and began to manipulate them.

Dancer watched the gambler a moment, then looking up, caught Florence watching him from across the room. He got up, looked down at Oldham a moment then, circling a table, bore down on Florence Peel.

She stood in the doorway of her office, watching him approach. As he came up, she said: "Afternoon, Marshal; haven't seen you around much lately."

"I'm here, now."

"So I see."

Dancer looked about the sparsely populated gambling hall. "Things are pretty quiet this afternoon."

"Yes."

"Has business fallen off lately?"

"Some. Why?"

"I was thinking that the herds haven't been coming in so fast lately. Another month and there won't be any."

"They'll come again in the spring."

"I know, but there won't be much doing in Lanyard during the winter."

"And Dave told you that I might close up for the winter? Is that what you're getting at, in a roundabout sort of a way?"

Dancer winced a little because of his bungling. "He mentioned that he might go to New Orleans."

She looked at him steadily for a moment then turned and walked into her office. When she reached the middle of it, she stopped and turning about, signalled with her head.

"Come in!"

He went into the room.

"Close the door," she said.

He swung it shut and stood with his back against it.

"All right, Jim," Evelyn said. "You asked for it."

"No," he said quickly.

"You wanted to know if I was going to New Orleans, with Dave?"

"I said Dave thought he might go there."

"I'm closing the Eldorado for the winter. I might even sell it. But I'm not going to New Orleans."

HER greenish eyes were on his so intently that he had to drop his own. He cleared his throat awkwardly and tried to say something, but did not know what to say. And Florence, the dam having burst within her, could not stop.

"Don't you know there's only one man with whom I'd go to New Orleans—or anywhere he wanted me to go?"

And still he could not speak.

Florence went on poignantly. "You're blind, Jim, or you're a fool."

"Yes," he admitted tautly.

"Yes, what?" she cried harshly. "Yes, you're a fool? She won't have you, Jim. She won't have you even as George Cummings and if she knew you were Jim Dancer, she'd cross the street to keep from passing near you."

"I know that even better than you, Florence," Dancer said tonelessly. "You see, it was her money that put the Pleasanton Agency on the trail of Jim Dancer."

"What?"

"She paid twenty thousand dollars to get—me!"

Florence was shocked out of her bitterness. She came toward Dancer and looked up into his face. "Why? Why should she do that?"

"Because I killed her father."

A low cry was torn from Florence's throat. Her hand reached out and involuntarily gripped Dancer's arm. "I don't believe it. You—you're not that sort of a man."

"It was in August '63."

"But that was during the war!"

"What Jamison and Anthony did in Independence was war; what Jim Lane forced Ewing and Plumb to do in Clay and Jackson Counties, that, too, was war. But they won the war and we didn't. So what we did in Lawrence . . ." He made an impatient gesture. "That wasn't war."

Florence let go of his arm and retreating to a chair, sat down heavily. "And she's lived with the hatred of a man named Jim Dancer for all of these years?" She shook her head and a tear splashed her hand. "And I've been feeling sorry for myself."

"Don't, Florence," he said, "don't feel anything—for me."

She laughed bitterly. "There's not much pattern to it, is there? Dave and me and . . . you. Maybe I'll go to New Orleans, after all."

Dancer opened the door and looked back at her. Her eyes met his. "And maybe," she said, "I'll go to hell."

He closed the door softly on her and went through the saloon. As he passed near Dave Oldham's table, the gambler looked up from a game of solitaire he had started. He looked at Jim Dancer—and looked through him!

Dancer walked out of the Eldorado and walked up the street to the Drovers' Hotel. He entered and Paul Hobson picked up an envelope from the desk.

"Cummings, here's a letter for you. From Bert Slocum." He handed the envelope to Dancer. "Leastwise," he added, "I suppose it's from Bert. His niece left it here a few minutes ago."

"Thanks," said Dancer, and climbed the stairs to his room.

Inside he closed the door and looked at the envelope Hobson had given him. His name was scrawled on the face of it. He stretched out on the narrow cot and putting his thumb under the flap, tore open the envelope. But even then he waited a moment before unfolding the note.

At last he opened it.

Mr. Cummings:

Won't you come to dinner this evening, so that I can apologize for this afternoon? Unless I hear from you otherwise, we shall expect you at seven.

                              Evelyn Slocum

Dancer re-read the note, then returned it to the envelope. After awhile he got up from the bed and finding a pencil and some paper, wrote a note:

Dear Miss Slocum:

Thank you for your kind invitation. I would like to accept but my duties will not permit.

                              Sincerely,
                              George Cummings

Two minutes after writing the note he tore it to shreds. He left his room and going out, stopped in at the barber shop where he had a shave and haircut. Then he returned to the hotel and in the lobby wrote a duplicate of the letter he had torn up; only this time he wrote with pen and ink.

He went so far as to locate a colored boy who worked as a swamper in a saloon, to deliver the message, but even as he put it in the

boy's hand, he changed his mind.

And at a quarter to seven he rode his horse out of the livery stable and started for the home of Bertram Slocum.

CHAPTER XVIII

IT WAS a big two-story frame house, the most imposing in Lanyard, as was to be expected of its foremost citizen. The house was located on the main road, leading west of town, approximately three-eighths of a mile from the center of Main Street.

As Dancer rode up, a man came around from the side of the house and took the reins from Dancer's hand. And then Bertram Slocum appeared on the verandah of the house.

"Good evening, Marshal," he said heartily. "I understand you're having dinner with us."

"Yes," said Dancer. He climbed the short flight of steps to the verandah.

"Dinner's almost ready," said Slocum. "But suppose we have a drink before we sit down?"

He held open the door for Dancer to enter. The latter stepped into the living room which was furnished like an eastern room. Beyond the living room was the dining room, where a colored maid was setting out plates.

In the living room, Slocum poured out whiskey into small glasses and filled a couple of tumblers with water. Slocum winked. "You can't buy stuff like this in town."

To Dancer, who was not a drinking man, it tasted no different than the other occasional drinks he had been forced to drink at one time or another. But he nodded approval.

Then Slocum said: "Evelyn tells me you were out riding on the prairie today and that

Harmer took a shot at you." He shook his head. "I'll have to fire that man."

"Not on my account."

Slocum chuckled. "A miss is as good as a mile, eh? You were in the war?" Before Dancer could reply, Evelyn Slocum entered the room. She was wearing a deep red velvet dress, cut low and trimmed with stiff black lace.

"Good evening, Mr. Cummings," she greeted him and held out her hand. "I'm glad you could come."

"Thank you for asking me," Dancer replied stiffly.

In the dining room the maid announced: "Dinner is ready."

They entered the room and seated themselves at the table, Slocum at the head, Evelyn on the right and Dancer directly across. The maid brought out the food, roast pork, a rarity in the cattle country, and vegetables that had come on the railroad from Kansas City.

As they ate, Slocum pursued the subject he had touched on before Evelyn had come in. "I'm fencing in some land out south of town. That is, I'm getting ready to do some fencing. Thought I'd wait to do the actual work until the drovers have gone home for the winter. They don't seem to like my fencing." He grunted. "Got an idea they can graze their herds wherever they please. They'll find out differently next spring."

"You're going to run cattle yourself?" Dancer asked.

"A few head." Slocum looked sharply at Dancer. "I don't see any reason to keep it a secret any longer. People'll find out soon enough. I'm planting wheat."

IT WAS apparent from her surprised expression that this was news even to Evelyn.

"Wheat?" she exclaimed. "Out there on this prairie?"

"Winter wheat," said Slocum. "You plant it in fall and it's ripe before the really hot weather comes along in the summer. T. C. Henry, over in Abilene, planted five thousand acres last fall and this summer harvested forty bushels to the acre."

Dancer lowered his fork and looked at Slocum in astonishment. "Isn't wheat selling for around a dollar a bushel?"

"That's why I'm going to raise wheat."

"How many acres are you going to put in, Uncle?" Evelyn asked.

"I've got twenty thousand acres of land."

"But you're not going to plant it all in wheat!"

"Why not?" Slocum saw the frown on Dancer's face. "This isn't cattle country, Cummings; no land is if it can be farmed. Food comes before anything else."

"Beef is food."

"Beef can be raised on barren ground; this soil is too rich to waste on grazing cattle."

"The same might be said of all the land east of here."

"Right. There'll be no herds coming east of Lanyard. But that's all right, the railroad's going to build westward during the winter."

"Even so, isn't this the closest point to the Texas Panhandle?"

Slocum shrugged. "What if it is? They'll just have to drive their herds a little further—and ship them a few miles more. There'll be just as many steers going on the trains—only they won't go from Lanyard."

"But suppose the cattlemen insist on shipping from here?"

"Insist?" cried Slocum. "What good would it do them to try if they can't reach the shipping pens? Why do you think I'm spending all that money on fencing?"

"And what happens to the town of Lanyard?"

Bert Slocum's face twisted in a cruel smile of power. "Lanyard's my town; I made it and I'll keep it going . . . but it'll be the kind of town I want it to be, without saloons and gambling halls. A few stores, the bank and hotel . . ."

As he talked, Dancer heard the drumming of hoofs outside come to a sudden stop. Boots pounded up stairs and someone banged loudly at the front door.

Evelyn Slocum pushed back her chair. "Excuse me," she said, and got to her feet.

Slocum did not even seem to notice. "Lanyard will exist because I'll need a town for the people who'll work for me. It takes a lot of men to farm twenty thousand acres and—"

He stopped as Evelyn re-entered the room, accompanied by the youthful night clerk of the Drovers' Hotel. "Excuse me, Mr. Slocum," the lad said, "but there's hell—I mean, things have popped in town. Milo Meeker's been killed and—"

Bert Slocum kicked back his chair. "Milo Meeker dead! How?"

"His store was held up by some men. Mr. Hobson thinks it was the James gang."

Dancer was already on his feet. "You'll excuse me . . ." He started for the door.

"Wait!" cried Slocum. "I'll ride with you."

BUT Dancer was going through the door. Outside, he sprang to the ground and ran around the house to the stables. He found the hostler rubbing down a couple of Slocum's horses.

"I've got to go back to Lanyard in a hurry," Dancer exclaimed.

"Sure," said the man. "I didn't know how long you'd be so I didn't unsaddle your horse."

Slocum came running up. "Amos, saddle Black Ben—quick!"

Dancer unhitched his horse from a stall, backed it out. "I'm sorry, Mr. Slocum, I can't wait."

He led the horse out of the stable, mounted and almost ran down Evelyn Slocum who was coming around the corner of the house. He pulled up his mount as she threw up a hand in a signal to stop him.

"I'm sorry we didn't get a chance to talk," she said. "I wanted to apologize for—"

"You already have," Dancer replied. "And thanks for—everything!"

He touched his horse's flank with his heel and the animal sprang past the girl. He sent it into a furious gallop and inside of three minutes was pulling it up before Milo Meeker's store.

It was dark on the street, but enough light came from inside the store to reveal a crowd outside. Dancer tied his horse to the hitchrail and pushed through the crowd at the door.

Inside Meeker's store were eight or ten townsmen. Hobson spied Dancer at once.

"Here you are, Marshal! A fine thing when you're needed!"

"What happened?" Dancer interrupted.

"The James gang!" Hobson exclaimed.

"How do you know it was the James boys?"

"Who else would it be? A half dozen men galloped into town, pulled up outside here and while a couple of them stayed outside the others charged in and—and killed Milo."

Dancer brushed past Hobson to where the merchant's body lay sprawled in a pool of blood, at the end of the counter. He had been struck by no less than three bullets; the killers had wanted to make sure.

Dancer turned back. "Was he in here alone?"

A man in shirt sleeves and wearing an apron pushed forward. "I was in here with him, but it was like Mr. Hobson said, they came in shooting—"

"What about money? Did they get much?"

The man's mouth fell open. "Why—uh—I don't know's they got anything. There was three-four of them inside here and they was all shooting . . ."

"At you, too? Or only Meeker?"

"I guess at both of us, although they didn't hit me. I ducked down soon's they began shooting . . ."

"Where did Meeker keep his money?"

"In the till."

"Where's that?"

The clerk went behind the counter, reached underneath and pulled out a drawer. He exclaimed. "They didn't touch the money!"

"Guess they didn't have time," a man said.

"The James boys take time," retorted Dancer. "This isn't their work."

"How do you know it ain't?" Paul Hobson cried.

DANCER did not even bother answering that. He brushed past Hobson and headed for the door. As he stepped through to the sidewalk, Bert Slocum dismounted at the hitchrail.

"Is it true, Cummings?" he cried.

"About Meeker—yes. But it wasn't a holdup. No money was taken. It was just—murder!"

"But who'd want to murder Milo Meeker?"

"I don't know." Dancer turned to the crowd. "Anybody see which way they went?"

Two or three men pointed eastward. "That way."

"How long ago?"

"Not more'n a half hour," someone said.

"A half hour!" exclaimed Dancer.

Paul Hobson had come out of the store. "Everybody in town was looking for you, Cummings. Seems to me we're paying you enough money so you'd—"

"He was having dinner at my house," Slocum interrupted sharply. He looked at Dancer. "Do you think we ought to organize a posse?"

"It wouldn't do any good tonight. They rode east, but once out of town they could have gone in any direction. I'll try to pick up their trail in the morning."

"This is a terrible thing," Bert Slocum said, "just as I was thinking that the town was tamed." He smacked his right fist into the palm of his left hand. "Some drunken Texas men, who had it in for Meeker."

Dancer caught sight of Dave Oldham standing at the edge of the crowd. Oldham's head moved almost imperceptibly and as soon as he could Dancer slipped away from the crowd. He joined Oldham near the entrance to the Eldorado.

"I heard the shooting," Oldham said, "and I was at the door when they rode off. They weren't Texas men."

"How do you know?"

"It wasn't quite dark yet and you know that I can spot a cowboy anytime, anywhere. They were riding northern horses—good ones."

Dancer shook his head. "Hobson keeps saying the James boys, but that's ridiculous. Stores aren't in their line and anyway, no money was taken."

"Too excited, Jim? I doubt it—those boys

knew what they were doing." He paused. "One of them was your old guerrilla friend, Yancey. I recognized him."

Dancer was silent a moment. "So he came back."

"The others were strangers, Jim. But they weren't cowboys."

Dancer said, "Meeker was a member of the city council . . ."

"That's what I was thinking," Oldham said softly. "Vedder was by a few minutes ago; said if I saw you to tell you he'd walk down to the courthouse in a little while."

Dancer looked down the street and saw a light in the second floor window of the jail building.

"He's there now." He started to walk off, then turned back. "If you're not busy, Dave, come along."

OLDHAM fell in beside Dancer and they crossed the street to detour about the crowd in front of Meeker's store. A few minutes later they climbed the stairs to the courtroom and found the door locked. Dancer knocked.

"Who is it?" called the voice of Charles Vedder.

"Cummings," Dancer replied.

The bolt was shot on the inside of the door and Vedder opened it. "You've been over to Meeker's?" Vedder asked.

"Yes."

Vedder frowned as he saw Oldham on the stairs outside. "Dave, do you mind? I'd like to talk to the Marshal."

"I'd like him to hear, Vedder," Dancer said quickly.

Vedder hesitated, then bobbed his head. "All right."

Dancer and Oldham went into the room and Vedder closed the door.

"Marshal," the prosecutor said, "I just got back from a trip to Kansas City. I went there because of Slocum. Do you know that six carloads of barbed wire have gone out of Lanyard in the last two weeks?"

"Dave and I know about that," Dancer said. "As a matter of fact, we took a ride out south of town today to see where the wire went to."

"Did you find out?"

"We turned back because someone took a shot at us with a rifle. But it's all right, the wire's Slocum's. He's told me all about it—and why he bought it."

"Why?"

"He's fencing in his property—to raise wheat."

"That's what I was going to tell you!" Oldham cried. "I found it out in Kansas City. He's placed an order for two hundred plows that are going to be delivered in a few days. They've never had an order like that in Kansas City and they think Slocum's crazy—but he's paid for the plows and for a lot of other machinery he's ordered."

Dancer said: "He told me about a man at Abilene who got forty bushels of wheat to an acre on five thousand acres. Slocum's going to plant twenty thousand acres."

Oldham whistled. "That's going to cost him something."

"Two hundred plows," said Vedder in a tone of awe, "at least four hundred good horses to pull them, discs, harrows, seed—at least three hundred men to do the work."

"Has Slocum got that sort of money?" Dancer asked.

"Nobody knows what he's got. He's made a lot off the town but still . . ." Vedder exhaled heavily. "If he wins he'll clear a half million in a single season."

"If he wins," Dancer said. "Do you think the town'll let him?"

"If he fences in that land," Vedder said, "he'll kill the cattle business for this town." He paused. "And I don't think the people in Lanyard will let him do that. That's why I called you over here."

"To stop Slocum? I don't see what we can do . . ."

"I've already done it." Vedder took a long envelope from his breast pocket and handed it to Dancer.

The latter looked at the envelope. "What's this?"

"Your appointment as sheriff of Bruno County."

"County!" exclaimed Dave Oldham.

"I've been working on it for several weeks," Vedder said. "The population of Lanyard alone is over one thousand and there are a couple of hundred people in Bruno."

"But how could I be appointed sheriff?" Dancer asked, puzzled. "Who appointed me?"

"Judge Currier of the Third District Circuit, who arrives in Lanyard tomorrow." Vedder smiled faintly. "And I'm county attorney. Of course the appointments are only temporary until county elections are held, but that won't be for several months yet. In the meantime, Judge Currier runs the county."

"And Leach?"

"Is a Justice of the Peace. He can perform weddings—and things like that." Dancer opened the envelope in his hand and studied the warrant that appointed him sheriff of a Kansas County. "Town marshal is one thing, Vedder," he said, "but sheriff . . ."

"Don't be silly, Cummings," Vedder said warmly. "There isn't a better man in Kansas for the job."

"He's right," Oldham added.

Dancer looked steadily at the gambler.

CHAPTER XIX

DAWN was scarcely breaking over Lanyard when Jim Dancer entered the livery stable. But early as it was the liveryman was up and already had Dancer's horse saddled.

"He's all ready for you, Marshal. Had a good feed of oats."

"Thanks."

Dancer started to lead the animal out when a voice spoke to him from the adjoining stall. "Morning, Marshal!"

It was Dave Oldham.

"Dave!" exclaimed Dancer. "There's no point in you getting up this early."

"I haven't been to sleep," chuckled Oldham. He led out his horse, saddled. "Don't argue—I'm riding with you." He tapped a rifle in a scabbard alongside his saddle. "And I'm a little better armed than we were yesterday."

They rode out of the livery stable and started down Main Street.

There was a well defined trail rutted by wagon wheels leading eastward but within a quarter of a mile after leaving the town, the trail became a dozen trails, each cutting off across the prairie land to wherever the Texas outfits that had made the trails, had camped. Both Oldham and Dancer realized the futility of trying to pick up the trail of a half dozen riders in the maze and ignoring the trails completely jogged in the general direction of the sodhouse where they had been stopped the day before.

They passed a trail herd of seven or eight hundred Longhorns. A range cook was making breakfast for a half dozen Texas men who were still wrapped in their blankets near the fire.

Dancer and Oldham swerved their horses so that they came up to the camp.

"'Morning," Dancer said to the cook.

"G'morning to you," replied the cook. "Coffee's just about ready if you want to light."

"Don't mind if we do," said Dancer and climbed down from his horse.

Oldham also alighted and the cook got out tin cups which he filled with scalding black coffee.

"That hits the spot," Oldham said.

"I ain't human until I've had my coffee," the cook said. He gulped down a mouthful of the steaming liquid. "Out pretty early, aren't you?"

Dancer nodded. "You didn't happen to see six men riding by this way yesterday evening, round about eight or nine o'clock?"

"Waal, no," said the cook. "I didn't see anybody, but I heard—"

"He didn't hear nothin'," said a voice behind Dancer. He turned and discovered that one of the cowboys was sitting up in his blankets. "He's deaf, so he couldn't hear a damn thing."

"Come to think of it," said the cook, "it was some Longhorns I heard."

"Six men who weren't from Texas," Dancer said, "they murdered a man in town."

"You're Cummings, the peace marshal," retorted the man on the ground. "I wouldn't tell a marshal what day of the month it was."

"That's your privilege," Dancer said coldly. He returned the tin cup to the cook. "Thanks for the coffee."

HE AND Oldham climbed back on their horses and rode off. Out of earshot of the camp, Oldham said: "I guess they passed this way, all right."

"There wasn't much doubt in my mind that they'd wind up down there," Dancer replied. "It was just a question of how directly they went. I guess they were in a hurry."

They put their horses into a canter and in about twenty minutes sighted the sodhouse from which they had been fired upon the day before. As they approached at a more conservative pace, Oldham said: "Quite a lot of horses inside that wire."

Dancer made note of the smoke coming from the stovepipe that stuck a couple of feet out of the roof. "And somebody's up, making breakfast."

"Well, what do we do—snipe?"

"No. There are enough of them so they won't be afraid of two men riding up. Come on."

Dancer put his mount into a fast trot and Oldham kept pace a few feet beside him. Dancer had an idea they were being watched from inside the house as they bore down on it, but there was no sign from within.

They pulled up outside the barbed wire gate and Oldham started to drag the long rifle out of the scabbard, but Dancer shook his head. "Too awkward for close use, Dave."

He put his hands to his mouth and hallooed the house. "Hello, inside!"

The door opened and a middle-aged man stepped outside. "Hello, yourself," he called back.

"Your name Will Harmer?" Dancer called.

"That's me."

Dancer gestured to the gate. "Like to talk to you."

"Sure, why not?"

He came forward and unlatched the wire

gate. Dancer and Oldham passed through and Harmer began fumbling to close the gate. "Go right in the house and make yourself at home," he invited carelessly.

"No hurry," said Dancer.

He stood aside and waited until Harmer had closed the gate, then he and Oldham fell in behind the caretaker. At the door, Harmer reached forward to open the door, then stepped to one side, but Oldham suddenly gave him a shove so that he went hurtling through the door. Then Oldham followed, reaching for his gun. He let go of it when he saw the guns in the hands of the six men who were ringing the room.

Dancer came through the door, hands swinging at his sides. His eyes picked out Yancey, the ex-guerrilla, as dirty as ever, more vicious-looking even than the last time Dancer had seen him.

"Hello, boys," Dancer said easily.

"You got a nerve bustin' in here," one of the men said.

Dancer retorted, "Harmer invited me in."

"This-un's the Marshal," Yancey said, pointing at Dancer with his Navy gun.

"Yeah?" said the first man. "Well, a marshal's got no authority outside his town."

"That's right," conceded Dancer, "but I thought you fellows might want to ride into Lanyard on your own account."

"We ain't lost nothin' in Lanyard," retorted one of the ruffians.

"No, but you killed a man there last night."

"Look here," began Yancey, "I know you from somewhere and I'm beginnin' to remember from where. It was a long time ago. . . ."

"In St. Louis?" asked Dancer, smiling.

Yancey scowled. "I ain't ever been in St. Louis."

"Maybe it was Chicago," said Dancer. He took a casual step forward and with a lightning blow struck down Yancey's gun hand with his left fist.

WITH his right hand he grabbed Yancey's left shoulder and whirled him completely around, at the same time circling the former guerrilla's neck with his left forearm. With his then free right hand, Dancer whipped out his Navy Colt and jammed it in Yancey's back.

"Anybody shoots," he cried, "and Yancey gets it first!"

"Don't!" choked Yancey. "Don't shoot—he's Jim Dancer!"

"Jim Dancer!" cried one of the ruffians, falling back.

"It came to me," babbled Yancey in sheer fright. "We was at Lawrence together."

At Dancer's side, Oldham drew a derringer with his left hand and a nickel-plated six-gun with his right. But the announcement of Dancer's real identity was what did the trick.

A gun clattered to the floor, then another. Dancer shoved Yancey away so roughly that the outlaw fell to his knees. Then he fanned the other outlaws in the room. One of them looked for a moment as if he would try to shoot it out, but when Dancer's gun came even with his eyes, he dropped his weapon hastily.

Dancer stepped to one side. "Start filing out!" he ordered, gesturing to the door. "And that goes for you, Harmer."

"I ain't done anything," Harmer whined.

"You gave shelter to a bunch of killers."

"Yeah, but you ain't got no authority outside of Lanyard. You said so yourself."

"This is enough authority," Dancer said, raising his gun. "Although you're wrong. I can arrest a man anywhere in the county. I'm sheriff of the county."

"Sheriff!" exclaimed a couple of the men.

"There's no sheriff out here."

"There has been since yesterday. I guess if you'd known it you wouldn't have stopped here last night."

"If I'd known Jim Dancer was the sheriff, I wouldn't even have come here," one of the men retorted.

"Outside," ordered Dave Oldham.

THE men filed out and Dancer and Oldham stood to one side, while they saddled their horses. Clear of the enclosure, Dancer and Oldham mounted their own horses and the cavalcade started for Lanyard.

They had gone less than a half mile when Yancey fell back.

"Stay up there," Dancer ordered.

"I want to talk to you, Jim," Yancey whined.

"I've got nothing to talk to you about."

But when Yancey still held back, Dancer let him talk. "Look, Jim, you don't want to go arrestin' me," the ex-guerrilla said. "We rode together during the war, you know, and since then I—" He dropped his voice in the hope that Oldham wouldn't hear. "I saw Cole Younger a few weeks ago. . ."

"Are you through?" Dancer asked grimly.

"No, I'm not through," Yancey said with sudden spirit. "But maybe you are, Jim. You're supposed to be dead and there's been talk for years that you been ridin' the night trails yourself. I'll bet they don't know in Lanyard that you're Jim Dancer."

"They'll know it after you sound off," said Dancer.

"I don't have to tell them, Jim. Just give me my gun and nobody'll ever see me around here."

"Or your friends."

"They'll go with me—and they won't say a word, Jim. I promise you they won't."

"There's a better way to keep you from talking," said Oldham. He drew the rifle from the scabbard.

Yancey bleated and spurred his horse ahead to catch up with his gang. Oldham looked sidewards at Dancer. "You know he's going to sound off."

"Yes."

"This way nobody'd know."

"You and I would, Dave. And I don't think you could murder seven men in cold blood."

"They killed Milo Meeker in cold blood."

"Even so."

Dave Oldham exhaled heavily. "Maybe you're right, Jim, but you know what this is going to do to you?"

"I've a fair idea. I wasn't cut out to be a sheriff."

"The hell of it is, Jim, I think you were."

CHAPTER XX

OLDHAM and Dancer had ridden out of Lanyard before five and a few minutes after seven they rode back into the town. There were only a few people on the streets and they stared in astonishment at the sight of seven mounted men being herded along to the jail by Dancer and Dave Oldham.

Romeike the jailer stood in the doorway as the cavalcade came up. The prisoners were herded into the cell at the rear of the jail and locking it, Dancer handed the key to the jailer. "Don't let anyone talk to them," he instructed the man. "I'm going to get some breakfast, then I'll be back."

He and Oldham remounted their horses and rode slowly back up the street. As he dismounted in front of the China Cafe, Charles Vedder darted out of his office; he lived in a back room.

"What's this, Cummings?" he cried. "Somebody just told me you got the men who killed Meeker."

"They're in jail."

"That's terrific, Sheriff!" Vedder's eyes lighted up with an unholy gleam. "Judge Currier comes in on the eight o'clock train. I'll run him right over to the courthouse and we'll show Bruno County some fast justice."

"All right," said Dancer. "Romeike'll bring in the prisoners and if you want me I'll testify, but before court opens I think you'd better give this back to Judge Currier."

He took the sheriff's warrant out of his pocket and handed it to Vedder, who exclaimed in surprise.

"What's the idea, Cummings?"

"That's the idea, Vedder," Dancer said. "It's made out in the name of Cummings and my name isn't Cummings."

"Well, what is it, then?"

Dancer drew a deep breath. "Jim Dancer."

For just a second Charles Vedder remained motionless, then he recoiled in horror. "Jim Dancer!"

"That's right," said Dancer, and walking away from the prosecutor, entered the China Cafe.

He seated himself at the counter and had given his order for ham, eggs and coffee before Dave Oldham came in and sat down beside him.

"It's going to be a warm day," Oldham said, after a moment.

"I expect so," replied Dancer, "but there's one thing a man can't do anything about—the weather."

They were almost finished eating when the train whoo-hooed, as it neared the terminus of Lanyard. Judge Currier was on that train; Judge Currier who represented the only real law within two hundred miles. Vedder would be down at the depot to meet him and then Lanyard would receive a shock—two shocks.

Dancer put two silver dollars on the counter and got up from his stool. The door of the cafe opened just then and Paul Hobson stormed in, his face bleak.

"Here you are, Marshal. We're having a council meeting over in Bert Slocum's office —an emergency meeting."

"Now?"

"They're waiting."

"Don't go," Oldham said under his breath, but Dancer pretended not to hear. He followed Hobson out of the cafe and across the street, neither of them speaking.

IN SLOCUM'S office were gathered Slocum, Chandler Leach and Carter Bullock. Slocum sat behind his desk, grim-faced. Chandler Leach was seated in an armchair fidgeting nervously, and Carter Bullock looked unhappy about the whole thing.

As Dancer and Hobson entered, Slocum grunted: "We're not going to wait for the prosecutor, in fact that's why we're holding this meeting."

"You're sure you want me here?" Dancer asked.

"You're still the marshal of Lanyard," replied Slocum. "Although you may not be when we get through."

It dawned on Dancer then that the group had not yet learned of his real identity, merely that he had been appointed sheriff of the newly formed county. He sat down in a straight-backed chair.

"Vedder," Slocum began, "thinks he's pulled a fast one. Behind our backs he's gone to the state authorities and had a county made of this territory with himself as county attorney and our friend, the marshal here, sheriff."

There were no reactions among the other members of the city council, so they all knew that already. Slocum went on: "There's a Kansas City judge coming out here this morning—in fact, he's probably arrived during the last ten minutes. He thinks he's going to tell us how to run this town. But he isn't. This is a legally elected council and Lanyard is a legally incorporated city. If this Kansas City judge knows his law, he'll know that he can't go interfering with city affairs."

"He can keep me from trying cases," Chandler Leach said morosely.

"To a certain extent, yes. We'll take that up later. First of all, there's some more important business to take care of—specifically, two things."

He drew a slip of paper from his pocket and consulted it. "I want to propose a new city ordinance, to wit: 'Because it has become a public nuisance, it is hereby ordered that the driving of cattle through the city streets of Lanyard be declared illegal, as of October 1, 1872.' "

He lowered the piece of paper. "That's a week from today."

"I move that we have a vote on that," Paul Hobson said quickly. "All in favor?"

"Aye," said Slocum.

Bullock, the banker, bobbed his head: "Aye."

"Aye," said Paul Hobson.

Chandler Leach looked unhappily about the group, swallowed hard and said: "Aye." Slocum fixed Dancer with a cold stare. "Cummings?"

"Opposed."

"The ayes have it," declared Hobson, "four-to-one."

"The driving of cattle on our streets is illegal as of October first," Slocum amplified. "We now come to the second matter of business." He paused but this time did not consult his slip of paper. "Because he has been found derelict in his duties, the city council hereby suspends Marshal George Cummings and relieves him of his duties."

"All in favor?" exclaimed Hobson.

THIS time Chandler Leach did not hesitate. He had made his choice a moment ago and voted promptly with the majority. Dancer unpinned his badge and dropped it on Slocum's desk. He headed for the door, but Slocum called to him.

"The keys to the jail, Cummings."

"Romeike has them."

"He's your man; tell him to turn loose the men he's got in jail illegally."

"Not illegally, Slocum," Dancer said quickly. "I arrested them outside the city limits—in my capacity of county sheriff. They're murderers and they'll go on trial before Judge Currier."

"That remains to be seen." Bert Slocum rose quickly. "Johnny!" he cried in a sharp voice.

Johnny Tancred appeared through a door that led to a rear room.

"Johnny," Slocum said. "You've been appointed temporary marshal of Lanyard. I order you to clear the Lanyard city jail of all people held there illegally. Now!"

Johnny Tancred grinned lazily at Dancer. "Going to stop me?"

"I don't know," Dancer replied. "But walk to the jail with you."

"Sure enough.'

Tancred winked at the members of the city council and followed Dancer through the door. Outside, a couple of men who had been loafing at the hitching rail fell in behind the two. And a hundred feet behind them came the city council.

The procession moved toward the log building that housed the jail and courthouse. From a distance, Dancer saw that a crowd had gathered outside the place and he saw Vedder, the newly appointed county attorney, standing at the top of the stairs that led to the courtroom. Dancer quickened his pace then and as they came up to the jail, the crowd parted to let him and Tancred through.

A tall, heavy-set man of about forty-five came out of the courtroom and stopped beside Charles Vedder.

"Sheriff," Vedder called down, "Judge Currier is ready to try the prisoners."

"There's a little difference of opinion, Vedder," Dancer replied. "Mr. Tancred, the new city marshal, insists that this is a city jail and that he has sole authority over it. He intends to turn loose the prisoners."

"What's that?" cried the man standing beside Vedder.

"You heard what the man said," Johnny Tancred said, smirking.

"And you listen to what I say," Judge Currier said savagely. He came down the flight of stairs. "I represent the state of Kansas in judicial and criminal matters and if you interfere in any way with the prisoners of this court I'll hold you in contempt of court. In other words, you'll go to jail—and it won't be this jail."

JOHNNY TANCRED'S cocksureness faded. He licked his lips uncertainly and looked about the crowd and saw only hostile faces. But then he spied the city council coming up.

"Mr. Slocum," he cried, "he says he'll send me to jail. What do I do now?"

Slocum, his face taut, pushed through the crowd. "You're Judge Currier?" he asked of the newly arrived judge.

"I am," snapped Judge Currier. "And you?"

"I'm a member of the city council."

"Then tell this fool marshal of yours what he's in for if he tries to defy this court."

Slocum also saw the hostile faces about him and knew that they would become even more hostile when they learned of the new city ordinance. He nodded to Tancred. "He's the boss, Marshal."

Charles Vedder, meanwhile, had come down the stairs. He indicated Dancer. "Here's the sheriff, Judge."

Judge Currier shifted his fierce eyes to Dancer. "Ah, yes, bring the prisoners into the courtroom, Sheriff."

Vedder nodded to Dancer. "All right— Sheriff!"

Dancer went to the front of the jail and discovered that Romeike had barricaded the door on the inside. But he opened it in response to Dancer's command.

Dancer went in and accepting the key from Romeike, unlocked the cell door.

Yancey popped forward. "So you're turning us loose, eh? Got your orders."

"You'll go outside, around the corner and up the stairs," Dancer said.

"Sure, sure," chortled Yancey, licking his lips. "Gotta make it look official, eh?"

CHAPTER XXI

THE prisoners filed out of the cell, went through the jail office and out through the front door. They hesitated a moment or two, in the face of the throng outside the doors, but with Dancer prodding them along they rounded the corner of the building and climbed the stairs.

In the courtroom, Judge Currier had taken his place at the "bench." Vedder stood in front of the table and the prisoners lined up at one side, facing several spectators on the other side of the room, the entire city council and few townspeople. More of the latter came in.

Judge Currier picked up a little wooden mallet and tapped the table. "Fourth District Court, County of Bruno, State of Kansas, now in session."

Charles Vedder took a step forward. "Your Honor, the case of the State of Kansas, versus seven John Does, on a charge of willful murder."

"Proceed," Judge Currier said.

Judge Leach stepped out from his crowd. "Just a minute, Your Honor, I'm Judge—ah—Chandler Leach. I—ah—represent the defendants and I ask the court to dismiss this ridiculous charge on the grounds of lack of evidence."

Dancer, looking at Yancey, saw the former guerrilla grin foolishly.

"Lack of evidence?" Judge Currier asked. Then, to Vedder: "What do you say, prosecutor?"

"Let me call just one witness, Your Honor," said Vedder.

"Objection!" cried Leach.

Judge Currier gave him a withering look. "Hold your objections until later, Counsellor."

Vedder said: "Otto Holtz!"

The clerk from Milo Meeker's store, stepped out of the crowd.

"Raise your right hand," Vedder ordered and as the man obeyed, "Do you swear to tell the truth, the whole truth and nothing but the truth, so help you God?"

"Yeah, sure," said Otto Holtz.

"Mr. Holtz, what is your name?"

The clerk blinked. "Why, Otto Holtz—you just said it."

"What is your occupation?"

"Why, everybody knows that I been workin' in Milo Meeker's store."

"You were working there yesterday?"

"Of course."

"What happened there yesterday evening, shortly before eight o'clock?"

Holtz looked at the prosecutor, puzzled. "Ain't that what this is all about?"

"It is, Mr. Holtz." Vedder drew a deep breath. "Perhaps you'd better tell the court—in your own words—just what happened at Mr. Meeker's store last night."

"Sure, that's what I'm here for. Mr. Meeker got killed by them—"

"I object!" cried Chandler Leach.

Vedder made an impatient gesture. "Perhaps you'd better just answer questions, Mr. Holtz."

"Huh? Did I say something?"

Vedder said patiently: "You were working in the store last night, Mr. Holtz?"

"That's right."

"And while you were there some men came in?"

"Yeah, sure, four of 'em. Like I told you last night. They come bustin' in and began shootin' and then they tore out again an'—"

"And after they left, your employer, Milo Meeker, was dead; is that right?"

"Yeah, sure."

"Thank you, Mr. Holtz. Now answer the next question carefully. Did you see the faces of these men who shot Mr. Meeker?"

"Of course I seen 'em. Them's them—"

"I object!" howled Chandler Leach.

"Objection overruled," snapped Judge Currier. "It is apparent that the state is endeavoring to make an identification. Proceed,

Mr. Veeder."

"Thank you. Now, Mr. Holtz—these men you saw shoot down Milo Meeker . . . do you recognize any of them here in this court-room?"

"I sure do." Otto Holtz moved across the room, let his eyes roam over the prisoners. "They was all shootin', but this man here," he pointed at Yancey, "his was the first bullet to hit Mr. Meeker."

THE smirk was suddenly gone from Yancey's features. His mouth fell wide open. But then it suddenly clamped shut. "Hey!" he cried. "What's the idea? I thought—"

He took a step forward to cross the room toward Bert Slocum, but Dancer, standing near, reached out and pushed him back.

Otto Holtz picked out three more men. "There three was also in the store with him. There was a couple of them outside holding the horses, but I didn't get a good look at them . . ."

"The state rests!" Charles Vedder announced in a loud tone.

Then Chandler Leach pounced forward. "Look here, Judge," he blustered. "I demand a jury trial for my clients."

Judge Currier banged his gavel on the table.

"You may think you're within your rights, Counsellor, and if this were Kansas City I would be the first to concede it. But it isn't; it is a raw frontier community. Only a few moments ago there was a discussion as to who had jurisdiction over this very building. This is a new county and it so happens that I have special judicial powers—which I assure you are not without precedent in this state. We have neither the time nor facilities for jury trials in clear-cut cases and your appeal is therefore denied. The four men who have

been identified by the witness, step forward."

The men remained where they were. Dancer waggled his finger at Yancey. "All right, Yancey, that's you."

Yancey moved forward in a sudden rush, past Dancer and Vedder, to the judge's desk.

"Looky here, Judge, I got somethin' to say that's goin' to knock you off that there chair."

Judge Currier banged down so hard with his gavel that he splintered its handle. "Order!" he thundered. "You'll get your chance to talk later."

"But, Judge . . ." still protested Yancey.

"Shut up!"

Yancey closed his mouth, but his eyes glowered dangerously. Dancer prodded forward the other three prisoners who had been identified by Otto Holtz.

"You men," said the judge, "have been identified by a proper witness of this court. The court finds you guilty of murder, and sentences you . . ." He paused for just a second. ". . . to be hanged by the neck until you are dead, each of you!"

A roar went up in the courtroom. Judge Leach shouted over and over that he objected, but his words were drowned out. Judge Currier, having broken his gavel, pounded on the table with his fist and after awhile the noise subsided.

He said then: "And in view of the fact that we have no facilities for keeping prisoners in this county, I order the executions to take place as soon as possible. Sheriff, I remand the prisoners in your custody."

"Sheriff, hell!" howled Yancey. "That's what I been tryin' to tell you all this time. He ain't no goddam sheriff. He's—Jim Dancer! It's him that ought to be hung, not me. He's Jim Dancer, the outlaw!"

FOR a moment there was a stunned silence,

then a roar went up that was even greater than the one that had followed the sentencing of the murderers. Bert Slocum, during the hubbub, moved up and gripped Dancer's arm. The latter tried to shake it off, but couldn't. And then suddenly the room became silent.

Except for Slocum's lashing voice: "Is that true, what he said?"

Dancer said evenly: "The part about my name being Jim Dancer—yes!"

Charles Vedder stepped up beside Jim Dancer. "Your Honor, the sheriff's real name has nothing to do with the case before the court."

"You're right, Prosecutor," Judge Currier said, "still, I would like to know if you were aware of the sheriff's true identity?"

"He told me this morning."

"This morning?"

"Yes. He—he gave me back the warrant you issued, appointing him sheriff."

"Where is it?"

Vedder took the document from his pocket. The judge examined it and laid it on the table before him. "This court is adjourned for an hour." Then he grimaced. "That is, it will be adjourned after the prisoners have been locked in the jail downstairs." He looked steadily at Dancer. "Lock them up, then come back here."

"Ain't you goin' to lock him up?" Yancey cried. "He admitted he was Jim Dancer!"

Judge Currier merely glared at him.

Dancer nodded to the prisoners. "Let's go."

Yancey drew back. "I ain't going with you, Jim Dancer . . ."

Dancer struck him a blow that smashed the former Quantrell man to his knees. He drew his revolver and Yancey bleated in fright and scrambling to his feet, hurried for the door. The other prisoners followed him quickly.

Going down the staircase, Dancer held his gun on the seven men and after two or three looked over their shoulders, they kept good order and marched quickly around the building to the front door.

Dancer locked them in the cell and handed the key to Romeike. "You may earn your pay today, Romeike," he said.

HE LEFT the jail office and reclimbed the stairs to the courthouse, which had been cleared of most of the spectators, although there were still eight or ten present, including the entire city council. Slocum was orating savagely to Judge Currier as Dancer came in.

"This is the most ridiculous situation I've ever heard in my life," he was saying. "Appointing as sheriff the most notorious criminal of our time."

"Just a moment," cut in Judge Currier. "I appointed a man named George Cummings, not Jim Dancer. However . . ." He fixed Dancer with a cold glare. "Let's get to the bottom of this. You actually admit that you are Jim Dancer?"

"Yes."

"The outlaw, Jim Dancer?"

"I'm the Jim Dancer you're referring to," Dancer said carefully, "but I'm not an outlaw. I never have been."

"That's absurd, Judge," cried Bert Slocum. "Everybody knows Jim Dancer's an outlaw."

"That's a matter of opinion," interposed Charles Vedder. "The Jim Dancer we've known in this community for three months has been anything but an outlaw. He's been marshal of this town and he's been a good marshal."

"He's a highwayman and murderer!"

shouted Slocum.

"You can prove those statements?" Judge Currier demanded.

"I don't have to prove them, any more than I have to prove that two and two is four. Everybody knows—"

"Everybody doesn't know," the judge snapped. "I'll admit that I've always heard Jim Dancer referred to as an outlaw—just as I've always heard that Jesse James is one."

"He's one of the James Gang!"

"You can prove that?"

"Make him prove that he isn't."

Judge Currier shook his head. "No, the burden of proof is upon the court. A man is innocent until proved guilty."

Slocum pointed a finger at Dancer. "Didn't you kill George Cummings?"

"No."

Paul Hobson leaped forward. "That's a lie! That's one thing I can prove. And so can two other people in this town."

The judge's eyes narrowed. "Who are these people?"

"A man named Oldham and a woman named Florence Peel, who owns the Eldorado. . ."

"Get them!"

BERT SLOCUM signaled to Chandler Leach and the fat justice hurried out of the room. Then Slocum nodded to Hobson. "All right, Paul, tell them about the first time you met," he pointed to Dancer, "him!"

"It was when I was coming out here on the stagecoach last May. He was sitting on the river bank with a dead man handcuffed to his wrist. He told us the dead man was Jim Dancer, the outlaw, and that he was George Cummings, a Pleasanton detective. I—I even helped bury the dead man after," he cleared his throat, "after we cut the man's

hand off because there was no handcuff key." Hobson sneered at Dancer. "You deny that?"

"No," said Dancer. "That part of it's true enough. I deny, however, that I killed George Cummings."

"Oh, he was drowned trying to swim across the river?" Slocum said sarcastically.

"The ferryboat capsized," Dancer said. "There were two horses on the boat and in the struggle one of them kicked Cummings. He was dead before we struck the water."

"And what about the ferryman?"

"He drowned."

"You expect us to believe that?"

"No. I didn't expect Arthur Pleasanton to believe it, either. That's why I assumed the identity of Cummings and went to Pleasanton's Kansas City office."

"Oh, you admit that part of it? Will you also admit that you met me in that office?"

"Of course."

"And why was I in the Pleasanton office?"

Dancer paused and saw that the eyes of everyone in the room were upon him. He said: "You were there because you had hired the Pleasanton Agency to run me down."

Triumphantly, Slocum turned to Judge Currier. "Is that enough for Your Honor?"

"Hardly," retorted Currier. "Anybody can employ a private detective. I could go to Arthur Pleasanton and tell him that you were an outlaw."

"All right," said Slocum, "then I'll tell you why I employed the Pleasanton Agency. As a matter of fact, it was on behalf of my niece." His eyes glowed with an odd yellow light. "Nine years ago this man Dancer shot down my niece's father, my own brother. He did it wantonly and in cold blood—before my niece's eyes. Ask him to deny that!"

Dave Oldham stepped into the room and said: "That was in 1863, during the war!"

The judge turned on Oldham. "Who're you?"

"My name is Oldham; I was told that I was wanted here."

"He's the man who was on the stagecoach," said Hobson, "when we buried the Pleasanton detective that Jim Dancer killed. But I must warn Your Honor that this man is friendly to Dancer."

"I gathered that," Currier said. "A moment ago, Mr. Oldham, you came to Dancer's defense."

"Merely as a former soldier, Your Honor. Jim Dancer's crime—if it was a crime—was committed during the war. The war has been over for more than seven years. History will decide as to the right and the wrong of it."

"Well put, Mr. Oldham," conceded Judge Currier. "I know a little about the war myself."

"Your Honor," cried Bert Slocum, "Jim Dancer was never a soldier. He was a murdering bushwhacker, no more!"

JUDGE CURRIER'S eyes gleamed.

"You rode with Quantrell?" he asked. And, as Dancer nodded, "I think we had a little brush with you the day before Westport. The Fourth Wisconsin Cavalry?" He nodded thoughtfully. "You fought very well, considering we outnumbered you about four to one." Then he suddenly caught himself. "This is not a War Commission trial; it's a civil court. It's not up to us to decide upon the war guilt of—"

"You're siding with him," howled Bert Slocum.

"I'm not siding with anyone, Mr. Slocum. You say your brother was killed by Quantrell?"

"By Jim Dancer, not Quantrell. He was foully murdered during the Lawrence Massa-

cre. The war had nothing to do with it. Any more than it had to do with Jesse James being an outlaw!"

"Jesse James isn't on trial before this court," declared Judge Currier. "Nor for that matter is Jim Dancer."

"Then I'll bring him to trial."

"If you can furnish sufficient evidence— actual evidence, Mr. Slocum, of any crime that Jim Dancer had committed since April 15, 1865, this court will consider the issuing of a warrant against Jim Dancer."

"You mean you're not going to do anything to him?"

"Until you furnish this court with proper evidence, no."

"You're keeping him on as sheriff knowing his identity?"

Judge Currier cleared his throat. "That is another matter. Whereas this court lacks evidence that Jim Dancer is an outlaw, there seems to be sufficient rumor, or perhaps I should say public opinion, which is unfavorable—although perhaps unwarranted— against Jim Dancer, which would make his appointment an unhappy one." He looked steadily at Jim Dancer. "An officer of the law must be above reproach. Mind you, I do not say you are not, Dancer, but public opinion is against you and I feel therefore that I must void this appointment."

Jim Dancer nodded. "Thank you, Judge."

He turned and walked to the door. As he passed through, Dave Oldham fell in behind him.

Dancer started down the stairs and Oldham clapped his shoulder. At the bottom of the stairs a crowd of forty or fifty people stood silently watching him. The expressions on their faces were not especially hostile. They'd all heard that George Cummings, the man who had tamed Lanyard was Jim

Dancer, the notorious outlaw. Curiosity was on most faces, pity on some.

As he reached the foot of the stairs, the crowd parted and made a passageway for Dancer. He walked through, started up the street in the direction of the hotel.

Behind Dancer came the drumming of a galloping horse's hoofs. A clear voice shouted at him: "Jim Dancer!"

DANCER flinched visibly but continued walking. A small caliber gun barked and a bullet whistled past Dancer, missing him by less than a foot.

Dancer stopped and slowly began to turn. Twenty feet away, Evelyn Slocum pulled up her horse so suddenly it skidded to its haunches. She bounced from the saddle, a riding quirt in one hand, a .32 caliber revolver in the other.

"Jim Dancer," she cried, "get ready to die!"

She raised the revolver.

Dave Oldham leaped out of the crowd and lunged toward the girl. She saw him coming and sprang forward to avoid him, firing at the same time.

The bullet seared Dancer's left side, but before she could fire again, Oldham had knocked the gun from her hand. She started to stoop to retrieve it, but Oldham kicked it clear across the street.

Evelyn leaped clear of Oldham, the quirt dangling in her hand. She rushed straight at Dancer.

He could have torn the riding quirt from her hand as she came blindly at him, but he didn't. The leather sizzled through the air and lashed his face and neck like a red hot iron.

"Maybe the law can't do anything to you, Jim Dancer," Evelyn cried hysterically, "but I can!"

The quirt went back again and again it seared Dancer's face. She struck a third time and a fourth and was in the act of striking a fifth time when Florence Peel stepped off the sidewalk and wrenched the quirt from her hand.

"Go home, you fool," Florence said. "Go home and ask the God that made a fool like you to forgive you. Jim Dancer's the best man you've ever known and some day you'll realize it."

She reached out and with the flat of her hand pushed Evelyn off balance so that she fell to one knee. From that position, Evelyn looked up at the proprietress of the Eldorado. The hysteria was suddenly gone from her and Florence, seeing that, threw the quirt contemptuously at her feet.

"Maybe you'd like to use it on me. Well, go ahead!"

Evelyn picked up the quirt, got to her feet and still staring at Florence Peel, walked to her horse. She got stiffly into the saddle and suddenly whirling the animal, galloped it away in the direction from which she had come.

Dancer, the blood trickling down his side and his face smarting from the blows of the whip, gave Florence Peel an odd glance and, turning, walked off.

CHAPTER XXII

FOR a moment that day, the city of Lanyard, Kansas, had known law and justice. Four murderers had been arrested, brought to a quick trial and sentenced to a death they deserved.

But the execution of the sentence was not carried out, for there was no one to perform it.

Judge Currier offered the post of sheriff, upon the recommendation of Charles Vedder, to a man named Kelso, who ran the livery stable and was known as a good man. Kelso almost accepted until he learned what his first official duty would be.

"No," he said. "Maybe they need it, but I'm not hanging four men."

The county attorney made a list of a half dozen potential candidates and went about the town and canvassed the men. He returned in a half hour to the courthouse and shook his head.

"I'm sorry, Judge," he said. "Nobody'll take the job—not when they have to begin with a hanging and the job only a temporary one."

"What do you mean, temporary? There won't be any election here until next year."

"By which time Lanyard will be a ghost town," said Vedder. "Bert Slocum played his trump card this morning; he put through a city ordinance making it illegal to drive cattle through the streets of Lanyard."

The judge looked at him in astonishment. "But that'll kill the cattle trade that made this town."

"That's what Slocum wants; you see, he's through with cattle. He owns twenty thousand acres of land and he's going to plant it all in wheat."

"And Slocum thinks he can get away with that? Bring him here!"

Charles Vedder hesitated, then shrugged and went to see Slocum in his office up the street. Johnny Tancred and a couple of his friends were loafing outside the office and followed Vedder into the building, where Vedder delivered the judge's order.

"So the judge wants to see me," Slocum said. "Well, I've been thinking things over and I don't think that I want to see the judge."

"He'll issue a warrant for your arrest if you don't come to him."

"And who'll serve his warrant?"

Vedder looked at Tancred and his associates, each of whom wore two guns on their hips and he turned and walked out. Tancred and his friends followed him.

"Going to get yourself a gun, Prosecutor?" taunted Tancred.

White-faced, Vedder went back to the jailhouse. At the foot of the stairs Tancred sent a last taunt after Vedder.

"Like to hire a good sheriff, Prosecutor?"

IN THE courtroom, Vedder told the judge of Slocum's defiance. Currier listened in silence, then got up and went to a carpetbag that he had brought with him directly from the train that morning. He got out a long-barreled revolver.

"Vedder," he said, "I followed the Union Pacific all the way across the country. I've seen fifty towns without law and I've known a lot of lawmen, some good and some bad. And sometimes I've seen bad lawmen who were better than the good. Tom Smith was the leader of the Bear River riots and two years later he was marshal of Abilene—the best lawman a boomtown ever had. We're going to call on Jim Dancer and beg him to become sheriff of this county." He headed for the door, but Vedder, his eyes shining in delight, beat him to the door. He started out and downstairs, the judge following.

From below, guns spouted fire and flame and death. Charles Vedder cried out and fell headlong down the stairs and after him came Judge Currier!

Johnny Tancred holstered smoking guns and said calmly to his two assistant murderers:

"They drew on us!"

He walked to the front door of the jail and tried the door. It was locked on the inside. He banged on the door with his fist. "This is Marshal Tancred," he cried. "Open up!"

"I don't take my orders from you," Romeike called through the door.

Johnny Tancred stepped back, drew one of his guns and placing it to within six inches of the lock on the door, fired twice.

Then he kicked in the door.

A shotgun roared inside the jail office, but Tancred, expecting that, had jumped aside and the full blast of the charge tore a huge hole in one of his men.

Then Tancred fired twice into the jail and, walked calmly into the room. He saw the cell key lying on the table, got it and unlocked the cell door.

"All right, boys," he said, "you're free."

The seven prisoners, four of whom had been convicted of murder and sentenced to death and three, to whom the judge had not got around, poured out of the cell into the jail office.

"Hold up your hands, boys," Johnny Tancred said jocularly. "I'm going to swear you all in as deputy marshals."

"What about the judge?" asked Yancey, a bit nervously.

Tancred laughed. "What the hell do you think that shooting was for? There ain't no more judge—and no law in Lanyard County except us."

"Where's Jim Dancer?"

"He got fired. Yeah, by the judge, before he died himself."

"I've got a score to settle with him," snarled Yancey, "and I don't mean for what he did to me today."

"Go ahead and settle it."

Yancey's face twisted in a frown. "You say we're the law in Lanyard?"

"That's right."

"Then why don't we all go and get Dancer? Make it legal."

Tancred looked sharply at Yancey a moment, then began to chuckle. "Legal, eh? Yeah! Dancer didn't like the way I worked the last time I was a marshal. Well, let's give him a sample of the way we're going to run things from now on."

THE nine men poured out of the jail and started up the street. But before they had gone very far they turned in at a hardware store and requisitioned a round of revolvers and ammunition.

"Charge them to the city," Tancred said to the cowed hardware store man.

As they came out of the store they were met by a frightened Bert Slocum.

"Johnny," cried Slocum. "You—you killed the judge and Vedder?"

"Sure," Johnny replied easily. "They drew on us. It was self-defense."

"There'll be trouble over that, Johnny," said Slocum, shaking his head in foreboding.

"Nothing we can't handle. Don't worry about a thing, Bert. We got plenty of law here." He winked. "I deputized the boys. We're on our way to arrest Dancer. Legal-like, too. Which reminds me, round up Judge Leach so we can give Dancer a quick trial—like he give the boys this morning."

Tancred winked again at Slocum and led his procession of deputies up the street.

As they neared the Eldorado, Tancred caught sight of Dave Oldham standing in the doorway. His eyes lit up in unholy glee.

"Well, well," he cried. "If it ain't the ex-marshal's volunteer assistant."

"Leave me alone, Tancred," said Oldham tautly.

"Why, I wouldn't think of bothering you, Mr. Oldham," Johnny Tancred said smoothly. "But I thought since you like to help marshals so much you might want to come along . . . while I arrest your friend, Dancer . . ."

"*You're* going to arrest Dancer?"

"He's an outlaw, isn't he? This is a law-abiding town and we don't tolerate outlaws."

"What about this rabble that's with you?" Oldham asked savagely.

"They're my deputies."

Florence Peel came through the door. "Deputies," she said scathingly, "that scum isn't fit to clean Jim Dancer's boots."

"Just for that, lady," snarled Tancred, "you can have a ringside seat at Dancer's hanging."

"The likes of you will never see Jim Dancer hang . . ."

"Oh, no? Where do you think we're going now?"

Oldham stepped out upon the sidewalk to block Tancred and his cutthroats. "They mean it, Florence. Go and warn Jim."

Startled, Florence Peel looked at Dave Oldham. What she saw in his eyes caused her to inhale sharply. She stepped out upon the sidewalk, started to run past Oldham, toward the Drovers' Hotel a hundred feet away.

Tancred cried out: "Here, you . . .!"

He reached for his guns. Oldham was already reaching for his own, but Oldham was an amateur gunfighter, Tancred a professional. Tancred's bullet slammed back Oldham, drove him to his knees. From that position Oldham fired at Tancred, putting his bullet through Tancred's left forearm. And then Tancred's second bullet caught Oldham between the eyes.

"The girl!" shouted one of the ruffians.

"She's going to warn Dancer!"

Yancey was already in pursuit of Florence Peel, but she was outstripping him. He stopped suddenly, whipped out his gun and fired. Florence broke in her stride and plunged to the sidewalk. The Tancred men, their leader among them, pounded up.

Tancred, blood dripping from his wounded arm, did not even spare a glance at the girl on the sidewalk as he ran past.

CHAPTER XXIII

THE group tore into the hotel, grabbed the young clerk who was in the lobby. With a gun in the boy's stomach, Tancred demanded the number of Dancer's room.

"N-number five," bleated the clerk.

Tancred shoved him aside and bounded for the stairs.

On the second floor, Tancred wasted no amenities. He kicked in the door of Number 5 and caught Dancer on the bed, just sitting up. His gun was in his belt which hung from a nail on the wall.

"You're under arrest, Dancer!" Tancred cried.

"And you're going to hang, damn you!" howled Yancey.

"So you let them loose," Dancer said soberly. "I guess that was the shooting I've been hearing."

"The judge, yeah," sneered Tancred. "And your friend, Oldham."

"Oldham's dead?"

"I never saw a deader man in my life. And that gambling woman friend of his."

"Florence Peel?"

"Yancey got her. She tried to run ahead and warn you we were coming."

Dancer looked steadily at Yancey. "I

guess that more than evens things between us."

Yancey shrank back from what he saw in Dancer's eyes. "I been after you a long time, Jim Dancer!"

"And now you've caught up with me?"

Yancey reached forward and struck Dancer in the face with the muzzle of his gun. The blow laid open a two-inch gash on Dancer's cheek. Blood trickled down onto his shirt.

Dancer said: "I expected that from you, Yancey."

Dancer's calmness enraged Yancey. "You're tough, Dancer, but you'll be down on your knees begging before this day is over."

"Let's get going," Tancred said impatiently. He shoved Dancer toward the door. Hands gripped him roughly and propelled him down the stairs and through the hotel lobby.

Out in front of the hotel, Tancred stopped his crew. "Where the hell's that judge?"

He looked up and down the street which was virtually deserted, except for four horsemen who were standing a few feet down the street.

Tancred swore roundly. "Yancey, take a couple of men and find the judge. Bring him here even if you have to drag him by the heels."

Yancey started to protest, but Tancred roared savagely at him: "I'm running this show."

Yancey touched a couple of his friends and the three trotted off up the street. Downstreet, two of the horsemen dismounted and giving the bridle reins of their mounts to the others, walked over to Tancred's crowd.

Tancred scowled at them. "What do you birds want?"

"Not a thing," said one of the men.

"We're strangers here and we thought—"

"Go and mind your own business," Tancred snarled. "It'll be healthier for you."

The two men held their ground. "We were only trying to pass the time of the day."

"You've passed it."

"All right, but you don't have to be so tough about it. We thought some of settling in this town, but if people are like this . . ."

"Look, stranger," Tancred said sourly, "we're law officers and we're about to hang an outlaw. We haven't got time to make a reception committee for strangers."

"Well," said the bigger of the two men, "a hanging, eh? I've always wanted to see one. When does it come off?"

"As soon as the judge tries him. We do things legal in this town."

"Good! Good!" said the big man. "There's nothing like a legal hanging."

A MUFFLED shot sounded in a saloon up the street and a moment later the door burst open and Judge Chandler Leach came running out as fast as his short legs could carry him. Behind him came Yancey, the former guerrilla, and his two mates. And behind them Bert Slocum.

Leach outstripped the others in his approach to Tancred's crowd.

"Marshal," he cried, "I can't do it. I haven't got authority to try a man on a hanging matter."

"You had plenty of authority before that Kansas City judge came here," sneered Tancred.

"Yes, but that was before we knew that a county had been formed."

"Well, it's been unformed," snapped Tancred. "And if you need any authority to try this man, here it is." He drew his gun and pointed it at Leach's stomach.

Slocum came up. "Johnny," he pleaded, "you've gone too far. You can't get away with this."

"But, Mr. Slocum," Tancred mocked, "I'm just a hireling—don't you remember? You hired me."

Slocum walked stiffly away from the group, crossing the street to the bank, which he entered. Johnny Tancred glowered after him a moment, then gave his full attention to Leach.

"All right, Judge, do you think you've got the authority now?"

Leach gulped. "Y-yes."

"The prisoner," said Johnny Tancred, "is a notorious outlaw and murderer, one Jim Dancer. That's him over there, the sick-looking bird with the blood on his face."

Judge Leach seemed to be trying to swallow his Adam's apple. Tancred poked the muzzle of his gun into the judge's ribs—not gently. "Can't you talk, Judge?"

"Uh—yes—uh—what is the evidence against this—this man?"

"Evidence, Judge? Why, I just told you he was a murderer; isn't my word good enough in this court?"

Yancey piped up. "I can give some evidence. I saw him kill a man once."

"There," said Tancred. "What more evidence do you want? Even Judge Currier took the word of only one man this morning."

The judge grasped at the straw. "That's right. I—I find the prisoner guilty as charged."

"That's fine, Judge, just fine. Now the sentence."

"Twenty-five dol . . . ." began the judge, then caught himself and shot a frightened glance at Tancred. The marshal's cold eyes caused him to drop his own.

"Death," the judge croaked. "Death by hanging . . ."

"Thank you, Judge," Tancred mocked. "You've done a good job—and there are plenty of witnesses here who heard you sentence the prisoner. Just in case there's any question about it later . . ."

"No, no," sobbed the judge.

"What's that?"

Leach tried to turn away but Tancred caught him roughly by the shoulder and turned him back. "I think you'd better put the sentence in writing. Andy—run into the hotel and get the judge some paper and a pen."

ONE of the deputies ran into the hotel. He returned in a moment with the required articles which were handed to the judge and the little man scrawled a few words on a sheet of paper.

"And now," Johnny Tancred announced, "we're going to have that little hanging party that the town's been looking forward to." He chuckled wickedly at Yancey. "You lucky dog; it couldda been you just as well."

"Don't joke about a think like that!" cried Yancey.

"I'm not joking; you had a close shave. And just to make you appreciate your good luck I'll let you tie the knot and slap the horse out from under him. How's that?"

"That's something I've been looking forward to!"

"All right, what do you say to that nice cedar at the end of the street? There's a branch just about eight foot off the ground that's just made for a nice hanging."

The crowd started up the street, herding Dancer along in front. From doors and windows townspeople watched the procession, but no one interfered. The law of Lanyard was gone; the town was in a worse condition than when Jim Dancer had first entered it.

And now—now Dancer, the man who had made law in Lanyard, was leaving. . . .

But the hanging party was going to have some spectators after all: the four strangers who were mounted on beautiful horses, followed the procession at a distance of about a hundred feet.

One of the marshals picked up a horse along the way and after awhile the hanging party came to the end of the street where a fine cedar tree stood alone at the side of the road. Ahead, less than an eighth of a mile, was the imposing residence of Bert Slocum, the deposed ruler of Lanyard.

And now that they had the tree and the horse, the would-be executioners discovered that they lacked the essential item, a rope. No one had thought to bring one along.

That was where the four strangers came in. They rode forward and one of them, a lean, sun-tanned young man of twenty-four or twenty-five, took a coil of rope from his saddle pommel.

"Here's the article you want, friends," he said, smiling crookedly.

TANCRED stepped forward to take the rope and looked sharply into the lean man's face. "Didn't I tell you awhile ago to mind your own business?"

"Seems to me you did say something like that, mister," retorted the lean young man. "But hangings don't come along every day, you know, and we hate to miss a good one." He suddenly smiled. "Besides, you're going to use my rope. That ought to be good enough for an admission ticket."

Tancred took the coil of rope and scowled. "You can stay, but keep clear, understand?"

"You bet!"

Tancred turned and tossed the rope to Yancey. "You said you wanted the pleasure of tying the knot."

But Yancey was suddenly standing as if petrified. His mouth was agape, his eyes threatened to pop from his face. He was staring at the lean young man who had given Tancred the rope.

"What's the matter with you, Yancey?" cried Tancred.

He whirled suddenly and looked at the lean man. The latter was smiling lazily and Tancred, puzzled, turned back to Yancey. He gripped the ex-guerrilla's shoulder and shook him.

"Snap out of it. You look like you'd suddenly seen a ghost."

The lean man on the horse said: "Takes nerve to hang a man. Maybe your friend's a little chicken-hearted."

"I told you to keep out of this," exclaimed Tancred. He grabbed the rope from Yancey's hands, shook out a length of it and began to tie a knot. By the time he had finished, Yancey had recovered somewhat, although his Adam's apple was moving furiously up and down.

Tancred gave him a disgusted look and walking past him, threw the clear end of the rope over the low limb. One of the "marshals" caught it and twining it about the tree trunk, knotted it securely. Tancred stepped up to Jim Dancer with the noose in his hands.

"Well, sheriff," he said, "you had a short run."

"Yours may be even shorter, Tancred," Dancer said evenly.

"Not as short as you think. I don't mind telling you that my plans don't call for me to hang around this territory." He grinned crookedly. "Old Slocum's going to get the surprise of his life when we run out on this and let him hold the bag—an empty bag. He's got a hundred and fifty thousand dollars in that bank of his that we're going to relieve him of."

The lean stranger suddenly rode his horse forward. "What's that, Mister? You're figuring to hold up the Lanyard bank?"

Tancred turned savagely to the mounted man. "I warned you to keep out of this . . ."

The lean man's horse was oddly restless; it moved so that it was sidewards to Jim Dancer and between him and Tancred.

The man on the horse said: "Hanging's one thing, Mister; that may be your job. But mine's holding up banks . . ."

"Look out, Tancred!" suddenly screamed Yancey. "*He's Jesse James!*"

And at that moment Jim Dancer reached up and grabbed the butt of the revolver that was so conveniently within his reach in the lean man's holster.

THE man on the horse didn't seem to mind; his own right hand had gone under his coat— and came out with a twin to the gun that Dancer had appropriated.

Dancer fired the first shot; he dropped to his knees and, firing under the horse's belly, caught Johnny Tancred with his gun only half drawn.

The bullet knocked Tancred backwards into Yancey, the former guerrilla, and spoiled his own aim. Jesse James' bullet caught Yancey in the stomach.

Yancey fell to his knees and took a second bullet in the back of his head; it was fired by the big stranger on horseback who had spurred forward.

"I told you to stay away from this town," cried the big man, who was Cole Younger.

That was all the shooting there was. There were nine more men in Tancred's group; one or two had gone for their guns, but the swift deaths of their two leaders paralyzed their hands . . . or perhaps it was the sudden knowledge of the identity of the four strangers . . . who were aligned with Jim Dancer.

Guns began dropping to the ground, to the great disgust of the young bandit leader. "Why, damn you for a bunch of chicken-hearted cowards," he raged. "You've got us outnumbered. Why don't you fight?"

"I ain't fightin' Jesse James," whined one of the craven crew.

"Then, if you' ain't fighting," cried Cole Younger, "start running!" He fired at the foot of the man who had spoken, his bullet clipping off a bit of the leather toe.

The man started running blindly—as did his friends. The outlaws fired a few shots after them.

Jim Dancer went around to the four horsemen and shook hands with each of them. He gripped the hand of Cole Younger, the longest.

"Sorry I had to break my promise to you, Jim," said the big outlaw. "I wouldn't have done it only we thought it would help you out." He smiled. "We got word in a roundabout sort of a way that you were having a lot of trouble here because of a man who owned the town and had too much money."

"Bert Slocum!"

"That's the man. Well, we were tipped off that this man wouldn't be so much trouble around here if he lost about a hundred and fifty thousand dollars that he kept in the local bank."

"What do you mean, you were tipped off?"

"He's telling you the truth, Jim," laughed Jesse James. "A big railroad man named Lanyard tipped us off." He made a clucking sound with his mouth. "He's got a good railroad too. May have to hold it up sometime."

Dancer, looking past the outlaws, toward the town of Lanyard, saw two riders come slowly toward them. At a distance of more than a hundred yards he recognized Bert Slocum and his niece, Evelyn.

Jesse James said: "Of course you're riding with us, Jim."

Dancer shook his head. "A man's got to play out the hand he's dealt . . . and mine is here."

"Jesse!" exclaimed a tall, mustachioed man. "We'd better go." He gestured toward the approaching riders.

Jesse nodded. "Right, Frank!" He looked down at Dancer. "Been good seeing you again." He grimaced wryly. "And maybe this makes up for the time you saved my life at Baxter Springs."

He gave Dancer a half salute and dug his spurs into his horse's flank. The animal sprang away, headed for the open prairie. The other outlaws followed Jesse James at a full gallop.

JIM DANCER looked at the gun he had borrowed from the outlaw chieftain and forgotten to return, and thrust it into the waistband of his trousers. Then he mounted the horse that had almost served as an execution block for him, and rode toward the town.

After a moment he had to pull up for the horses of the Slocums had stopped and were blocking the road.

"So you won after all, Dancer," said Slocum in a strangely dead tone.

Dancer made no reply and Slocum drew a slow breath. "I give you the town of Lanyard, Dancer. Carter Bullock ran off with all my money."

Dancer stared at him and the broken ruler of Lanyard rode past him. But the road was still blocked for Dancer, for Evelyn Slocum remained.

Dancer finally looked into her face and saw that it was heavy and dull.

"She loved you, didn't she, Jim?" Evelyn said slowly.

Dancer gave a start: "Florence Peel?"

"Who else? She died trying to help you and I—I tried to kill you."

Her impassive face suddenly broke and she buried her face in her hands. A sob shook her body and Jim Dancer, sitting his horse awkwardly, a half dozen feet away, felt as old as the plains of Kansas.

Then, finally, Evelyn Slocum stopped sobbing and lowered her hands from a tear-stained face. "A person can live only so long with hatred," she said.

"Or with death," said Jim Dancer. "If it helps any . . . I never forgot. Not for one minute of these nine years."

"You were only a boy," Evelyn said "What did you know about it all? I—I thought of that and fought it and today . . . today, I learned that there are things stronger than hate."

Dancer stared at her.

"I'm going away," Evelyn went on. "Maybe I can forget all this after awhile and then perhaps I can live a normal life and see people . . . as they really are."

She picked up her bridle reins. "Maybe I'll even come back to Lanyard." She looked squarely into Dancer's eyes "Will you be here?"

Dancer said hoarsely: "I'll be here."

She rode past him then, and after a moment Dancer rode into the town.

THE END

BETWEEN A ROCK AND A HARD PLACE

by S. Omar Barker

Whether it's a buck fight or a bullfight, Uncle Duff Mason never can stand to miss out on the excitement. That, as you'll find out, is why he happens to be still a bachelor—which doesn't seem to bother him much except when he plays with five-year-old Belinda Wheeler. And it's the strain of choosing in a crisis between the welfare of little Belinda and her big brother that leads to Uncle Duff's "arranging" a match between Ol' Champ, his dun-yellow longhorn, and Jace Wheeler's $500 Hereford bull.

I RECKON Uncle Duff was sort of a heller all right. Everybody said he was, and I never did hear him deny it. But nobody seemed to know just what they meant by it. He wasn't a drinking man, but he could help unravel a town with just as much whoop and holler as the next one. He was a crack shot with a pistol, yet in a time when most horseback men held it an obligation of honor to settle their differences with lead, Uncle Duff, moderate of size and slender, did his fighting by hand, and according to his own code.

"If it's an honest disagreement," he advised me, "fight it out fair. But if you've been jumped on unreasonable, wrastle him down an' git your thumb in his eye!"

He was a competent cowhand and a middling success in his own brand, but he was liable to waste half a day for a whole roundup crew matching bull-fights. If anybody ever needed a leg cut off Uncle Duff would have come a-running and brought his own saw— unless he happened to be too busy painting red stripes on a live horny toad to amaze little Belinda Wheeler with, the next time her ma let me fetch the kids over when I went after mail.

Mostly Uncle Duff and I rode together, but Wheeler's was one place he kept away from.

Even Ma said she would just as soon try to understand the ways of a wolf as she would Duffey Mason's, and she was his own sister. She seemed to think what he needed was a regulator. "Here you are," she would scold, "goin' on thirty-one, sound in wind and limb—why the dickens don't you find you a good, honest girl and get married?"

"Maybe I'd rather go fishin'," Uncle Duff would drawl, throwing me a wink. That always made me grin, because everybody knew the only time Duff Mason had ever gone fishing in his life was the time he turned up the bellies of a wagonload of mud-cats and suckers with a charge of powder in a hole on Bedalong Creek. He hadn't been fish-hungry; just liked to see the splash.

At 34 Ma was a strong-minded woman, else she couldn't have been kin to Uncle Duff. She refused to be sidetracked. "Women was created a-purpose so men could marry," she said severely. "It's the Lord's will, Duff

Mason, and you know it!"

"If that's what Gran'pa God was aimin' at," drawled Uncle Duff, "it's a wonder he didn't create more of 'em purty!"

That was another thing that made tongues cluck—this "Gran'pa God" talk that he had learned from the Mexicans the time he trailed a stolen horse all the way to Taos without telling anybody he was going—and didn't get back for two years.

"If you thought Becky McGuire was so tarnation purty," said Ma, thumbing straight for the supposed sore spot, "why in the name of creation didn't you marry her when you had the chance?"

This made Uncle Duff bat his granite-blue eyes a little, but if it sure enough quicked him he never let on.

"Ain't it funny," he chuckled, "how a man forgets things he ain't reminded of over two or three times a week?"

"Shame on you!" With Ma barking on your trail you might as well run for a hollow log. "My own brother! I just can't get over it!"

"Give yourself time, Sweet-Lickin'," grinned Uncle Duff, using the name Ma told me he had made up for her while licking a cake batter crock when he was a five-year-old. "It's only been ten or twelve years!"

"Eight," Ma corrected him with a sigh. "Little Jace Wheeler is goin' on seven. And to think that if you hadn't set more store by watchin' a couple of ol' surlies do battle than by gettin' to your own wedding, such a boy might have been yours!"

"Gran'pa God forbid!" said Uncle Duff. Although he was fond enough of Becky Wheeler's little girl, he made no bones about considering her son a pest. "If that little egg-sucker was mine, I'd drop him on his head an' shorten his neck a little. Besides, it wasn't bulls I was watchin' fight that time—it was a

pair of buck deer that I happened onto on Big Hump Mesa." He turned to me, and there was a gleam of excitement in his eyes just from the remembering of it. "Seven hours them bucks had their antlers locked, Bub, before they give out! If I hadn't been there to untangle 'em, they'd have laid there an' starved to death. A man don't git a chance at a sight like that but once in a lifetime, Bub!"

It must have been a fine, wild thing to see, and I wondered if I would ever have such a chance. At 13 the only thing I didn't admire about Uncle Duff was him calling me Bub. Ma had torn the wagonsheet by naming me Mansfield out of some book she'd read, so of course I needed a nickname. "Buck" would have suited me fine. But Uncle Duff took a notion to call me Bub, and he was a hard man to wean.

In the year since a stumbling bronc had sent Pa off to The High Pasture and Ma and me here to the Wagon Mesa country to live with Uncle Duff, I'd heard Ma wring him out a dozen times about leaving his bride-to-be waiting at the church while he watched a buckfight. Only Ma never could seem to remember whether it was a buckfight or a bullfight. Her mind ran more toward other things.

"Buckfight or bullfight," she continued her chiding, "it doesn't matter a whiff! You can't blame a prideful girl for getting mad and marrying another man!"

"You never have heard me blame her, have you?"

"Not out loud. But you won't neighbor with them. You won't—"

"Me an' Jason Wheeler just ain't the same breed of dog," said Uncle Duff curtly.

"I notice you make over that little daughter of his a-plenty whenever she comes over here to play!"

Uncle Duff blew a puff of smoke up past his nose, probably to hide the look that came into his eyes at the mention of five-year-old Belinda Wheeler, dark-eyed and sweet as a red velvet-flower.

"That proves what I'm tryin' to tell you," Ma persisted. "You ought to marry and have a little girl of your own instead of havin' to steal the chance to pet somebody else's because you're scared her pa might take a shot at you!"

That quicked him. Ma sure knew how to stir his dander.

"Scared hell!" he said with a sharp hardness like the cut edge of a piece of rawhide. "I'll play dolls with Mindy on her own front porch any time I take a notion to—an' who'll stop me?"

"Then why don't you?" Ma inquired sweetly.

"Because I ain't took a notion to—yet," said Uncle Duff.

Uncle Duff had paddled little Jace Wheeler once at our house for rubbing fresh cow sign in Belinda's hair, and the little booger had spread the word that his pa aimed to make a ge-bang business of it if Uncle Duff ever showed up on his premises. Maybe some folks got it in their heads that was why Uncle Duff kept away from there— except for the times I aim to tell about. But to me it was plain that whatever my Uncle Duff took a notion to do, no fear of either God or man ever stopped him.

Right now he took a notion to yank loose Ma's apron strings when she turned to stir a kettle of wild grape jam. "Don't you fret about me an' Jason Wheeler," he drawled with the perfectly sober face those oldtime cowhands knew so well how to put on when they was joshing. "If trouble busts loose, I can always run for the church!"

"Shame on you!" said Ma. But she had to hide a smile, and I laughed right out loud, because I had been there and seen it happen. There wasn't much of Uncle Duff's hell-arounding that I ever missed.

At that time Wheelerville was just Jason Wheeler's house and store, Frenchy Pinard's black-smith shop, and the little plank shack with a steeple on it that Wheeler had built for a church—preached in several times a year by some stray circuit rider, used the rest of the time by Wheeler himself to store grain in. Some said Jason had built the church as bait with which to promote a settlement around his store. But if he had it didn't work.

Uncle Duff claimed that all anybody needed in those days to start a town was a barrel of whisky and a gourd. But he had tried that himself, and it hadn't worked either. He had added another gourd and a little stock of goods to the whisky barrel and set up a store at the foot of Wagon Mesa, aiming "to git rich an' famous." But Uncle Duff was born to the saddle, not a prune counter.

He got into the habit of leaving the store open for folks to help themselves and leave the money in a cigar box while he was out with the cattle. Business might have thrived even on that basis, for it was 90 miles to Gap City and most range folks run pretty strong to honesty. But one day a cowhand named Jake Lang held a match to the bunghole to see how empty the whisky barrel was. Uncle Duff spied the smoke from not very far away, but he had a bullfight going, and by the time he found out which old surly could shove the hardest, his store was a pile of ashes.

The next day two wagonloads of goods unloaded at Jason Wheeler's place over on Bedalong Creek and Jace went into the mercantile business. It may have seemed peculiar to Uncle Duff that Wheeler was so ready to start a store when his own burned down, especially as Jake Lang was a Running W cowhand, but he never made an issue of it. Instead he hunted Jake up and thanked him.

"I'm built too short in the pockets for a damn counter jumper anyhow, Jake," he said. "You done me a favor by burnin' me out. But I ought to thumb Jace Wheeler's eyes out for puttin' you up to it."

"I tell you it was an accident, Duff!" Jake protested. "Wheeler never had no hand in it!"

"Sure," said Uncle Duff. "I hear he's goin' to sell everything from dog-irons to didies in that new store of his."

"He sure is!" Jake was enthusiastic. "Even got ol' Doc Roseberry to pick him out a shelf of medicines to cure everything from skunk bite to the hollow gut."

"Best cure for skunk bite that I know of," observed Uncle Duff dryly, "is to bite the skunk first."

"You oughta come over an' see what a layout he's got," Jake urged. "Beats haulin' from Gap City all to hell!"

"Maybe I will," said Uncle Duff, tilting his tall crowned hat over one ear while he scratched above the other. "Any of them new bulls of Wheeler's I might match a fight with for ol' Champ?"

"The Runnin' W don't buy high-class bulls just to git a horn run through 'em. If I was you I wouldn't mention matchin' a bull-fight to Jace Wheeler."

"If you was me," drawled Uncle Duff, "you'd shorten your lip a little before somebody steps on it."

It had been a few days later that Uncle Duff, Brazos Bill, Jug Johnson, and I cut out a little ol' pot-bellied dogie bull and drove him over to Wheeler's. You never saw such a sorry-looking burr-tailed scrub in your life,

but salty. The way he had gone on the prod when roped had tempted Uncle Duff to have a little fun.

Uncle Duff and Brazos Bill V'd their ropes on this little bull while Jug Johnson and I choused him from behind. He was plenty frothy by the time we stopped between Wheeler's store and the little plank church. There he sulled. Uncle Duff let out a whoop, and Jason Wheeler came stomping out of the store, followed by Jake Lang and several others. Jason was a tall, red-necked man, broad of hip and shoulder, with bristly red eyebrows.

"Howdy, Mr. Wheeler," drawled Uncle Duff in that dead sober way of his. "I hear you're in the market for hundred-dollar bulls. Now here's a high-class, purebred Scandinoovian sway-back, that I'll sell you for ninety-nine an' a case of prunes!"

"This scrub?" That Jason Wheeler was a humorless man was betrayed in the tone of his scorn, and the cowboys all began to grin. "Do you think I'm crazy?"

"If I did, do you think I'd come over here an' offer you this fine young male at half what he's worth?"

"Worth? Why, I wouldn't give a dime for him! Get him out of here!"

"I hear you're a good judge of cattle, Mr. Wheeler," urged Uncle Duff soothingly. "Prob'ly the best in the Territory. Before you miss this bargain, kindly step down an' feel the taller on this bull's brisket!"

The brisket was plainly pure hide and hair and cockleburrs, and the cowboys' grins widened.

Wheeler stepped down off the store porch. "Hup!" he growled, making a shooing motion with his hat. "Huy-yah! Get this scrub off'n my premises!"

He ought to have been around cattle and

cowboys long enough to know better. The scrub bull's tail gave a single switch, then arched a little up close to the root. His ears stood forward. He pawed at the earth, took a couple of short, stiff-legged steps, snuffed wind from his nose, and charged,

Uncle Duff's and Brazor Bill's ropes had looked fairly secure to the saddle horns, but now they suddenly slipped their dallies and fell slack. As Mr. Wheeler side-stepped, one of the scrub's stubby horns raked his hip pocket. By the time the little bull could whirl to charge again, the red-necked storekeeper was racing toward the open door of the little plank church, and it seemed to me that I could smell laughter in the whoops with which all of them, even Jake Lang, helped him run.

Whether the bull would have followed him on into the church without a little judicious guiding, no one will ever know. Looking in through the window I saw Mr. Wheeler treed on a pile of grain sacks and the bull having it out with a pair of plank benches and a tangled rope.

"Jake!" Wheeler yelled. "Fetch me my gun and I'll shoot the son of a so-and-so!"

It never was right clear whether he meant the bull or Uncle Duff, who was now standing in the doorway, rolling a smoke and giving no sign of amusement beyond a twinkle in his eye.

He turned to Lang. "Jake," he said, "hadn't you better fetch the man his go-bang?"

It was Becky Wheeler, still slender as a young girl, her long brown hair loose in the wind, who came running out of the house then and put a stop to the show. "Never mind the gun, Jake!" she said sharply, then bowed right up to Uncle Duff, her brown eyes flashing. "This is a fine thing, Duff Mason! Aren't you ever going to grow up?"

The look Uncle Duff gave her had something in it, I don't know what. "What for, Becky?" he said, and this time the soberness didn't look to be put on. He turned to the rest of us. "All right, boys, let's git this calf outa here before he busts a horn!"

The five of us worked him out without too much trouble, even with little Jace Wheeler in the way. Pretty soon we had the tow ropes fresh rigged on him, ready to go.

Nobody looked very mad now except Wheeler, and I thought Becky's presence had him tapered off a little, too. He waved a big hand toward the meeting-house, which was some messed up inside. "Who's goin' to pay this damage, Mason?"

Uncle Duff took time to lean down and give little Belinda Wheeler a willowbark whistle he fetched out of his pocket, then shrugged. "Why, if the bull won't, I reckon I will. How much?"

"Never mind it!" said Becky Wheeler quickly. "Only—please, Duff—I wish you wouldn't come here stirring up trouble!"

Without answering, Uncle Duff forked a couple of sawbucks out of his wallet and handed them to me. "Pay the man, Bub," he said. "An' look out you don't git bit."

I will say for Jason Wheeler that one of the tens was all he would take.

As we rode away, Brazos Bill had just started to rehash the bull sale for a warmed-over laugh, when a whizzer of a rock caught Uncle Duff behind the ear and like to knocked him out of the saddle. When we turned to look, we saw little Jace Wheeler cutting the dust for the house with his ma right after him.

"Gran'pa God!" said Uncle Duff, rubbing the bump, "I never knowed a mule could kick that high!"

That was the ruckus Uncle Duff had referred to when he told Ma that he "could, always run for the church."

It took a pretty good range bull to bring $50 in those days, so when Jason Wheeler shipped in a $500 white-face from Missouri, it gave folks almost as much to talk about as the epidemic of throat disease that came to plague the country only a few weeks later. It was a different kind of talk, of course, because Wheeler's bull didn't kill anybody's kids, but the diphtheria did.

I don't know whether Wheeler put the new bull in his west boundary pasture on purpose to tantalize Uncle Duff or not. But Uncle Duff he couldn't wait to go take a look at him. Brazos Bill and I rode with him down along our side of the stout four-wire fence between the two properties one evening, but the new bull was off in the scrubbery somewhere and we didn't sight him.

Uncle Duff never said anything, but the next morning he was gone before I got up, and toward noon Ma and I heard the doggonedest bellering you ever listened to, off down the draw.

"It's ol' Champ an' Wheeler's new bull talkin' fight!" I said.

"But I thought you told me Champ ranged over on Plum Creek!" said Ma, biting her lip.

"Oh, well," I told her, "bulls always drift around right smart."

That didn't fool Ma any. She knew as well as I did how come Champ to turn up all of a sudden over here next to the Running W fence. "I hope Duff don't cut Jason Wheeler's wire just to see two ol' surlies fight," she said uneasily.

"Uncle Duff never cut another man's fence in his life," I said. But I couldn't help wondering just how stout that four-wire fence of Wheeler's was. I rigged my pony and rode down there as quick as I could.

Ol' Champ was a high-hipped, dun-yellow bull about seven years old that had whipped every bull on Uncle Duff's range. In the longhorn breed, bulls never did grow great long horns like the steers did. Champ's were as thick as a man's leg at the butt, with an upswing that in about 15 inches tapered into polished black points as hard as flint and sharp as a bodkin. I doubt if he would have weighed 1000 pounds, but as Uncle Duff said, it was "all gristle an' go-git-'em."

Down on the first flat I came onto Uncle Duff sitting on his horse with one leg crooked around the saddle horn watching excited cattle putting on a parade up and down opposite sides of the fence. Strange cattle always act snuffy when they first come together and when a couple of bulls pair off and begin bowing up to each other, it reminds you of the way a crowd of human flock to a fist fight. That's the way it was there on the flat.

Wheeler's deep-loined new Hereford bull was mighty pretty. His red was the reddest I'd ever seen on a cow animal and the white of his head the whitest. His horns looked a little shorter than Ol' Champ's, and whitish at the tip, but plenty stout and sharp. With his thick, curly neck all bowed up, his nostrils blowing the dust, he was crowding the fence just about as close as Ol' Champ was. It surprised me to see a cowpen bull showing just as much fight as a longhorn of the range.

Either one of them was stout enough to have ripped that fence down, but you could see that neither was going to risk being caught off base long enough to do it. Bulls don't open a battle by trying to hook each other. They circle for position, then crash their heads together head on and push.

Uncle Duff didn't say anything when I rode up. I hooked my leg over the saddle horn, the same as his.

"Ol' White-Face looks mighty heavy," I commented.

Just then the Hereford ran his tongue out about a foot and let out a short rusty blast. Ol' Champ just stood there solid, snuffing wind through his nose but never batting an eye.

"I'll bet Ol' Champ can whip him," said Uncle Duff, with a calculating quirk of his head. "I'd sure give a purty to see him try!"

"You reckon that fence will keep 'em apart, Uncle Duff?" I inquired hopefully.

"It's a purty stout fence," said Uncle Duff. He stepped off his horse and picked up a stout-looking stick. He stuck it behind the top wire like a lever and put on a little pressure. "Staple seems plenty tight," he said— and at that moment Jason Wheeler and Jake Lang rode up out of a gully a few yards away. Uncle Duff didn't move away from the fence.

"Mason," said Wheeler, lofty as all get-out, "I paid five hundred dollars for that bull. If you turn that scrub longhorn of yours in on him and get him hurt there'll be trouble."

"When there is," said Uncle Duff, "I'll be there."

"I'm just warnin' you," said Wheeler.

"Mr. Wheeler," said Uncle Duff, shucking his coat, "which side of this fence would you rather fight on?"

Wheeler's answer to that was to give a single significant slap at the butt of his gun and ride away. Jake Lang sort of grinned and followed him.

I never did see anything eat on a man more than the idea of matching a fight between those two bulls did on Uncle Duff. Sometime almost every day White-Face and Ol' Champ would rendezvous at the fence line for a spell of "paw and beller," and Uncle Duff didn't often miss being on hand to watch them.

But when Ma tartly suggested that somebody might saw off a few posts so the fence could accidentally fall down, and get all this foolishness over with, Uncle Duff spoke up pretty sharp.

"That white-face is valuable property," he said, and it sounded to me as if he was mainly laying it on the tawline to himself. "Gittin' him hurt would be might' nigh the same as stealin'!"

It wasn't very long afterward that we heard that a sickness which Doc Roseberry called diphtheria had broken out in Gap City. Next it was spreading out among the nesters. We heard that two Ramadeaux children over on French Creek had died with it, quick. It gave us something more vital to talk about than Jason Wheeler's new bull. We heard that Doc Roseberry had a medicine called antitoxin which needed only a single dose to cure the disease if he got to it in time. But it was a medicine that had to be shot into you with a needle, and with people living so far apart, old Doc Roseberry was having a hell of a time trying to answer every call.

Then the word got around that Jason Wheeler had bought a batch of the stuff to sell at his store, and the nester-folks were buying it and shooting it into their ailing children themselves whether they knew how or not—even whether they knew for sure that it was the diphtheria. To make it easier for country doctors, or for folks who weren't doctors, to use, the antitoxin was put up in single doses, each supposed to be sufficient for one case, not measured out in units according to need as it is now. But there were cases where the child died anyway, and some parents feared the medicine almost as much as they did the disease.

Uncle Duff got the notion that maybe

folks weren't using it right, and rode all the way to Gap City to get Doc Roseberry to show him "the right way to squirt them hooperdamics." After that he rode far and often, but came home often, too, always with anxiety in his eyes.

"Any news?" he would ask, and Ma would shake her head, meaning that neither her young'un or the Wheelers had come down with it yet.

Even with all his going and coming, Uncle Duff still found time once in a while to take a *pasear* down the fence and speculate on the forbidden pleasure of matching that bullfight. That's what he and I were doing the morning that Frenchy Pinard, his rheumatic legs comfortless in the saddle, came riding over.

"Those Wheeler keeds," he said, "they go seeck in the night. All cowboys out on the works—the Papa ride for the Docteur heself. But Meez Wheeler afraid they die before he return back. She like you to come—queeck!"

That was how we went—quick. Uncle Duff ordered me back to the house, but I didn't mind him. After that I don't think he noticed whether I came along or not.

Becky Wheeler's face was as gray-white as wet paper when she came to the door. "Duff," she said, "we're in a fix. Jason sold out all the antitoxin. He couldn't refuse folks, and he expected to get more. This morning I looked again—and found one dose, back of the shelf."

"Well, one dose is better than none," said Uncle Duff.

"But—but don't you see, Duff? It's enough for one of the children—but not for both! They choke so bad, and their fever's so high! Duff—I'm scared!"

Uncle Duff put the needle in a saucepan and poured boiling water from the teakettle over it. "Becky," he said quietly. "I reckon you'll have to tell me which one to save—an' which to risk."

"I can't! Oh, God, I can't!" Becky's voice had a faraway, whispery sound to it. "Duff—I want you to go in there—alone—and do what God tells you is right. And whether they live or die, promise me never to tell me—or anybody—which one you gave it to!"

Duff looked at her a long time without batting those granite-blue eyes of his. "I'm afraid me an' Gran'pa God ain't on close enough speakin' terms for that," he said finally, "But I reckon I'll promise you."

I didn't suppose he even knew I was there, but as he went into the bedroom, he turned in the door, "You git back outside, Bub," he ordered sharply. "Don't you know this damn stuff is ketchin'?"

I went outside quickly and slipped around to the bedroom window. Uncle Duff must have found the room too hot for his liking, for I had to duck down below the sill when he came over and opened the long-faced lower sash a few inches.

When I peeked again he was still standing there, his head turned sidewise and a little up, like he was talking to somebody taller than he was.

"Look here, Gran'pa God," he was saying, as if speaking to a friendly neighbor, "if this was a bullfight I'd know what to do. But the way it is, it looks like you've got me between a rock an' a hard place."

Then he went over to the corner where the bed was, and I never could crane my neck enough to see which one of the sick kids he shot the medicine into. Ornery as he was, I couldn't help feeling sorry for little Jace.

Uncle Duff was a long time coming out. I was waiting on the front porch when Becky came to the door with him.

"I've done all I can do," I heard him tell her. "The rest is up to Gran'pa God. But I'll stay till Jason gits back with the doctor if you want me to."

"You look all wore out yourself, Duff," she said. "Jake and the cowboys will be in off the work, and Mrs. Pinard's coming to stay with me. Whyn't you go on home and get some rest?"

I'd seen Uncle Duff in many a mood, but never tight-strung and drawn around the gills like he was as we rode back toward the ranch. Once my pony stumbled and bumped into his a little.

"Gran'pa God!" he said, sharper than he had ever spoken to me before. "Can't you hold that damn nag's head up?"

As we rode up the boundary fence, there were those two bulls up along the wire again, talking fight. At first I thought Uncle Duff was going to ride right on past without even looking at them. Then all of a sudden he reined up.

"Bub," he said, "let's you and me match us a bullfight!"

The sound of it somehow put me in mind of the way I've since seen men with a bad case of the drooptail reach for a bottle of whisky.

With a couple of stout sticks and a rock it didn't take us long to loosen staples and let down the wire. To my surprise it was White-Face that made the invasion, bowed up and snuffing to beat the band, while Ol' Champ took time out to paw some more dirt up on his narrow back.

By the time we got back on our horses, they were stiff-tailed and circling for position. Then their big bony foreheads crashed together and their backs began to hump up with the strain of a mighty pushing that budged neither one of them a foot. A couple of frolicking steers bowed up and blatted and pranced around them, but the battling bulls paid them no attention.

"Purty well matched!" said Uncle Duff, and something of the old gleam was back in his eye.

Then the Hereford's superior weight began to tell, and Ol' Champ began to give ground.

"He's goin' to git licked, Uncle Duff! I cried, with very real concern. "That white-face has got him goin'!"

"Ol' Champ's been pushed before," said Uncle Duff.

In another moment I saw what he meant. Instead of losing footing and letting himself get hooked down when he had to back up too fast, the wiry longhorn broke free, sprang sideways with incredible nimbleness and whirled to horn the white-face in the shoulder as he surged past. It was a vicious gouge, but it did not down the Hereford. With a grunt he arched around with his meaty neck bowed and again the head-on battle of the push began.

Time after time in the next hour White-Face seemed to gain an overpowering advantage, only to have Ol' Champ's spry footwork beat him out of it. Then finally one of Ol' Champ's horn thrusts found a soft spot between two ribs, and the white-face went down, never to get up again.

"I love to see 'em fight, but I hate to see 'em git horned down an' killed," was Uncle Duff's comment as we rode on home. "That white-face put up right smart of a battle!"

It had been an exciting but not a pretty thing to see. I felt shaky and sort of sick inside. I was scared, too, wondering what Wheeler would do when he found out what had happened to his bull.

At the ranch Uncle Duff stopped only to

swallow a cup of coffee, then allowed he would take a *pasear* over to French Creek to see how the sick folks over there were making out, and Ma didn't try to stop him. He seemed in mighty good spirits.

"There's a young widow woman over there," Ma said sort of to herself after he left. "Who knows?"

It was some after sunup when he got back the next morning.

"Saddle me a fresh horse while I see if I can beg your Ma out of a cup of coffee, Bub," he said. "I'm goin' to ride over an' see if Wheeler's back with the doctor yet. You recollect he said there'd be trouble if anything happened to his bull—an' I promised him I'd be there."

I didn't ask whether I could go along or not. When I climbed my horse Uncle Duff looked at me mighty hard but didn't say anything, so I went.

Jason Wheeler and old Doc Roseberry came out on the porch as we rode up. Both of them looked pretty gaunt in the face.

"Duff," said Wheeler, "I don't know as it matters a damn now, but I can't help wantin' to know which one—"

"Which won?" broke in Uncle Duff. "Why, that longhorn whipped him four ways from the jack! Your white-face put up a purty fair fight for a cowpen critter, but—"

"I ain't talkin' about bulls, Duff," cut in Wheeler. "I want to know which one of my children you give that medicine to?"

"Gran'pa God!" said Uncle Duff, sort of quiet. "You mean one of 'em died?"

"The kids," said Doc Roseberry, squinting through his pipe smoke, "are both doin' all right. My godfrey, what you fixin' to do with all that money, Duff? My fees ain't that high!"

Uncle Duff had dismounted and was stiff-legging it up the porch steps with a thick wad of bills which he shoved into Jason Wheeler's hands. "Payin' for a bullfight, Doc," he breezed. "An' by the Gran'pa it was worth it!" He turned to bat his granite-blue eyes challengingly at Mr. Wheeler. "I'm buyin' me a dead bull, Wheeler," he said. "If five hundred ain't enough, come over an' see if you're man enough to pull my whiskers for the balance! So long, gents!'

Jason Wheeler stared at the money in his hand, then at Uncle Duff's back as he reached for his horse. "Hold on here! I don't ask no money from you, Duff!" he began. "I—"

But that didn't stop Uncle Duff. Becky Wheeler came out the door, just as he swung into the saddle, her lips parted as if to call to him; but that didn't stop him either. And whatever Uncle Duff was a-notion to do was good enough for me. We left out of there in a fog of dust.

"Sure 'nough, Uncle Duff," I asked him. as we loped away, "which one did you give the medicine to?"

"That, Bub," he grinned back at me, "is between me an' Gran'pa God!"

And so it might have remained if old Doc Roseberry hadn't later told Ma in confidence that he had noticed hypodermic needle pricks in the skin of both little Belinda and Jace. Half a dose of antitoxin each, he figured, had somehow been enough to stave off the strangling till he got there.

Maybe Gran'pa God had something to do with that, too.

THE END

BORROWED BULLETS

by Ralph Berard

Cutting sign on a notch-hunter of the Jack Rabbit Kid's calibre any Range City son but Race Gordon would have thought first of the two thousand dollar reward offered for the bandit dead or alive!

THE body was sprawled face down in the dust, arms outstretched. Blood stained the dead man's shirt. The stiff whitness of the clutching hands in the early sunlight told young Race Gordon even before he dismounted that the man was dead. His horse, a nervous-looking high-bred grey mare, grazed some fifty feet from the short-cut trail to Range City.

Race hesitated a moment, standing there looking down at the still form. He finally stooped and turned the body over, then stepped back, startled, a wild scatter of disconnected thoughts chasing through his brain.

Anyone living within a hundred miles of Range City would have recognized the Jack Rabbit Kid from the reward posters stuck up all over the country. Most anyone except Race Gordon would have thought first of the two thousand dollar reward offered for the bandit dead or alive.

But Race thought of something else: Of the Kid's reputation, of how the Jack Rabbit Kid had fought and killed. Every man within a thousand miles was afraid of the Jack Rabbit Kid.

All of his nineteen years Race had wanted to be feared and respected like that. And in the last four years he had had a specially good reason.

When Race had been only fifteen, he'd heard his father tell how Gatz Blemming and three hired killers had seized control of Range City and started to drive the small ranchers out of the valley. Even then Race had sometimes brooded over the thought of riding to Range City and shooting it out with Gatz Blemming. But he'd known, of course, how foolish and impossible it was and the best he could do was to borrow his dad's gunbelt without his permission and sneak to a draw in the hills where he practiced his draw and his aim. His dad, hearing the shots one day, had ridden out and surprised him there.

"Who're ya planning to kill?" Jake Gordon had asked sternly.

Race had drawn his skinny six feet up an extra inch and swelled out the strong frame of his sinewy thin chest and said, "When I grow up, I'll kill anyone who steals from you or Mom or Ritzy."

"You're mighty young for guns," his dad had said, "but it's a hard country. Don't reckon ya can learn your shooting any younger." Jake Gordon had swung his horse and ridden slowly away without looking back. Race had stared after him for a moment then had returned resolutely to his practicing. That same evening Jake Gordon had given the lad the guns and the belt and his blessing.

Now it had been just two years since Cal

Fetters, the loyal foreman of Jake Gordon's Four Bar spread who had stuck by them through a long siege of drouth and rustling, had found the honest old rancher's bullet-ridden body far out on the north range and the full responsibility of the Four Bar had been thrust suddenly on Race's youthful shoulders. Fetters had told Race, "I know it was Gatz Blemming's men who killed your dad. We saw the whole thing but it wouldn't be no use me claiming that. I'd likely just get killed for my trouble."

Race had understood how things were and he hadn't blamed Fetters for not talking. But as long as Jake Gordon was alive, the Range City Bank which Gatz Blemming had also got control of, had pretended leniency in regard to a past due payment of fifteen hundred dollars against the Four Bar. Hardly, however, had Race's father been buried before the bank filed foreclosure notice.

"It means we'll lose everything," Race's grief-stricken mother had said. And when he looked at her haggard face he had felt a hot dagger of passionate hate stab him deeply. He'd watched his kid sister, Ritzy, trying to comfort his mother and he'd sworn in tight-lipped silence that he'd settle with Gatz Blemming regardless of what happened to himself.

He had started this day for Range City to make what he knew would be a last futile appeal to the bank. Then he would try guns. Blemming's hired gunmen, Drag Shanto, Kale Bletsin or Jake Fundy, might kill him. But somehow it hadn't seemed to matter. He'd looked into his mother's anguish-filled eyes and seen the pleading hopelessness in his little sister's face and nothing much seemed to matter except the need to satisfy a kind of blind madness like a red burning passion that spurred him on and augmented the reckless determination of his youth and increased his deep faith in the rightness of his cause.

RACE recalled, as he looked down at the Jack Rabbit Kid, how his father had once said, "As long as the Jack Rabbit Kid lives us small ranchers has got a chance. The Kid ain't really against what's right even if he is on the owlhoot. If ya notice right close ya'll see his depredations is against them what got their positions by robbing and killing. They say the Kid's dad owned a ranch that was lost almighty mysterious-like when his old man died."

"Just like me," Race Gordon thought now as he looked at the corpse. Then he let his bridle strap drop and he kneeled by the Kid's body. It was still warm. The Kid hadn't been dead very long. Race straightened the legs and the arms so that when the body was cold it could still be put on a horse. A sort of wild scheme was finding shape in his mind. He gave up the useless idea of talking with Blemming's banker again.

Race unbuckled the Kid's guns, a pair of perfectly matched pearl-handled weapons. He unbuckled his own, then took off his trousers and shirt. It was a dank unpleasant business, this stripping the outer clothes from a corpse and putting them on. He folded his own things neatly and laid them on the ground. Then he tucked them under the Kid's head so they wouldn't blow away and so they'd be there when he came back. He grinned at himself mockingly: *"When he came back."* What he meant was, *"If he came back."*

He straightened and practiced a couple of times drawing those guns of the Kid's. They balanced in his long fingers and leveled out fine. Race grinned, a hard chiseled grin like men sometimes wear when they die. He clamped his teeth tightly together and walked with slow, determined steps to where the Kid's grey horse was grazing.

The mare raised her head and moved her ears forward. Race spoke to her softly and it seemed odd how calm and even his own voice sounded. It was like he'd always been a killer; as if he knew the horse would stand still and welcome his weight in the Kid's empty saddle.

He mounted then and rode toward Range City leaving his own horse grazing nearby. He fashioned a mask for his eyes from a black cloth he found in the Kid's pocket. The Kid was a tall skinny fellow like himself . . . and men were afraid of the Kid.

It was noon when Race Gordon rode into Range City with the black mask over his eyes. He sat straight in the saddle and kept his face forward. The horse kicked up grey dust that lay in the street and it drifted heavy in the hot air like a thick ominous cloud forecasting a storm.

The few townspeople who were about ducked out of sight because they thought Race Gordon was the Jack Rabbit Kid. Race rode to the Wildcat saloon and dismounted. It seemed to him as if there wasn't much air in the town and he moved along easily as if walking in a subconscious dream. The batwing doors seemed so light he strode through hardly knowing he'd pushed them.

Inside, it was dark and suddenly cool. It occurred to him then that maybe he'd seen the last of the sunshine but he still kept a grin on his face down under the mask and he looked a lot like the Jack Rabbit Kid.

There was the long bar on the right with Blemming's spying white-sleeved barkeep behind it. Empty chairs and tables cluttered the place. Perhaps a dozen men were sitting about. Bletsin and Fundy sat at a far corner table. He didn't see Blemming or Shanto any place about.

Race knew that every eye was on him and he vaguely wondered why. He'd even forgotten the mask on his face and didn't realize now that men who peeked in from the crack of the door were watching to see what the Jack Rabbit Kid was going to do. There was no more sound in the place than in a graveyard at night.

Race kept looking for Gatz Blemming. But the man he'd come to kill for drygulching his father was not there. Race moved forward with measured steps and stopped by the bar, then turned his back, hooking his elbows on the hardwood, unmindful of the pale-faced, taut-lipped barkeeper behind him.

But he heard the faint click of metal and knew it was the hammer of a gun being cocked.

Instinctively he whirled on his toes. A shot sounded and lead whistled close. Only his sudden movement had saved him from the barkeeper's lead when he had tried to shoot Race in the back so he could claim the reward for the Jack Rabbit Kid.

ONE of the ivory-handled guns came into Race's hand as Fundy jumped up from his chair with a weapon raised. Fundy's gun blazed as Race leaped and rolled over the counter. He pumped lead into the barkeeper's stomach as he dropped to the floor. He had drawn his second gun in the same movement. He fired. Fundy stared, gulped and pitched forward.

Bledsin's gun kept flashing. Lead thudded into the counter. The barkeeper rolled over and was still. Race saw blood on the front of the shirt he was wearing. But the blood was dry. It was the blood of the Jack Rabbit Kid. Race had sprung from the floor and rolled over the counter in the same Jack Rabbit movement that had made the Kid famous. The set grin was still on his face and he hadn't been hit.

He hunkered along behind the counter now. The shooting stopped. Bledsin couldn't see him. Then Race stood erect, got Bledsin squarely lined in his sights and fired. He fired again. Bledsin clutched at his waist. His gun spun in the air as he fell.

New bullets hailed across the bar now. Glass from the mirror and from broken bottles showered down. Men crouched behind overturned tables. All who weren't cowards were trying to kill the Jack Rabbit Kid and claim the reward.

Race hunkered along toward the rear. He reached a rear window and felt a bullet burn through the flesh of his hip as he toppled through in a shower of glass. He came to his feet in the alley and found himself laughing crazily, laughing and running. He'd done for two of the men that he wanted; he'd have to come back for the others.

A shower of late lead whistled around the corner of the building as Race got safely around it. He holstered his guns, ran along the far side and stopped at the corner. He stood there a split second to straighten his mask.

A dozen men came running, yelling wildly, after the reward for the Jack Rabbit Kid. Perhaps they thought they had winged him.

Race held the Kid's guns firmly, one in each hand. He stepped around the corner and faced them with the guns leveled deadly. Taken by surprise, the men stopped as if they'd run into a wall.

"The first man t' level a weapon dies," said Race Gordon. He appraised them a moment with calm deliberation and knew they were afraid. Sheriff Ballard wasn't among them and Race was glad of that because he didn't want to mix with the law or kill any innocent person. He held them off with one pointed gun while he got to the Kid's grey mare and climbed up into the saddle. Bullets followed as he rode out of town but he was low and skinny in the Kid's saddle and none of them reached him.

In the first ravine that would hide himself and the horse he drew up. His wound was only a scratch and had almost stopped bleeding. But it made him feel stiff and it pained. Still he was grinning and what he had done didn't seem anything great.

Race waited there in the ravine. He kept thinking of his mother and of his kid sister and of how his job was only half finished. He wasn't much afraid of a posse because it seemed the sheriff had been out of town. If anyone did follow him they'd never expect him to stop this close to town.

Just after dusk he spurred the horse out of the ravine and rode back to Range City. It was pitch dark when he tied the grey mare behind an abandoned building on the outskirts of town. He ran eagerly to the rear of the Wildcat and found, as he'd expected, that the window he had leaped through had not been repaired.

Peering through the broken glass he saw that the place had been cleaned up. There was a larger crowd inside than there had been at noon. A new barkeeper was serving the drinks.

Race could only see behind the counter and a little past the end of it. Outside the building, he was in shadow and there was little chance of them seeing him. Suddenly he realized some men were sitting at a table to his right. He couldn't see them but he could hear their words.

"You weren't here during the fight at noon, still ya got a bullet wound," an authoritative voice accused. "How'd it happen?"

"I tell yuh, Boss, I shot it out with the Jack Rabbit Kid just before daylight."

RACE strained closer, held his ear to a glass next to the one which was broken.

You've always boasted, Shanto, about getting the Jack Rabbit Kid. Suppose you killed him this time?" A low satirical laugh followed the words. Then Race's teeth snapped together and his right hand clutched a gun handle. He recognized Gatz Blemming's voice.

"Don't guess I killed him," Shanto was saying. "But he swayed a lot in the saddle and he didn't follow . . . he spurred out o' range mighty pronto."

Blemming's mocking laugh rose louder. "Ya slipped, Shanto. Ya almost admitted he didn't follow when ya ran away."

The Jack Rabbit Kid's guns came into Race's hands again, their ivory handles feeling warm and friendly in his grasp. Their long barrels crashed the remaining glass of the window. He stepped inside and faced the men at the table.

Shanto's coal black eyes flashed mixed hatred and fear. He saw the black mask. He recognized the Jack Rabbit Kid's guns.

The roomful of men stood watching. Tense. Eager. But hesitant. Gatz Blemming was watching, his hand near his gun, but making no effort to raise it.

Race let a quick glance sweep the room. He saw the crowd standing silent, motionless, like tintype pictures of men. Sheriff Ballard stepped suddenly out from the others and began to move forward.

Race swung around to face the lawman. He let the muzzles of his guns drop down, dropped the weapons themselves back to their holsters. He felt the cold crease of his grin come back on his face as a plan came to his mind and he watched with the tail of his eye to see Shanto slowly snaking out his gun. He felt rather than saw Gatz Blemming shift in his chair. The sheriff was still a dozen paces away and Blemming didn't want the Jack Rabbit Kid to be taken alive.

Shanto's gun came up almost level. Blemming's weapons were ready in his hands. And when Shanto would have fired Race jerked himself back as a jack rabbit crouches before it leaps forward. As Shanto fired he threw himself downward and forward and came to his knees answering the fire both Shanto and Blemming had started. Race's weapons spoke again and again. They spat out the hate and lust for vengeance that sprang from inside him. While his leads drove deep into Shanto and deep in Blemming he felt their leads seeking his own flesh. He stumbled, fell, and rolled back through the broken window.

He got somehow to those few quiet blocks at the edge of town where he'd tied the Kid's horse in the blackness. Shouting and the sound of horse's hoofs came from in front of the Wildcat. Race didn't spur the horse into flight. He held it in check and let it pick slow steps between the dark buildings that cast no shadows in the absolute blackness. The little sound his horse made was lost in the greater noise of the sheriff's hastily organized posse. Race was a mile away before the posse was ready, and then they didn't know which way to follow because of the darkness.

BUT the first streaks of dawn found the posse

close on his trail. In daylight it wasn't a hard trail to follow. The tracks of his horse led along the short cut to the Four Bar Ranch. Streaks of blood marked the way.

They were less than half way when Sheriff Ballard halted his party. Two horsemen were riding toward them. As they came nearer they saw that one man was slumped and stiff. He was dead, his body tied to the saddle of the grey horse. A thin, tall youth on a cow-pony came leading the grey. The youth looked familiar to Ballard and a moment later he recognized Race.

Race said weakly, "Had quite a fight, Sheriff, but I killed the Jack Rabbit Kid. I'm claimin' the reward."

Ballard's eyes narrowed. "Yeah," he said doubtfully. He rode up to Race and yanked his guns from his holsters. Then he drew alongside the dead man's mount, drew the ivory handled guns from the Kid's belt and frowned. Then he fingered curiously the red ribbons of the Jack Rabbit Kid's torn left shirt sleeve and raised clear, honest eyes to meet Race's. "You were wearin' the Kid's clothes when you got yer hand busted up," he accused.

But Race's eyes had fluttered shut. He reeled in the saddle and a deputy whose horse stood nearest barely kept him from falling.

He got back his senses on the way into town. He was riding in front of somebody's saddle and that was about all he could tell. The jerking of the horse jarred his head and he couldn't get coherence into his thinking. Pretty soon he passed out again.

Then he was sitting in old Doc Reynold's office and someone was sponging his face. Sheriff Ballard sat beside him. He felt pain in his hand, in his arm, down in his leg and in his hip.

"You're not going to die," the doctor said.

Race tried to grin. He thought vaguely about Billy the Kid and the luck that went with fighting for a good cause. "Didn't figure I would," he said, then turned toward the sheriff. "Did you send word to my folks?"

"I sent a deputy," Ballard said. "They ought to get here after a little."

Race raised on his elbow. He was weak but he felt a little excited. "I killed the Jack Rabbit Kid, Sheriff. I shot him in the right side under the arm. You'll find a hole in his shirt where there isn't one in my body. I took his clothes and rode into town and I killed four men that every honest man in town wanted killed. And I never killed one of them till he shot at me first."

The sheriff's face was stern. "You impersonated an outlaw which gave 'em a right to shoot you on sight."

"They had their rights," Race grinned. "Only they're dead and I ain't. I'm still claiming the reward. I've got to have fifteen hundred dollars down to the bank by tonight to save the Four Bar for mother and Ritzy."

Doc Reynolds put a kind hand on the lad's shoulder. "Son," he said, "Sheriff Ballard asked me to examine the Jack Rabbit Kid and say how long he's been dead. I haven't told him yet but I just came across the street and I saw people standing in little groups and I heard them talking. They're saying, lad, that the outlaw was the best friend this town ever had. They're planning to give him a mighty fine funeral. They think the shooting you did was done by the Jack Rabbit Kid. It's better I think that they shouldn't know any different. You could have killed the Kid after he did his shooting here. That way you'd be entitled to the reward and folks couldn't stay mad at you long for killing an outlaw with a price on his head." The old sawbones sighed deeply and turned to Ballard.

"Sheriff," he said, "no doctor can tell exactly how long a man's been dead. If Race Gordon here says he killed the kid, I don't see how you can prove that he didn't. The Kid was killed with a .45 bullet and that's the caliber of Race's guns."

Ballard smiled slightly and nodded his understanding. "Guess maybe you're right, Doc. Race ought t' have the reward."

Race lay back then with a little sigh of relief. He had a feeling as if the Jack Rabbit Kid were there in the room saying, "It sounds all right to me, Partner. It's the way I'd want it to be."

THE END

"I think you've had enough, Pete."

"Ain't that always the way it is? When you need a lawman there's never one around!"

WESTERN FICTION MAGAZINE

Writers & Artists Guidelines

Send all fiction submissions as a Word Document (.doc) file attachments via email to fortunapublications@gmail.com.

Fiction:

We are looking for Western Adventure stories in the 1800's. Fiction may range from 1,000 to 40,000+ words. We pay $.001-.01/word on publication for First North American Serial Rights.

Artwork:

Submit samples (jpg) to the email address above. We are seeking detailed, realistic work. We pay $25 for full-page (8.5 x 11 inch) B&W interior illustrations and $75 for full-color cover art.

TENDERFOOT

by E. Hoffman Price

He's only a kid and he has a lot to learn about women but he knows horse flesh
and he can make a delayed draw with the speed of a side-winder.

HE HAD A coffin-shaped face, and like the thoroughbred he rode, his legs were long; but while the horse was graceful as a panther, the rider was gangling, slightly stooped, and his oversized hands did not know what to do with themselves when he dismounted at the hitching rack in front of Squint Eye Morgan's Sabine Palace, a dive so named because of its proximity to the river which separates Texas and Louisiana.

A .45 single action Colt was awkwardly strapped to his thigh, and its owner looked as though he must have picked a lucky day for his very recent first shave, otherwise he would have cut his own throat; yet somehow, he did not stumble over the hand-hewn planks as he strode to the bar.

Squint Eye Morgan winked broadly when the boy piped, "Whiskey, if yo' please, suh." Then, voice suddenly going bass, he boomed like a yearling bull, "I'm Simon Bolivar Grimes, suh, lookin' fo' my uncle's ranch in Crockett County in the next day or two."

"Not unless yuh kin fly," was Squint Eye's mock serious answer. "It's nigh onto eight hundred mile from here."

And that exchange gave everyone a chance to notice that the horse at the hitching rack was worth a thousand dollars of any man's money; that the buckskin poke from which Grimes took a gold piece to pay for his drink weighed at least four pounds, and none of it silver.

One of the half-dressed girls lounging on the bench at the edge of the tiny dance floor thought he was awfully cunning. The others had more practical thoughts, and debated initiating the yokel to what few mysteries their low bodices and short skirts contrived to conceal.

Grimes decided he might as well spend the night in Orange and rest up a spell befo' going on to the Box-A ranch; and then, after a cross fire of whispers, one of the players slid from his place at the poker table and raked in his winnings. Keno Charley, white-fingered and debonair house gambler, invited the boy to sit in.

"Thank yo' very kindly, suh," Grimes declined, "but my pap'd lambast me if he ever heard of me playin' cards."

Which gave the girls a break, and Grimes a thrill. Thus far, he had never more than vaguely suspected white women of having legs; just skirts and feet.

A SWEET-FACED Creole with great black eyes and a passionate mouth was the first to reach the hillbilly. Her skin was pale olive, and her half bared breasts were exquisitely rounded and firm. While Grimes reddened at the lovely stretch of silken legs, and a glimpse of thighs momentarily revealed before her short skirt settled almost to her knees, he was eager with the eagerness of youth.

It was entirely optional at the Sabine Palace whether the girls merely danced and hustled drinks, or took time out to show guests through their upstairs rooms, though such fine points never occurred to Grimes. He knew his elementary biology, but where he came from, it didn't apply to white women—not as far as boys and bachelors were concerned.

"Want to dance, honey?" she invited, betraying none of the hard calculation of her companions.

"I'd love to, m'am," and she was lost in his long arms, a sweet parcel of tawdry spangles and warm flesh.

Lorette managed to dodge his heavy boots; and though she had to tiptoe to get her eyebrows to his shoulders, somehow that seductively writhing body, those swaying hips, and shapely legs all clung to the best advantage . . . .

Grimes was breathing hard when the fiddle squeaking ceased, and tingling from tow head to cowhide boots. He was flushed and sheepish from knowing that she knew his eager glance was probing the scented shadows between her breasts. He gulped his whiskey and was shocked when Lorette drank hers. He didn't know she was taking tea at a dollar a drink.

Lorette's eyes had softened, and a little ghost of a smile sweetened her mouth. That gangling boy was reminding her that she was about his age, even though she did feel so much older. Her soft-voiced dance hall chatter died out, and she also began fumbling for words.

He did not know she was thinking, "Some night, I'll take too much real liquor, and forget to say no to Muddy Hawkins . . ."

She shuddered, then laughed bitterly when Grimes rumbled, "Are yo'all chilly, m'am—"

He checked himself; he couldn't add, "with so much of you uncovered."

"Maybe you're right, honey." She caught his hand. "Come along, and I'll get a shawl."

BUT THE TRAILING of her voice, and the clinging caress of her fingers hinted things that made Grimes' heart rise and choke him. The smokey, oil lighted room seemed all awhirl. He did not hear the scrape of a chair, a man's angry mutter behind him, and another man taunting, "Keep yore shirt on, Muddy. That button won't know what to do with her, nohow. An' she never did want none of *you!*"

"Nor you neither!" was Muddy Hawkins' retort to Pinwheel Smith—the other one of a vicious pair whose friendship centered in Lorette's despising them both.

Grimes followed twinkling ankles and swaying hips up the narrow, one-way stairs. He was afraid of Lorette, so frail and dainty.

She did not light the bracket lamp on the wall. A pencil of moonlight made a blur of pillows, picked highlights from crude furniture. And then all that band of glamour centered on the shimmering ivory splendor that appeared as spangled silk rustled down about Lorette's ankles.

She was now quite close, and his awkward hands were conscious of the filmy stuff that still clung to her skin. Women were very wonderful and mysterious . . . he was glad he didn't have to speak . . . he'd not have known what to say.

Then her lips found his mouth, and her arms insistently drew him toward her. . . .

LATER, THOUGH his voice still cracked at times, it was a full grown man who told Lorette about Uncle Carter and the Box-A ranch.

"An' I'd sho' love to have you'all come along with me, m'am," he concluded.

"You foolish boy," she whispered, swallowing a catch in her voice. He meant it. "You don't know what you're saying. I'm . . . why—" There was no malice in her gentle mockery when she added, "Your pap would lambaste you, and me too."

"M'am," he protested, following her to the door, "I'd jest bust anyone's haid what said a cross-eyed word to you."

Lorette was composed when she reached the foot of the stairs leading to the bar room, but Grimes walked more erectly, head higher. His face was a revelation; and Muddy Hawkins knew that the girl had not even thought of rifling the buckskin poke. His fingers twitched as he snarled, "By God, he did—"

"Shet up!" Pinwheel Smith chuckled maliciously. "Jest shows he's a better man'n you be!"

His calculating glance shifted toward the thoroughbred horse at the hitching post, full in the glow of the front lights. When Pinwheel turned back, Muddy, now half way across the floor, had Lorette by the arm.

"You dirty ____! You an' yore pertendin'!"

Lorette understood the cut throat's wrath, and her face whitened as she saw Pinwheel in the background, grinning evilly, waiting. Muddy thrust her against the door jamb before she could retort. Grimes growled in wordless wrath, swung an awkward fist that no more than grazed the ruffian's cheek; but chairs scraped, and men scrambled for cover. They knew that Muddy would blast the boy loose from his eye teeth, and get away with another plea of self defense—which he could, since Grimes was armed.

Pinwheel, however, had not moved. The kid wouldn't get a chance to draw, and he had to be handy for a deft grab at that poke of gold.

AS GRIMES recovered, there was a glint of blued steel, and the muzzle of a short barreled revolver blotted out all but those rattlesnake eyes. Time ceased in the Sabine Palace, and so did sound. Death face Grimes—then the murky air burst into hell roaring flame, and something jerked at his arm.

Before he knew it was the blast of his own Colt, he wondered why Muddy suddenly spun, clutching his stomach, unfired gun

clattering to the floor. He least of all realized that nature, and years of boyhood hunting had given him the quick reflexes to make a delayed draw and win by an eyelash.

Lorette screamed, first terror, then quavering relief. Grimes half turned, but instinct warned him. He jerked back jest as another blast shook the room. But Pinwheel Smith's lead only raked the boy's shoulder; and his second shot was muffled by the thunder of Grimes' portable siege gun. A hammer blow knocked him sprawling, stomach tangled with his spine.

"They's mo' fo' any of you'll what wants some," announced Simon Bolivar Grimes,

unshaken by the wild shot. "Raise yo' hands—you, there—"

The gangling boy's face was grim as his granite eyes. In feuds at home he'd seen men killed aplenty, but never by his own hand. He still could not quite believe he had done it; but as Lorette drew closer, he remembered he was now a man.

"Git upstairs, woman, an' fetch yo' clothes," he commanded. "We're goin'. Quick!"

"But—" She gasped, blinked, still incredulous.

"Git!" he repeated, and she obeyed. Grimes remembered only his home traditions: there was now a feud between him and the friends of the dead, regardless of his just self defense.

"Listen, kid, take it easy," protested Squint Eye Morgan, to whom a shooting was just part of the night's work. But though his hands wavered harmlessly enough, Grimes had a single track mind which was still reeling.

Wham! The back bar mirror spattered. Squint Eye, however, was untouched except for flying glass. He had ducked in time. The tension of waiting for Lorette was robbing the deadly youngster of his accuracy.

A stocky man with a horse-shoe shaped gray moustache came clumping in from the front: Mark Ferrell, the town marshal, who had been drawn by the thunder of the guns. Age and seasoning had made him confident. He arrived with holstered weapons, and when he saw a dozen uplifted hands, it was too late.

"Raise yo' hands!" piped the boy behind the long barreled Colt.

"Better do it, marshal!" croaked Keno Charley, and another added, "He's killin' us all—he's crazy—he done shot Squint Eye—"

Two men twitching in pools of blood made it convincing. Ferrell, despite his star, lifted his hands; but he warned, "Yuh kain't do it, boy. Ef I don't git yuh, they's enough deppities to chase yah plumb to Pecos."

A STIRRING at the end of the bar warned Grimes, but not in time. He whirled as half a whiskey bottle, top shattered by his shot, drenched his face with bits of glass and stinging rotgut. The marshal's arrival had given Squint Eye his chance. Grimes' smoke pole roared, but harmlessly; blood and whiskey blinded him. A hurled cuspidor crashed against his head. That distraction gave the law its chance.

"Git on yore feet!" growled Ferrell, kicking the smoking gun into a corner and seizing Grimes by the collar.

Then he learned that conversation was out of order. Howling his wrath, the dizzied lad ploughed in, but boots and fists were too plentiful.

"He grabbed my poke!" yelled the vigilant Squint Eye, playing up the main chance; and once the hangers on had their cue, they gave the marshal an improvised story of a daring hold-up. That'd settle the yoke!

With what Ferrell had seen on entering, that was plausible enough; so when pistol whipping had put an end to resisting arrest, he and a tardily arrived deputy dragged Grimes toward the door.

"I ain't held no one up!" he protested; then, recognizing futility, he added, "But yo'all feed my hoss, yo' hear?"

"What hoss?" grumbled the panting marshal.

"That hoss there—" Grimes blinked the blood and sweat from his eyes. The thoroughbred was gone, and not even hoof beats lingered.

Once at the town jail, Ferrell demanded of the accusers, "Now, where's that dinero this kid grabbed?"

"Search him, marshal," answered Squint Eye. "Et's in a buckskin poke—don't know jest how much, but—"

But the bag was gone.

"Ain't no gold," frowned the marshal. "Mebbe he drapped it."

"Drapped, hell!" chorused a dozen voices. "We done looked fer it."

"Git that Lorette!" snarled Squint Eye. "Bet she grabbed it offen the floor whilst he was shootin' us up jest before yuh got here."

"Yo' kaint call her a thief!" raged Grimes.

Then he began to remember. He'd laid it on Lorette's dresser, and the thrill of the girl had made him forget it. "Yo'all go git her. She'll prove it ain't his'n. I done left it in her room, and that proves I didn't take it offen this here skunk. An' it's got my pap's name branded on it."

"Find the gal!" snapped Ferrell to a deputy. "But fust lock this jaybird in the hoosegow. Though mebbe 'tis his dinero!"

The door slammed on a battered but triumphant Grimes.

The accusers, muttering and plucking tobacco stained moustaches, pulled long faces. Ferrell, though rough, was just in his own way; but Squint Eye Morgan, resenting a cut face and shattered mirror, was racking his crooked brain for a story to counteract the marked buckskin pouch, a kink that he had not expected, seeing that gold was gold.

"Yuh'll git yores yet," sneered Morgan, pausing for a final word before dashing back to the Sabine Palace. "Shootin' up two of my best customers."

And that left Grimes to brood over the loss of his horse. If his pap didn't lambaste him, his Uncle Carter would, when he got to Crockett County, where he was to learn how to run a ranch. His father's brother was along in years, and a younger Grimes had to go

west to carry on.

Sweet mess he'd made of it, thus far; then he consoled himself, "But I'd not dast admit I'd ever let that skunk hit a woman, or he'd sho' disown me."

Presently Ferrell returned, and his iron face was grim.

"Listen, jasper—that gal's done gone, and her hoof prints leads right up to the hitchin' rack where yore hoss was tied. Purty smart, havin' her sashay with the plunder, so's we kaint prove yuh took it."

He paused, spat a jet of tobacco juice at the bars of Grimes' cell, then added, "So we're holdin' yuh fer murder. Got plenty witnesses to swear you shot down two citizens an' tried to smoke out the owner of our leadin' barroom."

Grimes' indignant protests echoed in the emptiness of the corridor, as the marshal made an impressive exit.

MURDER! The Grimes had in the past six or seven generations done a fair share of killing, but they'd been honest feud shootings, not murder

And now, if they stood him on the back of a mustang, looped a rawhide *riata* about his neck, fastened the free end to a limb of a tree, and smacked the temporary mount across the rump, he'd be left dangling, with never a chance to prove to pap that he'd killed two skunks for hitting a woman—even though she was a woman who'd stolen his poke and his horse.

That last was what really hurt. It took the edge from his newly found manhood; that, and the unjust accusation. Twice in a flaming moment he had beaten doom, which was a man's share of chances; and his breed was too stoical to fear the mere extinction of death. But the disgrace!

Morning came, and without any sign of Lorette. The greasy, pendulous breasted Mexican wife of the town marshal bought Grimes his breakfast. Pity marked her fat face as she watched him stare frostily at the coffee, beans, and sow-belly she slid through the bars.

"More better you eat," she wheedled. "They don' hang you till the trial. Maybe tomorrow, an' you should not die hongry."

A suggestion of vanished winsomeness brightened her smile. Grimes nodded, forced a half grin, and said, "Thank yo', m'am. Sho' looks good."

He wolfed it down, and the broad hipped Mexican, picking up the plate, cheerfully added, "Sooch a nice boy. An' eef they hang you, I weel make you the tortillas weeth chili for the las' meal, no?"

Greasers were funny people, saying "no" when they meant yes. He didn't know that tortillas were corn cakes tough as leather, and that the chili would blister his throat like fire, but it was nice to get a friendly word. He fumbled in his pocket and found a five dollar gold piece among his loose silver.

"Take it, ma'm," he said. "I won't have much use for it much longer."

She could hardly understand his words, but his meaning was plain. She left, shaking her head. Loretta's treachery could not help but arouse a touchof feminine indignation at another woman's work.

The jail was of brick; but even if Grimes had had a knife to work on the crumbling mortar, he would have had no chance to use it. The incredible killing of two cutthroats by an awkward hillbilly made him the sensation of the town.

The inhabitants came to gape; and while the better element muttered about there being contradictory angles, they were true to form and did nothing about it. That left Squint Eye Morgan and his clique to stick to their accusations, hoping that the criminal, trying to save himself, would give some hint as to Lorette's hiding place. They had the marshal in a bag.

They were sure he and the dance hall girl had agreed to meet somewhere. The disappearance of the thoroughbred horse convinced them. And if Lorette returned, Grimes' buckskin pouch of gold could be seized for damages to the Sabine Palace, or as a fine for disturbing the peace.

THAT FORENOON, twelve men, neither good nor remotely true, made up the frontier jury. After a frantic scramble for a Bible, the witnesses solemnly swore that Grimes had held the place up and smoked out "pore Muddy an' Pinwheel."

The execution was set for sunrise. The delay was to give Lorette a chance to repent and return with the gold.

As Grimes was marched from the court, there was much applause and talk about the marshal's valor in subduing the outlaw; and that, with the close packing of the crowd, gave no one a chance to notice that the Law's Mexican wife slipped a Bowie knife beneath the prisoner's belt. Grimes himself for a moment wondered at the chill of steel against his skin; but he did not betray his surprise, and his manacles kept him from rashly using the weapon.

Porky McTeague, a pot bellied deputy with three chins, planted himself on a bench in the jail corridor to guard the condemned. He was glum, being forced to miss the preparations for the barbecue that was to precede the hanging; but that evening, slightly after sundown, he brightened; and not entirely because of the pint bottle he had sullenly guzzled.

Heel clicks—woman's heels—sounded in the corridor. Grub for the prisoner; spicy, pungent food, reeking of chili and garlic and cumin seed. However, it was not the marshal's hay-bag wife who brought it, but a girl—slender, with glistening black hair and hazel eyes that were strangely lovely against her cream colored skin. Even in the face of the hangman, Simon Bolivar Grimes knew a rare armful of feminine flesh when he saw it.

Now that he knew women had legs, his imagination told him what must be above the girl's trim ankles; and though he got but a peep of the lamplight glow reflected from the curves in her bodice, he reckoned that what she carried there would repay further study.

"My mother sent me weeth the supper," she explained to the prisoner.

The marshal's daughter flashed an angry eye at Porky who chuckled drunkenly and patted the elegant roundness south of her hip, and flared, "Peeg! I weel not give you wan bit of thees chili. Ees for Senor Grimes."

One spoonful made the captive think he had swallowed a volcano in full eruption. He gasped, blinked tears from his eyes; but he couldn't offend that sweet creature, so he said, "M'am, this is sho' good, but lookin' at yo'all jest takes my appetite. I'm a-seein angels a-fore they hangs me."

And that, coming from the damned, touched Catalina's half-Latin heart. "Do you, really?" She wedged her lovely face between the bars. "Kees me, joost once—"

And that burned Porky to alcoholic fury.

"If you like him, have at it!" he snarled. He had the door unlocked before Grimes, dazzled by hot lips and a cloud of black hair, could sense what was happening. And when the grating swung in, smacking him back and off balance, it was too late. Then the girl pitched head first into the cell, driven by the jailer's paw.

"Yo' low down skunk," roared Grimes, recovering; but Porky's gun drove him back.

He locked the door, then, face to the bars, taunted, "Now see how she likes yuh!"

GRIMES, gentleman by instinct, snatched the big bowl of chili colorado and hurled it. The stuff, hot from fire and even hotter in its own excoriating right, poured into the piggish eyes and gaping mouth. Porky's gasp drew in a lungful of caustic gravy. It would have raised blisters on a packsaddle.

"Oooow!" howled the tortured jailer. "Hell on the mountain tops—you damn'—, yuh've killed—"

But the rest was lost as Porky, rubbing his burning eyes and making them infinitely worse, ran screeching into the darkness; and with the rest of the town preparing for the barbecue, he found neither advice nor spectators.

"That peeg 'ave run away weeth your supper," commiserated Catalina. "An' now I can not get some more. I am lock in the jail, no?"

She eyed him, and had to tilt her head well back to do so. Then she sighed, remembering Grimes' valiant slayings, the dance hall girl's treachery. Her mother's account of the hillbilly had led to her guilefully suggesting that maybe mama was too tired to feed the captive.

The result of that was that Grimes forgot he had a knife which he could now use to chop out enough mortar to make a getaway. The more he saw of Catalina, the more he did get that way. He lifted her up to the bench which he had mounted, attracted anew by Porky's groans and a prodigious splashing.

For a moment they watched the jailer's vain struggles in a horse trough. Then, as Porky emerged and set out at a full gallop, Catalina laughed, and said, "Ees going to hunt the doctor. For the eyes, no?"

Catalina was nice lifting, if you grabbed her in the right places, and there wasn't a wrong one between her shapely shoulders and her dimpled knees. Even a man facing execution couldn't miss that; and when she remarked that she'd rather never be kissed unless some one other than Porky McTeague did it, Grimes lost no time.

In the meanwhile, he had lifted her from the bench, and moved it into a corner. And with a bit of privacy at his disposal, Grimes remembered things he'd learned about women. He was bolder than a nice girl like Catalina approved of, even though she was warm blooded . . .

She said, "No." Grimes, a born gentleman, would have stopped, but these greasers, mother and daughter alike, meant yes when they said no. So he didn't stop, and pretty soon, Catalina was warmer than Porky McTeague's eyes, and her little breasts were trying to keep her heart from pounding them out of place. But Grimes held her tight enough to prevent that.

So Catalina sighed and liked it . . . and anyway, it was sort of romantic, brightening the last hours of a condemned man . . .

BUT she didn't have as much time as she had hoped. They did not hear the tramp of heavy feet; not until two men stopped at the cell door. It was not Porky returning; that law man, sobered up by pain, realized how he had mishandled the marshal's daughter, and borrowed a horse to head west. The new arrivals were the marshal himself, and Amos Brunton, the sheriff of Orange County, summoned to take charge of the hanging.

He arrived early, eager for a look at the

incredible condemned; but what he saw made him envy the prisoner.

"Porky, dad-bust yore—damn' hide!" roared Ferrell, who saw much more of his daughter's' sleekly curving legs than her skirt was ever meant to display. "What the—damn' tar-nation hell's this—yuh gol-blasted skunk—whar air yah, Porky?"

The sheriff stroked his beard and muttered something about seduction as well as murder, and delicately turned his head.

"Seduction, is it?" bellowed the outraged marshal. He drew his gun, but Brunton seized his wrist. "I'll seduct him!"

He stormed out of jail; the sheriff after him. Catalina was hysterically laughing, crying and trying to induce her skirt to meet her ankles. Grimes felt foolish; and then, having

succeeded in soothing the distracted girl, he heard a soft, grating sound that startled him.

Something was scraping at the high, barred window of his cell. His first thought was that jealous Porky had returned to kill him secretly. He remembered the Bowie knife in his pocket, but as his fingers closed on the butt, a small hand gripped the bars. Then a woman murmured, "Honey, I've got a file to cut a bar, an' you can bend it open."

"Git away!" cried Grimes, horrified and confused by Lorette's whisper. "Yo'll wake the jailer."

Metal clinked on the floor; a heavy file thrust between the bars. But Catalina had heard enough.

"*Cabron!* You still love her?" she screeched, slapping and clawing him.

Grimes froze as from without he caught an incredulous gasp, then the muted pad-pad of a horse's muffled hoofs. Worse and more of it! Lorette, he now knew, had slipped out at the marshal's arrival at the saloon the night before, not realizing she could help him by remaining to prove he had not held up the Sabine Palace. Now, having heard Catalina's jealous fury, she had gone. There would be no horse waiting, even if he could file a bar.

"Shut up, woman!" he growled, wrenching the Bowie knife Catalina had snatched from his pocket. "I'm gittin', an' I don't want to throttle you lest I has to."

Grimes, gentleman by instinct, forgot himself so far as to shake her till her teeth rattled. Then he slapped her in the only place women ought to be slapped. That quelled Catalina, and she calmed down; frowned, suddenly brightened as it dawned on her that anyone as popular and deadly as Simon Bolivar Grimes was a man among men.

"That ees right, *querido mio*," she fondly murmured. "We weel escape, and leave her here, no?"

"No," agreed Grimes. Oddly enough, that was the wrong answer, but Catalina did not hear, being already busy gouging out mortar.

AFTER what her father had seen, a trip with Grimes would not be so bad. So she plied the knife till her little hands were blistered; and the file rasped valiantly. Maybe he could make it before the marshal found a sober deputy.

But he didn't. Footsteps echoed in the corridor, and his heart sank to his cowhide boots. Ferrell was returning. Grimes snatched Catalina's knife, crept toward the door jamb, and whispered, "Yo' file, an' they'll think it's me."

The window, though not entirely out of the line of vision from the door, was not the first thing visible from the dim, lamplit passage.

Two men accompanied the marshal: Sheriff Brunton, and a solemn person in a black frock coat.

"Quit that filin' and come out, Grimes!" bellowed Ferrell. "Quick a-fore I blast yuh!"

A shotgun barrel reached in between the bars. Grimes dared not snatch it, lest the startled marshal jerk the trigger and blow Catalina to ragged bits. He pocketed his knife and answered, "I'm here, and what yo'all want now?"

"Git busy, parson," boomed the marshal, ignoring the defiant query. He opened the door, then, shifting the double-barrelled shotgun to point at Grimes' stomach, he added, "Ain't goin' to be no hangin', yuh dad-gummed skunk. Yo're marryin' my daughter, right now, or I'm a-blowing yore belly around yore spine."

Not long ago, that would have been a reprieve; but Lorette's unexpected loyalty had touched him deeply, and anyway, she was his first girl. More than that, Grimes was pig-stubborn, like all his kind. In spite of the pleasant things he had learned about Catalina, he wasn't being herded into a wedding.

"Listen, yo' ornery sculpin," he growled, as parson, witness, and father of the bride-to-be entered the cell, "ain't never been a Grimes married with a shotgun, and ain't never goin' to be. Anyhow, I didn't seduct yo' daughter."

"Yuh warn't tellin' her fortune when I come in, yuh dad-blasted scum," raged the marshal. "An' now they will be a hangin'. After the weddin', yuh ongrateful ruffian."

"Yo'all try it!" challenged Grimes, arms akimbo, fingers almost touching the Bowie knife in his right pants pocket. "Lynchin' an honest man fo' trying to keep what's hisn. Ain't no parson'd have a thing to do with a thievin' disgrace to the law!"

Ferrell's face darkened. Death again commanded silence in the jail house; and this time Grimes had no revolver, nor could he hope to duck the double muzzles almost against his stomach.

"Brother Ferrell," quavered the parson, "Miss Catalina—"

"Not even if the priest married us!" shrilled the indignant girl, bounding from her corner. "I weel not marry that peeg!"

From one side she pounced like a panther to claw Grimes; and the marshal's hair trigger nerves were ready for anything. He had heard more than enough of the boy desperado that afternoon. The double charge of buckshot, however, only tore the skirt from the parson's long coat, and the flame set it smouldering. Catalina's reckless fury at her lover's repudiation had brought her hip against the gun barrel. Thus she saved the man she tried to claw.

The sheriffs gun danced out, but in the dense cloud of black powder smoke and the fumes of burning cloth he dared not fire; not without the risk of riddling the horrified man of God, or the frenzied girl. And Ferrell, dropping his empty shotgun, had no chance to go for his holsters. The prisoner saw to that.

GRIMES, maddened by the gun blast, exploded in a blind rage, great fists hammering, shoulder driving through. In the confusion of descending pistol barrels and the parson's flailing boots, he jerked loose Ferrell's gun belt, bellowed his triumph, and broke from the tangle.

The sheriffs gun blazed, but an instant after Grimes snapped a shot into the overhead lamp. Flaming fuel poured to the floor; and as the enemy ducked, he cleared the angle of the corridor.

Men, drawn by the fusillade, were running toward the square. None knew what it was about, but some poured lead at the lanky fugitive as others, more prudent, flattened behind a watering trough and tried to drop the fugitive as he raced toward a hitching rack packed with horses belonging to visitors from out of town.

A slug nicked Grimes. He dropped; three heads and shoulders cropped up, gun barrels gleaming in the moonglow. Then Grimes' borrowed Colts blazed. A man jerked up, clutching his throat; another howled. The survivors flattened out of sight, deciding, "Ain't our hosses, nohow!"

Then the sheriff burst from the red glare of the jail front, and after him came Ferrell, reloaded shotgun in hand, and daughter trailing him.

"A thousand dollars, dead er alive!" he bellowed, leveling the gun.

Grimes, rounding the cluster of panicky horses, missed the screaming pellets; but a dozen mustangs, rumps riddled, stampeded in every direction. For a moment he hesitated. He was on foot, and a price was on his head. He'd better have married the girl. Or could he make the outskirts of the town, capture a horse whose fright had subsided?

Not a chance. They were coming, now. He bounded into the narrow space between two deserted houses, guns ready. Moonlight shooting might be tricky, but they did little else, back home in Gawgia.

"*Smack-smack-smack!*" He held them at bay; and then the heavy blast of a .60 caliber Sharps shook the tumult. Half the siding was torn from the shack as the heavy slug spattered him with splinters. Someone was trying to pick him off with an old fashioned buffalo gun.

Some stampeded horses were coming to a halt, but far behind the attackers, not where Grimes could mount up.

A pistol crackled behind him, though he did not hear or feel the bullet. A yell. They were flanking him. He whirled, desperate. A horse was stretching long legs up the narrow space behind him. A familiar horse—his own thoroughbred, and a woman mounting him. Lorette!

"Quick, honey!" she gasped, boosting herself backward over the cantle. "They're chasing me—they caught me hiding—"

He piled on the gallant beast, who stood fast, though snorting and quivering. Another shot from the rear. A shrill, quavering cry, and the thoroughbred soared incredibly into the moonlight and searching gun-fire of the square. Panic nicked his high strung nerves, and raking lead had stung him; but Grimes,

holstering an empty .45, used hand and knee, wheeled and rode for it.

Lorette moaned as she clung to Grimes, hunched low in the saddle. The beast was wounded, overloaded, and he was hampered by clumsily tied hoof-mufflings; yet his whip-cord muscles stretched in mighty strides, carrying him westward.

But the respite was brief; and soon they heard from behind the drumming of hoofs on the hard soil. The pursuit was gaining, and the thoroughbred's stride was failing. Grimes wheeled him about.

"Ease up," he panted, trying to shake Lorette's arms a bit looser. She coughed, moaned softly, relaxed. Grimes' borrowed Colt crackled savagely, and before the pursuit came within *their* firing range.

A saddle emptied; a horse dropped; but Grimes had shot his last shell, and one man charged on alone. It was the marshal, on a racing pinto pony.

"Let's git, boy!" panted Grimes, urging the thoroughbred into action.

He made a valiant effort, but he was losing. His great heart could not carry him much further. The following hoofbeats became stronger, and punctuated with pistol blasts. Lead sang, first wild, then nicking Grimes.

"Oh, Gawd, if I had a gun," he groaned as his horse stumbled, recovered, then reached out with a killing stride. His last effort, and Grimes knew death was gripping that gallant heart.

Lorette tried to say something, but it was lost in blended hoofbeats and a man's hoarse yelling. Then the thoroughbred pitched in a heap, and his riders with him. He had been dead in his last two strides.

"Here's a gun, honey," gasped Lorette, crawling toward Grimes. She fumbled in her bosom. Her hand came out with a little derringer, short, deadly—but now red as her own tiny hand. "Your money's in—the saddle—bags—go back—an' marry—her—"

She crumpled, and Grimes himself wounded and dazed, lurched to his feet, still clawing for the derringer with its two murderous barrels. He heard the snorting mustang, and Ferrell's exclamation. He wondered why the marshal didn't shoot.

"Yuh dad-bloomed scoundrel," rumbled Ferrell, misunderstanding the sobbing gasp and shudder that racked the man who lay near the girl whose blood frothed face smiled at the moonlight.

His drawn pistol drooped. Lack of answering fire proved Grimes was nearly dead, or had no more cartridges. But Ferrell did not know of the derringer, of the slaying wrath and grief that made Grimes thresh and shudder in the dust. Then he did get an instant of understanding.

That was when both barrels coughed lead, driving his nickeled star half way through his heart. Grimes' feud was settled, and he at last clambered to his knees, weak but intact. Now that it was over, he was sorry for that old man; he'd rather not have shot him, but one of Ferrell's men had killed Lorette . . . .

He took the saddle from the thoroughbred and put it on the pinto; then, gathering Lorette into his arms, he choked, "I got him. An' they wasn't no weddin' after all . . . ."

He had some difficulty in mounting a horse skittish from the smell of blood, but he finally made it, and with a dead woman in his arms.

"Uncle Carter," he half sobbed, spurring his pinto westward, " 'll lambaste me fo' losin' that hoss . . . honey, I didn't really care nuthin' for Catalina, nohow . . . ."

He blinked, swallowed; and a full grown man rode on, looking for a place to bury his first girl, whose pale face still half smiled up at him.

THE END

GUN WHIP LAW

by Jack Anderson

Bullets were ballots for law and order when young
Jeff Hacknew tried to enact a new brand of gun-blazing
justice for the down-trodden nesters.

JEFF HACKNEW sucked nervously at a cold, bitter cigar, his ears tuned to the big clock on the wall of the chamber. Slanting his eyes, he saw Dede Holmes staring at him, her big blue eyes anxious and wondering.

Two hours more, and Nebraska's first legislature would be feed for talk down at the Last Chance—and folks in Omaha would sneer at his feeble tries. He squirmed when two more legislators brushed by, shuffling past the squatting Indians in the hallway, headed for the door on the east side of the building. That cleaned the chamber of members except for Smed Tester and himself. And Smed Tester's smile gave him the idea that something big was brewing.

"You look nervous since legislators began leaving their seats." Big, handsome Smed Tester's voice flowed like sand in front of a light wind. "I suppose they figure a bill a fellow don't understand himself isn't worth voting on." There was mocking laughter in his sharp eyes.

"Who don't understand what?" Jeff demanded, gruffly, whipping the cigar from his jaws. Sweat dropped against his side from under the armpits.

"I presumed you didn't, since I know a lawyer friend of yours wrote the bill." Smed Tester chuckled dryly, and Jeff cringed inwardly. "The same lawyer that's teaching you the three R's and telling you all about government three nights a week."

"Why you—" Jeff clenched his fists. Lights were dancing in Tester's gray eyes as he went on.

"And after all, pudgy little Loon Larkins had to drag the bill up to the speaker."

Smed Tester looked and talked smoothly, and it burned Jeff, reminding him of himself: of that darned beard that wouldn't stay trimmed and where he could find a few strands of tobacco any time he ran low in the pocket; of hands and feet that couldn't find the right place to be; of his woolen shirt and blue jeans washed out by the sun. His voice sounded as polished to his own ears as a pay-night cuspidor.

"All I'm saying in that bill is common sense—something you wouldn't understand! I'm saying that folks who come out to this wild prairie and broke the ground and built themselves a sod home have the right to that claim, even if the territory ain't been opened by the government. And anybody who jumps the claim, after the government opens up, is breaking the law!" Jeff was excited, and tobacco burned its way into his stomach. "I understand *that!*"

A wall shot up in Tester's sharp gray eyes. "That isn't what Federal law says. And it isn't what Nebraska law will say." His eyes darted toward Jeff's hips. "Packing guns won't do

The gun danced in Jeff's hand, giving him a savage feeling of satisfaction.

any good here. It's brains here. You'll find that out, soon." He swept aside his coat, exposing his hardware. "Of course, we all carry a gun—just in case." He nodded toward the spectators' section.

Jeff didn't have to look; he knew. There were a dozen grim gunhawks there, and they were Tester's men. They were fur thieves, drifters, claim jumpers. They were led by a big, black-bearded fellow Jeff knew as One-Eyed Grunson.

JEFF SWALLOWED, knowing that if his bill didn't pass, these men would jump claims, and there'd be open war. He was restless inside, felt like he was swelling up. Smed Tester's eyes were cold, mocking. Then the big fellow turned and went outside. He tripped over the blanketed Indian buck in the

hallway and kicked the fellow in the ribs. "Damn' lazy bums!" he spat, moving on.

Scratching his beard, Jeff scanned the small chamber, chopped into two sections by a railing to divide legislators from spectators. Emptiness hung like a dead weight, and he bit his cigar in two and threw aside the charred end. He missed the members who had shuffled around, whispering, passing out tanglefoot if you'd vote for this bill or that; missed the jaw-chawing about some little thing, that even the fireman, sergeant-at-arms, door keeper and spectators chimed into. The ticking of the clock got louder.

He was fishing around for some kind of plan when Loon Larkins puffed in, smelling as if he'd crept from the inside of a whiskey keg.

"We're licked! Plumb licked!"

Jeff shifted his chew, his nerves like a nest of hornets that had been poked with a stick. His barrel-bellied, legislator friend wasn't any big brain, but he had a grain of common sense and wasn't easy excited. Jeff watched the big, bulging eyes.

"You know where everybody's gone?" Larkins rasped into his ear. "They're over to a saloon Smed Tester's opened acrost the street! He's hung out the red underwear—right next door to that crazy Women's Temperance League office!"

Jeff swore under his breath. So that was it! On the frontier, the red underwear was the signal for free drinks. A numbness crawled through his body. Tester was playing on the weakest spot of the men—their love for fire water. To waste time, and keep Jeff's bill from going through.

Bitterly he gave his gun belt a hitch. It looked as if his bill was stomped, and that would mean he'd round up the squatters and they'd back their rights with gunsmoke. Loon Larkins moved close to him.

"That ain't the worst!" His pudgy friend threw a side glance toward One-Eyed Grunson and his men. "I found Tester's got a bill of his own in his pocket, right now!" Jeff was being twisted inside. "I got it from the barkeep, who didn't know I was your pal. Tester's bill is putting squatters outside the law! Squatters not only won't have legal rights to their homes—they'll have to run off from the law!"

Jeff almost swallowed his chew. "He won't get nobody to listen to nothing like that. Never!"

"That's where you're wrong," Larkins said. "He's gonna slip it in easy. He's serving up drinks to get permission to pass his bill by a committee of three. Then he'll get the committee drunk. They'll pass that bill even after the legislature closes!"

"Can they do something like that?" Jeff demanded. "Can they now? Loon, this ain't no time for any of your fool notions

"It's the truth!" Larkins exclaimed.

His firmness tore Jeff apart inside. Larkins wasn't fooling; he was serious as death. If Tester's scheme worked now, the squatters were through. They would be hunted men.

Suddenly the clock was squeezing Jeff, knocking him off balance; he didn't have any idea what to do. He felt as helpless as a day-old kitten.

She was mighty pretty in her sunbonnet and long, light blue cotton dress. He'd heard folks say a time or two she wasn't so pretty, but to him she was the finest girl in Nebraska. His heart couldn't seem to get settled when she looked up at him with eyes that put him in mind of a clear sky after a summer storm.

"That one-eyed fellow went around to a few legislators and said something," she said, drawing her brows into two soft, worried clumps. "Right after, everybody started moving out. I don't like it!"

JEFF looked into her soft face. Her father had died a couple of weeks ago, leaving her alone on her place ten miles out of Omaha; she was his personal reason for the fight to pass the squatter's bill. But now, knowing he had no chance . . .

Her voice was thin, brittle as glass. "Jeff, you know something. You're worried. What is it?"

Jeff cussed the folks who had put him up for election and voted for him even after he told them he didn't belong in any part of the territory government. Her anxious face drove home the fact he'd been nothing but a fur trapper, freighter, and buffalo hunter, and had followed the notion all his life that fists and guns were the only real ways to reason. She knew how feeble he was; she's seen him trying to get his long legs under the schoolboy desk and finally give up and sit on top, whittling with a Bowie knife while affairs of state were discussed. She'd seen him eating hard-boiled eggs with his knife while Loon Larkins brought up his bill. Jeff shuffled around and then told Dede, in a thick voice while he looked at the floor, about the red underwear and about how things were looking. Suddenly she swept by him and tramped down the hallway.

Surprised, he turned. She held her skirts from the dusty floor. He wanted to yell out, but didn't. He just stood, listening to her tiny footfalls.

"I hope I don't know women," Loon Larkins said in a graveyard voice. Jeff was cold inside as his fat friend curled his lips and shook his head. "If I know women, that's the last you see of her. She's put up with your drinking, fighting, swearing and lying. But you let her down."

You could always depend on Loon Larkins for the worst! The clock was ticking louder as Jeff turned from his friend. A horse thumped down the street outside, and he wanted to be on it, riding as far from Omaha as he could get. He thought of Smed Tester and most of the legislators, stuffed in calico boiled shirts and dark coats, with two rows of frills jammed between shirt and coat; and he felt suddenly sick.

Maybe he belonged to riff-raff like One-Eyed Grunson, smiling up at the clock, over there. At least his kind packed guns openly, not under cutaways and coats. He spat his chew on the floor and paced, his boots pounding but not breaking the steady clicking pace of the clock . . .

IF ONLY he wasn't the only man in the legislature who knew about Smed Tester's past and knew he'd stop at nothing, Jeff thought. Tester had got in the legislature, the *Palladium* had said, on the brag he'd been in Iowa's legislature and knew government inside and out. Jeff had grinned at first about that brag, but didn't think it was funny any more.

He'd seen Tester on a steamboat, coming up the yellow Missouri from White Cloud to Omaha. Jeff had been a deck passenger while Tester had had a stateroom, but he remembered wondering whether the handsome fellow in cutaway and high hat was a senator or what, the way he'd swung his gold cane and walked around with his nose up in the air. Jeff recalled another passenger had told him Tester was supposed to be a count or something, that he was slicking everybody at cards and dice, and that every lady aboard ship had her eyes on him. Tester had ridden high until the boat snagged on a sand bar off Nebraska City.

The captain had bragged his boat would float on dew, but he had soon given up trying to pull off the sand bar and called for help. It had been a deck hand off the rescue boat that had snarled at Smed Tester.

"That's the coyote, there!" His face had gone white as death. "He had a gang of claim jumpers out near Eureka. Got all the mill sites, fords, and best land gobbled up that way. Then he bled us dry till we bought back his claims!" He had pulled out a gun, trembling as if he had the fevers. "I been looking for him for two years!"

Tester had laughed in the fellow's face, hid as he had been behind the captain. They'd dragged off the deck hand, and the passengers, a ragged lot of land speculators, gamblers, adventurers and merchants, who'd seen fights till they'd gotten dull, forgot the whole thing.

Then later, up in Plattsmouth, Jeff had come down the street on the tail end of a shooting. That same deck hand had been stretched in the street, and Smed Tester had stood over him with smoking gun. Jeff recalled the words of the sheriff. "Can't figger it out. Hark here was a good man. Been around here before. Never knowed him to lose his haid. He went crazy and attacked this feller on sight. No doubt he was shot in self defense—"

Curious, Jeff had stuck around. Drifters had come in Plattsmouth, on horseback, by stage, by steamer. One-Eyed Grunson had been one of them; the rest of that crew sitting now in the spectators' section had been the others.

There wasn't a bit of doubt, Smed Tester meant to make another clean-up. And those damn' fool legislators—

Jeff knew now why he hadn't felt in place here. It had been more than the walls and more than the poise. These people didn't speak his language. They worried and stewed about the legal way to do things. He didn't care a hang about anything except which was right and which was wrong—measured by common sense. Common sense told him that squatters had done the work and the fighting for their land and that it belonged to them, no matter what Washington said. Dede Holmes and folks like her were entitled to a square deal.

And how far will you go to see they get a square deal?

He heard the distant tinkle of glasses, heard buzzing voices, laughing. Heard Smed Tester's voice, booming: "Fire and fall back! Give the next man his turn for a shot!"

Jeff was curled up inside, pacing the floor. How would going over there and shooting things up help the squatters? His jaws tightened as he looked up at the clock. One hour more—

One-Eyed Grunson and his men were grinning, watching the big hands . . . Jeff had to decide. Quick. He banged his fist into the palm of his hand. A loud crack answered his slap, but it was distant, outside the building. He stiffened. Anxiously he listened to the far-off scrape of chairs. He jumped inside as glasses crashed and the voices of women buzzed angrily.

He sensed how much he'd been holding in him when he rushed for the door. He squeezed through in front of Loon Larkins, whose eyes were bulging. The Indians had vanished from the hallway. Jeff's hand dropped on the cool butt of his holstered gun.

His broad face flushed with excitement. Loon Larkins stumbled past and then wheeled in the doorway.

"The Temperance League!" he bellowed, grinning. "Dede must have rounded 'em up!"

SHOCK ripped through Jeff like a knife when he reached the steps of the capital building. White-faced legislators poured from the saloon building, their hands laced over their heads, each pair or so followed by a club-swinging, red-faced female. Their gruff protests and pleas for reason were lost under the angry screeches of the women.

The excitement was spreading fast. The horses spooked and tugged at the hitching racks. Indians shuffled down the street, rolling startled eyes across their shoulders. A stream of curses turned Jeff's gaze upstreet. A drunken bull whacker crawled up on his wagon and turned his team, his wide eyes poking back through the dust. A couple of dogs yapped and danced around in the confused tangle of legislators and women.

Dede Holmes, standing apart, watched with tiny fists resting on her hips. The way her lower lip was hooked over her upper, showed a grim and business-like mood.

Jeff didn't know whether to laugh or get sore. One old lady dragged the speaker from the saloon by the ear, spilling whiskey from an up-turned bottle with her other hand. His cries of "Ouch! Leggo me!" ended suddenly in gurgling and sputtering as the old lady dropped the bottle before the horse trough and dunked the speaker.

The speaker came out coughing and gasping, and after he took a quick look at the tight-lipped old lady, started down the street. Jeff saw sudden danger and glanced at Loon Larkin's wide, grinning face.

"Come on, we got to hold these guys here! Take the upper end of the street!"

Hooking out his six-gun, Jeff leaped down the stairs. The legislators and women kicked up little pods of dust, through which bounced the excited dogs. Across the way, a crowd of curious people were gathering.

Jeff was determined as he ran ahead of the speaker and faced him with the gun. The beefy fellow's face was bloated and red, and his mouth was open. He stopped short, puffing, a puzzled look on his face. Jeff stood ready. The old lady swung from behind, catching the speaker behind the ear with a loud, ringing slap.

"Get back till we vote on that squatter's bill!" Jeff barked hoarsely. "On the run!"

Without a word the speaker turned and waddled toward the capital steps. Jeff was tight-lipped, keeping his six-gun levelled as he herded other legislators toward the building. They were confused and beaten, and it wasn't much of a job. Jeff didn't bother with Smed Tester, remembering One-Eyed Grunson and his men inside; he crossed the street at a run and took the capital steps, three at a time. Out of the corner of his eye, he saw Loon Larkins and Smed Tester both following him.

He blinked as he got out of the sun and into the gray hallway. When he burst into the chamber he smelled whiskey and sweat, and things seemed to be squeezing in on him.

But Jeff forgot everything else when he saw One-Eyed Grunson running from under the big clock. One of the legislators roared, "Them damn' fool females! That looney fat Larkin! It's time to quit anyhow!"

A glance told Jeff the story. One-Eyed had moved the hand of the clock past adjournment time!

Anger pounced on Jeff like a coyote on a sick calf. He was no match for Smed Tester and his cronies, playing their own lousy and crooked kind of game. But from now on, he was going to play his way!

As he rushed forward, he told himself this was the end. He'd be in boothill tomorrow. But by damn, here was one legislator who'd see that squatters got a square deal, or else!

HANDS on the butts of his guns, Jeff wheeled under the big clock. His heart was pounding like hoof-beats in his chest and the blood was kicking him in the temples.

"I'll drill anybody tries to get out that door till we've voted on my bill!" Jeff said hoarsely.

That, he saw quickly, was the spark that robbed Smed Tester of reason. With a curse, the big fellow clawed for his gun.

"Duck, Loon!" Jeff shouted.

Men spilled away on all sides. Crawled for cover like animals. As Tester's gun levelled off, Jeff's bullet caught and spun him. Tester dumped against the wall.

Out of the corner of his eye, Jeff saw Loon Larkin drawing and firing from a crouch. A warning turned him. "Tester's men!"

The blasts deafened in the little, closed room and the smell of powder was strong. Tester's men spattered bullets at him. His gun crashed once, dumping One-Eyed Grunson.

Then his lips tightened and breath rushed from him as lead slapped into his body. He tried to hold his feet but staggered and fell against a desk.

Things clouded up pretty bad and he wasn't sure what was going on. Muzzle-blasts flashed like torches and the smoke rolled in like a prairie fire. The roar was in his head, heavy and terrible. But one thought shot home.

Tester's gunmen were in the open. And legislators had out their hardware and were backing him up.

Suddenly Jeff felt as if he was part of the legislature. The members talked his language. And he had to get back in this debate. This was talk he understood!

He felt sick. Dizzy. Braced his arms on something, the desk maybe. Threw his weight over his arms. Collapsed back to his knees, cursing slowly.

The roar—the smoke—the blasts of six-guns. Shadows wrapped around him. He fought to bring things into focus. To shake off the shadows. But he couldn't. He couldn't—

Someone was crawling toward him. Bleeding. Trying to get out of the line of fire. He fought to see.

Smed Tester!

And Tester saw him.

It was the biggest job of Jeff's life. The gun was a big hunk of lead. His hands wouldn't grip, his arms wouldn't lift.

Blood was gushing from Tester's lips and his gun was like a wavering, hollow finger . . .

The gun danced in Jeff's hand, giving him a savage feeling of satisfaction. Tester's head snapped back, turning at a crazy angle on his shoulders. He slumped forward. . .

Then the chamber was quiet as death, and very dark after the muzzle blasts. Smoke crept in like a thick fog. Jeff saw movement in the smoke, but he turned away—toward the speaker's desk.

There was only one thought in his mind, but that desk seemed a mile away. He staggered toward it, groping, an iron band across his chest. He sighed as the rough wood was under his hand. He saw the white paper—*his bill*—and clutched it.

The speaker's voice blasted from the shadows. "You don't need no more votes on that bill, Jeff! That bill done past! That's gun whip law!"

Fading swiftly, Jeff slumped forward. He recalled trying to hang on but knew he hadn't and wondered where he was. There were dim cheers; then he heard feet running toward him, and he saw a movement of skirts.

He wasn't out cold, though, because somebody said, "Oh doctor! Is he hurt bad? I—I think an awful lot of him. Tell me—"

Dede Holmes! He wondered whether he was smiling; he wanted to smile. Then he was dimly, but pleasantly, surprised.

"Shucks, don't you worry none. He ain't gonna die. Bullet didn't get his lung, noway. Sides, God ain't gonna let a good legislator die now, when the territory of Nebraska's needing him so right bad!"

Jeff felt awful peaceful-like, as clumsy hands ripped open his wet, sticky shirt.

THE END

THE LONE RANGER

JIM HATFIELD, TEXAS RANGERS

WESTERNS

Available from Fiction House Press
www.FictionHousePress.com

ZANE GREY